MIRIAM VERHEYDEN

The Homeowner's Association

A Novel

Christmas 2024

Miriam Verheyden

**QUARTER
CENTURY
PUBLISHING**

Dedicated to Nicole,
therapist extraordinaire, wise woman, cheerleader, life changer.
Without you, I wouldn't be where I am today,
and this book wouldn't exist.

"Don't ask why the addiction, ask why the pain. To understand people's pain, you have to understand their lives."

Dr. Gabor Maté

Contents

Prologue

L uke opened the door to his visitor. "Come in," he said shortly, turning around and leading the way into the living room. He sat down on the sofa and gestured for his guest to take a seat.

"Thanks," the visitor began. "As I said on the phone, I'm here to bury the hatchet. This feud has gone on long enough, and I think it's time we make peace."

"Fine by me," Luke said, arms folded. "I'm not the one who started it."

A flicker of anger crossed the visitor's face, disappearing as fast as it had come.

"You are right. It's water under the bridge now, right? Can't we just move on?"

"I was under the impression you were going to do some apologizing. I have yet to hear an apology."

The fury on the visitor's face was unmistakable now.

Luke smiled. "I'm waiting."

Seconds ticked by. They looked at each other, dark eyes boring into blue ones.

Finally, the visitor looked away. "Alright, alright, I'm sorry. We went too far. I apologize."

For a moment it looked like Luke was going to push it, but

then he relented.

"Thanks, I appreciate that. You'll leave us alone from now on? My wife and I can get on with our lives?"

"Yes, we won't bother you anymore. Now, what do you say we drink to that? I brought something special to toast our newfound friendship."

The visitor pulled a bottle of Scotch out of the bag by their feet. "This is a twelve-year-old Glenlivet. Bought it years ago on vacation in Scotland and kept it for a special occasion. What do you say?"

"Sure, sounds good. Let me get some glasses."

"No need, I brought glasses as well," the visitor said. "If you could just get some ice, I'll pour us each one."

Luke rose and disappeared into the kitchen. As soon as he was out of the room, the visitor pulled a small bottle out of their jeans pocket and emptied its contents into one of the glasses, adding Scotch and stirring it with a small swivel stick they'd kept in the other pocket. Luke returned with the ice just as the liquid stopped spinning.

"Here we go," he announced and set the bowl with the ice cubes on the coffee table.

The visitor added a few cubes to each glass and handed one to Luke.

"Cheers," the visitor said with a smile. "To good health."

* * *

Hours later, the visitor was woken by the sound of sirens. The other person in the bed stirred. "I wonder what that's all about," they murmured sleepily.

"Don't worry about it," the visitor whispered back. "Go back

2

to sleep."

The visitor smiled into the darkness.

The plan had worked.

Chapter 1

D read filled Valerie's stomach as she drew near the community mailboxes. She carefully checked the rear-view mirror, peeked up the hill and then in all directions to make sure there was nobody around before stopping her car in front of them. Heart pounding and feeling slightly nauseous, she had to force herself to unclench her hands from the steering wheel and to open the door. She left the car running in case she needed a quick getaway before tentatively approaching her box. It looked just like the others from the outside, unmarked and innocent. But then again, even if there was a ticking bomb inside, it would be impossible to know until it was too late. With her hand trembling she unlocked the box and peered inside. There was a small pile of letters, and as Valerie reached out for them, she felt bile rise up in her throat. What if there was another one of those letters?

She swallowed the bile back down, determined not to vomit in public. Even though there was nobody on the street, Valerie imagined several sets of eyes on her, watching her from behind drawn curtains, waiting for a sign of weakness. Without looking at the mail in her hand, she slammed the box shut and hastily retreated to the relative safety of her car.

At home she kicked off her shoes, threw the mail on the

kitchen counter, poured herself a large glass of wine from the box in the fridge, and emptied half of it in one gulp while still standing. She then refilled it to the brim, grabbed the mail, and plopped down on the couch in the living room. Tears were pricking her eyes, and when Smokey came purring into the room and jumped lightly on her lap, she let the tears fall freely, burying her face in her cat's soft fur.

"Oh Smokey, I'm too scared to look at the letters," she sobbed, hugging her cat so tightly that he gave an indignant meow.

"Sorry, baby. What if they've sent another threatening letter? I don't think I can handle it. Why are they so awful? And why did Luke have to die? I can't cope with them without him."

Valerie was aware that having a full-blown conversation with her cat might be cause for concern, but she didn't care. Ever since her husband Luke passed away a year ago, she felt that she was slowly losing her grip on sanity. Frankly, she was looking forward to the day when it would slip out of her fingers entirely and she could enter a state of certifiable madness. Being declared mentally incompetent and sent to a mental institution sounded like a nice break from the nightmare her life had become.

Luke had died suddenly of a heart attack. Valerie would never forget the awful day when she came home from work and found him dead on the floor in the living room, his body already cold, vacant eyes staring blindly into space. His dear, familiar face had looked like the mask of a stranger and haunted her in her nightmares ever since that day. It was the first image that popped into her head when she thought of him, a fact that made her want to despair. They had been together for twenty-four years, and all she saw in her mind's eye was his dead face. It was so unfair.

Luke had been diagnosed with heart disease a few years before, but they thought he had the condition under control with medication. Valerie couldn't help but wonder if the stress they had been under before Luke's death had contributed to his heart attack. Whatever the reason, he was gone, and he had left her behind, all alone.

The aftermath of his death was a blur. There was the funeral she was heavily medicated for, a meeting with her boss to arrange time off work, and a brief phase where people kept offering help and awkward condolences, followed by the gaping void she'd found herself in ever since. Her life had lost all colour and purpose, the well-meaning people had disappeared, and all she was left with was a cat, a growing drinking problem, and a group of people who seemed determined to destroy her.

* * *

Valerie and Luke met when she was nineteen years old and he twenty-eight. She was a student, living in a dorm, eating ramen noodles, and stacking shelves in a grocery store on weekends. He drove a Mercedes, had a place overlooking the ocean, and wore designer clothes. He was charming, confident, and devastatingly handsome; she thought of herself as plain, awkward, and boring. Everything about her was average: she was of average height, average build, with an average face. Valerie was neither fat nor skinny, neither ugly nor pretty, with dishwater blonde hair that was neither long nor short, ending just below her shoulders.

She was surprised when he asked her out on a date, and even

more surprised when he told her soon after that he had fallen in love with her. She wasn't sure how she felt, but everybody told her that he was a catch and that she would be crazy to turn him down – so she didn't.

Valerie hadn't looked for a relationship. She had been excited about living on her own for the first time, away from her preacher-parents who had monitored her every move and constantly reminded her to behave herself in a way that wouldn't reflect badly on them. "People are looking at you," they repeatedly told her, and she was expected to be at church every Sunday, in youth group every Friday, to sing in the choir, and to help her mom at women's circle. Her parents were kind but strict, and being the pastor's daughter wasn't exactly a ticket into the popular kids' ranks. She felt shackled by her parents' vocation, resentful of always having to behave but too obedient to rebel.

She had been looking forward to making new friends, sleeping in on Sundays, and trying to figure out who she was as a person. It felt to her like she had only been a preacher's daughter thus far, and she wanted to add another description to the sadly lacking "about me" section she kept in her head.

Valerie had first realized that she had no idea who she was when she had been interviewed for her first summer job at sixteen. She sat nervously in front of the owner of the local grocery store, and when he prompted her to "tell me about yourself", she hadn't had any idea what to say. She went to school, to church, and she liked to read – what else was there?

Valerie couldn't remember what she'd said, but ever since the interview she was obsessed with trying to find an answer to that question. She envied other girls who came with a ready-made list: daughter, sister, friend, ballet dancer, horseback

7

rider, future astrophysicist. She had neither the ambition nor the confidence for such a lofty career goal, she had no siblings, didn't feel like she fit in with her youth-group friends who all seemed to actually believe in God while she had serious doubts, and there had never been time or money for expensive hobbies.

One thing was certain: Valerie wanted to leave her small town behind and move to a big city where she could experience the freedom of living in a place where nobody knew her. She decided to go to nursing school and convinced her parents that Vancouver was the best place to learn how to become a nurse. She was excited to be eight hours away from the suffocating scrutiny of her overprotective parents and small-town life, and couldn't wait to live the life of a college student.

However, college wasn't how Valerie had imagined it. Instead of finding her tribe of like-minded friends as she had hoped, she once again felt like the odd one out. Groups formed, but somehow she didn't manage to join any of them, either because of her shyness or, her greatest fear, because she was too awkward. After a week of getting lost, eating lunch alone, and fighting back tears more than once, a curly-haired girl marched up to her on a Friday afternoon as she was sitting underneath a tree after class, doing homework and wondering what to do on the weekend.

"Hey, you are in my set, aren't you?" she asked in a business-like tone. Valerie looked up at a skinny girl with huge glasses, short brown hair, and the worst case of dandruff she had ever seen. White flakes flecked her dark hair, a fine layer of white dust had settled on the girl's narrow shoulders, and Valerie watched in amazement as the girl brushed off her shoulders impatiently and a white cloud drifted lazily to the ground, pretty as snow. She must have been staring, because the girl said: "Would you like to take a picture? It lasts longer."

Valerie blushed furiously and stammered: "I-I'm so sorry, I didn't mean to, I-"

The other girl smiled. "Relax, I'm just teasing you. I have psoriasis, it's not contagious. It's particularly bad right now, I got a flare-up because of the stress of starting college and everything. It doesn't always look that extreme. I'm Hattie, by the way." She stuck out her hand and Valerie automatically shook it. "I've seen you on your own all week, is that on purpose? Do you prefer to be alone? If you do I totally understand, just say the word and I'll bugger off. If not, do you wanna hang out?"

She looked at Valerie expectantly. It took Valerie a moment to respond, having momentarily been rendered speechless, before asking the first question that popped into her mind: "Sorry, what?"

Hattie laughed and plopped herself down next to Valerie. "What's your name?"

So began her friendship with Hattie. Fast-talking, smart, and bossy, Hattie took her on as if Valerie was a lost puppy, and from that moment on they did everything together. It wasn't the group of friends Valerie had been dreaming of or the college experience she had hoped for, but she was grateful not to be alone anymore. Hattie also lived on campus, and it was wonderful to have someone to study with, hang out with on the weekends, and most importantly, walk in a pair instead of alone. Valerie always felt like a huge letter L was emblazoned on her chest whenever she did anything alone, thinking that everyone must think she was too unlikable to have friends.

Still, even though she was glad for Hattie's company, she couldn't help but feel like she was missing out. Hattie was a passionate crafter, scrapbooker, and movie aficionado, and Valerie went along with it even though none of these activities were her jam. But because she still didn't know what she'd rather do and Hattie's force of will was much stronger than hers, it was easiest to go along with what her friend wanted.

Valerie yearned to realize her fantasy of living like they did in *Friends* with a group to hang out with every day, going in and out of each other's places, and knowing you could always find them at the same coffee shop if you wanted company. She also wanted to go out and party but didn't know how to make that happen. Hattie had no interest, and Valerie was too shy to ask others to tag along. As for going alone? Unthinkable. She'd die of shame and embarrassment.

And then the end of the first semester came and with it the invite she'd been waiting for.

"Hey Valerie, we're all going out on Friday after we're done with our last exam, you and Hattie should come!" Trish called over to her as they were waiting in front of a classroom to write their second-to-last exam. Some students were doing last-minute revisions, others sat with their eyes closed in an effort to calm their nerves, and the group of popular kids stood around, discussing where to go on Friday. Trish was one of the popular kids, but she was nice to everyone.

Valerie blushed with pleasure and surprise. "Sounds good!" she managed to say without stuttering. "Where are you going?"

"The Roxy," Trish replied. "We're getting a party bus from campus; it leaves at eight. Let me know if you're coming and I'll put your names down!"

Hattie was going straight home after the exams and politely declined the invite. But Valerie had planned to stay the weekend before driving the 700 kilometres to her parents' house, knowing she needed to get a proper night's sleep before that long drive. Without a moment's hesitation she beamed at Trish and said: "Yes, I'm in."

Valerie floated into the exam as if on clouds.

* * *

That Friday night changed her life. A few people had smuggled bottles of cheap champagne into school, and as soon as Valerie walked out of the exam room, a guy whose name she didn't know pressed a red plastic cup into her hand. "We're done!" he sang, grabbing her other hand and giving her a twirl. "Let's party!"

They drank on school grounds until they were chased off, moving to someone's common room where the party really kicked off. They drank, danced, sang, and laughed, and then Trish pulled Valerie into her room to get ready together with a bunch of other girls.

"You know, you're actually really fun!" Trish said at one point and gave Valerie a hug. Buoyed by the alcohol and being in the midst of the realization of her dream, Valerie hugged her back tightly.

"So are you," she said, and then added, "thank you for including me."

"Aww, you are welcome," Trish said. "Let me do your make-up, okay?"

When she walked into the club two hours later as part of a large group, Valerie felt on top of the world. *This* was the college experience she had been waiting for. Trish had done her hair and make-up expertly, and talked her into borrowing one of her dresses, a fitted little number with a short, flared skirt. Valerie felt like she was wearing a costume, playing someone she was not, and this new person was all the things she wasn't: pretty, popular, and uncharacteristically daring.

As she was dancing with people that weren't her friends, wearing clothes that weren't hers, made-up in a way she usually never made herself up, and brazen in a way only alcohol and pretending to be someone you are not could make you – that's when she met her future husband.

Luke was tall, dark-haired, and incredibly charming. He would later always claim that it was love at first sight for him, that he knew as soon as he laid eyes on her that she was the woman for him. All Valerie could honestly say was that she had been flattered by the attention. This person that wasn't her had flirted outrageously with him, but it hadn't seemed real, just like everything else that night wasn't real. Underneath the buzz and the high of the night, Valerie knew that she was playing out a fantasy, and she hadn't expected to see him ever again after that night.

But he surprised her. She had given him her number, and the very next day he called. Hungover and too stunned to overthink it, she had agreed to meet with him for dinner the following night, and then spent the next thirty hours panicking about what to wear, what to do with her hair, and what they would talk about. When she returned Trish's dress she told her about the date, and Trish offered her another outfit to wear and to do her hair again. She suspected that Trish saw her as a project, something to do now that the exams were over and they didn't need to study anymore, but she didn't care. She needed all the help she could get, because if she remembered correctly, Luke was *hot*. What he saw in her she had no idea; she hoped it wasn't beer goggles that made him want to take her out. What if he took one good look at her in the sober light of day, turned on his heel and left?

Decked out in a slip dress and unfamiliar high heels, and with Trish's advice— "If you're worried about what to say just ask him questions and let him talk, guys love to talk about themselves" – fresh in her mind, she nervously awaited Luke's arrival.

He came in a silver Mercedes, dressed in a suit jacket, crisp white shirt, designer jeans, and expensive-looking shoes. He held a bunch of flowers in his hands, and to her immense relief he didn't run away screaming upon seeing her but said: "You are even more beautiful than the other night, which I didn't think was possible". It should have sounded cheesy, but she was thoroughly charmed by him. He opened the car door for her, courteously held open the restaurant door, pulled out her chair for her, and asked her questions about herself. Luke seemed genuinely fascinated by her small-town upbringing as the pastor's kid, and laughed at her anecdotes. He made her feel witty and interesting, because he had a way of concentrating all of his attention on her alone, as if she was the only person in the room.

She learnt that he was the youngest of three brothers, worked in finance, liked golfing, skiing, and travelling, and that he was looking for a serious relationship. "I don't want to scare you away," he said gently, taking her hand in his and looking deep into her eyes. "I know that you are young and still in school. But I want to be upfront about what I'm looking for, so we are not wasting each other's time. I want to be married by thirty and start a family. If you're not ready for a relationship just say the word, and you'll never see me again after tonight."

Valerie was startled by his ultimatum but decided that she liked his decisiveness. At twenty-eight he was pretty old, so it made sense that he didn't want to wait around. If it was up to her she would have preferred to take it slow, date for a while and see where things were going. But since that option didn't seem to exist for him, she took the only other one that allowed her to keep seeing him and said: "I'm all in if you are."

She was going home the next day because she had a job lined up, and for the next few weeks they were talking on the phone every day, getting to know each other. Luke knew who he was and what he wanted, and Valerie, who didn't know either, was deeply impressed by it. She wondered what it would be like to be so confident, to know one's place in the world. Would she ever find hers? Maybe with him by her side, she could?

* * *

He met her parents a month later, visiting her in her hometown, and they were charmed by him. Without their prompting he asked to sleep in the spare room, earnestly telling them that he knew how young she was, that he respected her, and that he would never do anything she didn't want him to. He expressed his desire to get married, casually mentioning that he was financially secure and that he regarded it as his responsibility to take care of a woman.

"Your dad and I really like your young man," Valerie's mom said to her later in the kitchen as they were doing the dishes.

"He's great, isn't he?" Valerie asked, needing the reassurance. Then she voiced the concern she'd had since the beginning: "You don't think he's moving too fast, coming here after knowing me for only a month?"

"Not at all," her mom said dismissively. "If you know, you know. Besides, we appreciate him making the effort. Your father and I like that it's important to him to meet us. We want to know who you're going out with. We are very impressed by him."

"You don't mind the nine-year age gap?"

"Not at all, honey. Men mature so much later than women, having an older man is much better, trust me. Dad and I are five years apart, and let me tell you, I've sometimes wished it was more."

Her mother kissed her on the forehead. "Trust me, he's a catch. You couldn't do any better."

Nine months later he proposed, after having asked her father for her hand, and a year after that they got married. She graduated three months later, and they settled into their lives together. Valerie got a job at a hospital and Luke left for his office in a suit and tie every morning. After a year of marriage they tried to get pregnant, but when it didn't happen they went to the doctor and found out that Luke was infertile, probably due to an injury he'd had as a child. She brought up adoption, but Luke was vehemently against it.

"I don't want to raise somebody else's kid," was his attitude, and he wouldn't budge.

Instead they travelled extensively, went on skiing holidays every winter, and entertained regularly. Luke was an outgoing guy with a large group of friends, and even though they were all very nice to her and seemed to have accepted her, Valerie couldn't help but feel that she didn't belong. She was the youngest of them, not a mother, and she always felt left out somehow, as if there was a secret password you needed to enter the inner sanctum that she had never been given. When she tried to explain to Luke how she felt, he laughed it off, telling her that it was all in her head and to stop overthinking. "They love you!" he assured her. "Stop worrying so much!"

She loved her husband, but he just didn't get it. Luke didn't know what being insecure felt like – he never doubted himself or his judgment. He was utterly confident and truly didn't seem to care what others thought of him. "I can't change it anyway, so why even try? I only worry about things I can change, everything else is a waste of time."

Try as she might, Valerie couldn't stop worrying. She worried about global warming, getting fat, about people not liking her, about dying before she found her purpose. She still carried her "about me" list in her head, and was dissatisfied with what was on it thus far: daughter, wife, nurse, traveller – what else? She hesitated to put *friend* on it because even though Hattie and her had stayed friends and she and Luke technically had a large friend group, she felt inadequate. She worried about not investing enough time into friendships but didn't have the energy to do more. Having a job dealing with people, plus looking after her husband was more than enough human interaction for her most days. She had to force herself to schedule get-togethers with her friends, to check in regularly, and to remember to send birthday and Christmas cards. It was all so much *work*.

Valerie knew how lucky she was and felt guilty for being dissatisfied. Why did everything feel like too much? And why did it also feel like something was missing in her life?

Three years ago they decided to move. Valerie had been working through the first wave of the pandemic and she was exhausted. Case numbers of active COVID-19 cases were rising, and in August of 2020 they were higher than they had been in

March before the lockdown. Living in a big city and working in a big hospital didn't feel safe anymore.

They'd lived in Vancouver their entire marriage, but Luke had made enough smart investments that he could retire at fifty, and with the sale of their house they would be able to afford something amazing in a smaller town away from the chaos, traffic, danger, and the grey weather in the winter.

"Honey, look at this," he said one evening as they were sitting beside each other on the sofa, scrolling on their phones. He handed her his and she looked at the screen: it showed an image of a picturesque town studded with trees, snow-capped mountains in the distance, and a bridge crossing a sparkling river. Superimposed on it in large, looping font were the words:

Summerfield
Where Dreams Turn into Reality

"What is this?" she asked.

"Our future!" he said excitedly. "It's a small town a few hours away from here, and it has everything we want: lakes, rivers, mountains, snow in the winter, warm weather in the summer, tons of hiking trails, a bookstore, boutiques, coffee shops, a handful of decent-looking restaurants and *very* affordable houses. If we sell our place and move we'll never have to work again!"

Valerie clicked through the photos on the town's website. She saw pictures of live concerts in a park, a farmer's market, a beautiful town centre decorated for what looked like a fall festival, fit-looking seniors cross-country skiing under an azure-blue sky, and lots of photos of fall foliage, rivers, people fishing or water skiing, and gorgeous sunsets.

"This looks amazing," she breathed, smiling widely. "When can we go and check it out?"

They did the very next weekend, and both of them fell in love with Summerfield. They stayed in an old-fashioned B&B with a grandmotherly hostess who cooked them a hearty breakfast of bacon, eggs, French toast, homemade muffins, and strong coffee, and happily told them stories of the town and people. She also gave them the number of a real-estate-agent friend of hers who agreed to show them a few houses for sale that same afternoon.

"This is Pleasant Hill, one of the most desirable areas in Summerfield," the real-estate-agent informed them as they were driving through a pretty neighbourhood of well-maintained houses with neatly manicured lawns, tidy front yards, and tree-lined streets. "The people here are house-proud and really care about their community," she continued as they pulled up in front of a gorgeous two-story house, painted green with brown shutters and a large front porch.

The house was beautiful: polished hardwood floors, state-of-the-art appliances, a lavish kitchen, and spa-like bath-rooms. It was airy and filled with light, and the big windows showed incredible views of the valley. The large backyard was expertly landscaped and came with a hot tub, fireplace, and gazebo. Valerie closed her eyes and pictured Luke and herself in this yard, hosting a barbecue for the new friends they would make here. *A fresh start*, she thought to herself. Maybe a new town would help her find whatever it was that was missing in her life.

Chapter 2

Holly Kent stepped out of her front door into the sunshine, giving the doorknob a quick polish with the cloth she kept in her pocket for this very purpose. She let her sharp eyes roam over the front yard critically, making a mental note to tell her husband Homer that the lawn needed cutting today. On the way down her pretty garden path she frequently stopped to snip off a wilted flower here, stray twig there, and to pick up any leaf that had dared to fall onto her pristine lawn. She frowned when she spotted the plastic bag that had blown into her yard. "Idiot people," she muttered disapprovingly at whoever had littered, or hadn't paid attention when they lost their grip on the bag.

That was the problem with people: they didn't care. They didn't care about order and cleanliness, they didn't care about keeping things tidy, and they certainly didn't seem to care about living in a well-kept neighbourhood. Holly couldn't understand it. Why didn't people have pride in their environment?

Once satisfied with the state of her own yard she set off on her daily inspection of Pleasant Hill, her notebook at the ready.

Holly was sixty-three, but you wouldn't know it. She moved with the purposeful, quick stride of a much younger woman, and she did what needed to be done to keep herself presentable. In Holly's opinion it was every woman's duty not to let herself go, and she took keeping her body slim and her hair free of greys as seriously as she took keeping up the neighbourhood.

Walking through what she considered her domain never failed to fill her with pride. Holly loved seeing the uniform white picket fences, the neatly kept lawns, the houses all painted in the approved suburban traditional palette, and to enjoy the litter-free and regularly swept sidewalks. The street lights had been updated five years ago to historic area lighting, and Holly was pleased to see that the hanging baskets were in full bloom and thriving. But then her gaze fell on the Fowler's front yard, and she frowned. "That dog hasn't been approved," she muttered and made a note in her notebook. Pets were strictly regulated to no more than two dogs per household, and Holly knew that they already had two, a yappy little thing she'd very much like to kick if she could get away with it, and a mutt of indeterminate origin that growled at her. This dog was new, and she couldn't wait to issue them a warning.

By the end of her inspection she had found seven lawns that were too long, three yards that needed pruning or weeding, one house that needed repainting (the rule was to repaint every five years), an unauthorized RV parked in a driveway, and no less than eight houses that were violating the appearance of property covenant by being messy, having garbage lying around, and one by flying a non-approved flag.

Holly was the president of Pleasant Hill's homeowner's association, and she took that role seriously. Her and Homer had founded the HOA thirty years ago, shortly after they moved into the area. Back then, Pleasant Hill wasn't nearly as prestigious as it was now; on the contrary, there were several run-down houses, one of which was rumoured to be some sort of unofficial halfway house, with shifty-looking people going in and out at all hours of the day and night. It was scandalous and brought down the value of the entire neighbourhood. But far from being discouraged by this, Holly was determined to change her community, to either get people to follow her vision or get them the hell out.

And a vision she had: Holly wanted to make Pleasant Hill greater than it had ever been. She imagined it to become a picture-perfect utopia of immaculate houses with matching white picket fences, meticulously maintained lawns, regularly pruned hedges, and sidewalks free of dirt, leaves, and litter. She pictured housewives who chatted companionably to each other while washing their windows, stoops that shone after a weekly scrubbing, and husbands who mowed the lawn every Saturday. In Holly's opinion, home ownership was a privilege that needed to be earned, and because too many people didn't take it seriously enough it needed to come with rules and regulations.

Soon after they had moved into the area, Holly set out to find allies and locate potential troublemakers. She went from house to house with freshly baked muffins, ostensibly to introduce herself, but more importantly to get to know her new neighbours. Holly carried a notebook with her, and as soon as she left a house she would retreat out of sight and make detailed notes. Name, marital status, how many children, how many pets, how many vehicles and what state they were in, was she invited in, what did they offer her if she was, what did the inside look like, how clean was everything, and about a dozen more items.

She invented a complicated points system: points were given

when she was invited into the house, but deducted if she wasn't being offered refreshments. There were extra points for good coffee and home baked goods, and points taken off for being offered alcohol before 5 pm, particularly when it was boxed wine or beer in cans.

Holly appreciated seasonal decor, tasteful furnishings, tidiness, and having no more than two children. She disapproved of parents who had more than two, deeming it unnecessary. What on earth for? It led to too much dirt and chaos, toys and sports equipment strewn across the front yard, and kids running wild because both their parents had to work to afford their frivolous amount of children.

* * *

That's how she befriended Mary Potter, her neighbour across the street. When Holly visited Mary with her muffins to introduce herself, a mousy, nervous-looking woman of indeterminate age opened the door wearing yellow rubber gloves.

"Hello there!" Holly said warmly. "I'm Holly Kent. My husband Homer and I just moved across the street, and I wanted to introduce myself. Here, I made you some blueberry muffins, they're still warm." Holly proffered the basket, tied with a ribbon, to the woman in front of her. She had limp hair, a pale, narrow face, and was wearing baggy jeans and a colourless sweater.

"Oh, w-wow, that's so nice," the woman stammered, a dull flush creeping into her hollow cheeks. "Um, you caught me cleaning the toilet − " she flushed deeper− "er, I mean, the bathroom, and I probably smell like bleach, and I don't want to get bleach on your wonderful muffins ..." She trailed off,

22

looking mortified.

Holly took over. "Why don't I take the muffins inside the kitchen for you?" she suggested with a smile. "Just show me the way."

The woman nodded uncertainly, opened the door wider, and motioned for Holly to come in.

The kitchen was a 70s nightmare with dark wood cabinets, avocado-green laminate countertops, and yellowing flowery wallpaper, but it was immaculately clean and tidy. Holly put the muffins down on the round tablecloth-covered kitchen table and turned around, looking expectantly at the other woman. Was she going to introduce herself or offer her something to drink?

Apparently not. She had finally taken off her rubber gloves and was now vigorously scrubbing her hands under running water, her back turned. Holly got the impression that her neighbour was either pathologically shy or socially awkward – probably a mixture of both. No problem; what those people needed was guidance and someone telling them what to do, and Holly was just the woman for the job.

"Hey, listen, why don't you sit down, and I make us some coffee? You look like you could use a break." Holly started opening cabinets in the search of coffee grounds, glancing over her shoulder to see the other woman's reaction. She had whirled around and opened her mouth, most likely to protest, but Holly didn't give her a chance to speak.

"I insist," she said firmly, and having located the coffee, she swiftly scooped a few spoonfuls into the coffeemaker and switched it on.

"So, what's your name?" she asked, taking out plates and cups she had found while looking through the cabinets.

23

"Mary," came the subdued reply.

"You have a beautiful home, Mary," Holly lied. "And it's so neat and tidy! You can tell a lot about a person by the way they keep their house, and what your house is telling me is that you care about the way you live. You take pride in order and cleanliness, and I admire that. I feel the same way."

"Thank you!" said Mary, looking pleased. "Albert – that's my husband – likes a clean house. He works so hard all day, the least I can do is make it comfortable for him at home. I've been a homemaker all my life, and now that the boys are out of the house – I have two sons – I have no other responsibilities than looking after Albert and our home." She stopped talking to catch her breath, and noticing that the coffee was ready, she jumped up to get the carafe and pour them each a cup.

"I'm so sorry I was so inhospitable at first," Mary continued, pulling cream out of the fridge and sugar out of the cabinet. "You caught me off guard. I don't get many visitors, particularly not unannounced." She quickly glanced at Holly. "Sorry, I didn't mean to offend you."

"No offense taken," Holly assured her. "I never usually visit anyone without arranging it first, but I didn't have your phone number." She had been taking mental notes while Mary was talking, and she was delighted at her score. Married, two grown children, working husband, houseproud housewife, and a push-over – Mary was perfect.

From that day forward Holly carefully cultivated a friendship with Mary. She called her once or twice a week, always making sure she was charming and complimentary.

"Mary, your hydrangeas are flourishing," she'd say one day, "you have such a gift for gardening!"

"What's your secret for getting your windows so spotlessly

clean?" she'd ask the next time, even though she secretly swore by using vinegar mixed with filtered water and wouldn't be swayed to use anything else.

"I'm so glad that it's *you* who lives across from us and not some of the other neighbours." She lowered her voice. "That halfway house is such a disgrace; I wish there was something we could do about it."

Mary fell for it hook, line, and sinker. Soon she was a loyal friend who unquestioningly did whatever Holly asked her to do. Which was handy, because Holly had a plan: she wanted to create a homeowner's association, she wanted to be the president, and she needed a wing woman to help her achieve that goal.

She used her comprehensive notes on everybody in Pleasant Hill and made a list of like-minded people, neutrals, and problem cases.

"I'm throwing a party!" she announced to her husband once the list was done. Homer wasn't involved in her plans except for when it came to the topic of the board. He'd dared to voice the opinion that he should be president, but she quickly disabused him of that idea. She was doing all the work; she'd be damned if she gave him the big job. Besides, he neither had the same ambition as her nor her vision. Holly had big plans for Pleasant Hill, way bigger than her husband's tiny imagination would allow.

The guest list for the party was put together after much consideration. Holly sent out invitations to twenty carefully chosen houses, requesting their presence at a "community-building gathering to mingle, get to know each other, and plan improvements to Pleasant Hill". She had decided to get the people with the highest scores together, people who thought like her and would be on board with her ideas. She also included people whom she judged to feel neutral about it, so the like-minded people could convert the neutral. She was certain that they could be convinced to see things her way once they had good food and wine in their bellies and she had painted a glittering picture of a spectacular future for Pleasant Hill. After all, who didn't want to make their neighbourhood better?

The party was a big hit. Everything worked out the way Holly had planned: together with Homer, Mary, and Mary's husband Albert, the four of them subtly steered individual conversations towards how nice Pleasant Hill was now, but that it could become great if only they'd work together to make it so. They all brought their conversations to the halfway house and other ramshackle houses in the neighbourhood, making sure everybody felt the same way they did. Once they'd been sufficiently primed, Holly went in for the kill. In the lull between the main course and dessert, when everybody was pleasantly full and in an agreeable mood, she got up and delivered a rousing speech about how Pleasant Hill could become the most desirable neighbourhood of Summerfield, winning prizes for its outstanding gardens and best Christmas decorations, not to mention the increase in property value which would lead to attracting "a certain class of people".

"Every community requires a set of rules to function properly. Without rules, nations would collapse. So will neighbourhoods. Run-down houses reflect poorly on all of us, lower the property value, and bring in unsavoury characters. Do we want to raise our children in a neighbourhood with drug dealers, people with loose morals, and hoodlums that may break into our homes? Do we want loud noises at all hours of the night? Do we want cars with broken mufflers that make a racket when

26

they come down the street?"

Enthusiastic nodding of heads and exclamations of "no way!", "enough is enough", "but what can we do about it?" greeted her questions.

Holly smiled to herself. She had them.

"I have a proposition for you: let's start a homeowner's association."

They all agreed unanimously.

* * *

The next few years were the happiest of Holly's life. Once she and Homer had officially set up the HOA and had been appointed president and vice president, they drew up the covenants, conditions, and restrictions (CC&Rs). Their first priority was the appearance and maintenance of the properties, and they included everything from approved house colours, how often to repaint, which holiday decorations were permitted, to fence regulations, lawn maintenance, and rules for landscaping.

They created rules for how many different people were allowed to live in a house; how many vehicles could be parked in front of it; the condition they had to be in (rusty and/or loud were not allowed), and that boats, RVs, and other recreational vehicles were only permitted to be parked at the street for the purpose of loading and unloading.

Pet restrictions were introduced as well as strict guidelines on the removal of feces and how to properly dispose of them.

They set up regulations about noise, parties, and, on Holly's insistence, personal conduct, which was vaguely defined and wide open to interpretation – exactly the way she wanted it.

When the CC&Rs were in place, they went about getting as many residents as possible to join. Most signed the documents willingly, and the ones who were reluctant could usually be persuaded either with gentle bribes or, if that didn't work, with veiled threats. Unsurprisingly, the owner of the halfway house – an unmarried woman named Taylor Kirby who offered drug addicts who'd finished rehab a room until they could afford their own place – didn't join. She also wasn't willing to upgrade the exterior of her house, and flat-out refused to stop housing drug addicts. "They are *recovering* addicts, you bigot-bitch!" Taylor yelled at her and added: "These people have been hurt enough. They deserve a chance like everybody else. Why don't you try being compassionate for a change? It will be a new experience for you." Then she slammed the door in Holly's face.

Holly was fuming and swore to Homer that she would get them out, no matter what.

How to get rid of an obstinate woman with her band of hardened druggies? It was infuriating that Holly couldn't use the HOA's rules and regulations against Taylor, but since she'd lived here before its existence, Holly couldn't legally do anything against her. It was too late for a civilized conversation over tea, companionably handing out methadone to the addicts while discussing options. Besides, Taylor was one of those women who opposed good sense and common courtesy out of principle. There was no appealing to one's reason if they didn't have any. No, people like Taylor didn't understand subtlety. Threats were the only language they were fluent in.

Holly started sending anonymous letters that told Taylor and her drug addicts that they weren't wanted here and that they should leave. She signed the letters "an upstanding citizen", hoping it conveyed the message that they were not. The letter campaign spanned over a year, in which she'd sometimes send one a week, sometimes none for several months. The irregularity of the letters, she figured, was probably more effective than sending them at some sort of schedule.

It didn't work. Taylor must have known that it was Holly who was behind the letters, and evidently Holly didn't scare her.

"What should we do?" she asked her husband in exasperation. "We can't have her stay, but I don't know how to get rid of her."

"Leave it to me," Homer replied, an evil glint in his eye.

Holly was disconcerted by this but shoved it away. She knew firsthand that her husband could be dangerous, but she didn't want to think about it.

She didn't know how he did it, but within weeks of telling him about her Taylor problem, the "For Sale" sign had gone up in front of Taylor's house. Holly had been waiting so long for this moment that she should have been elated, but instead she was deeply unsettled.

What had her husband done?

Chapter 3

C lementine Harrison needed a change. As she was gazing out at the grey January sky from her cozy apartment on the nineteenth floor in Toronto she took stock of her life. She was fifty-two, single again after a recent breakup, and she felt out of sorts. Clementine was a social documentary photographer who loved her career, but lately she was unable to pick up her camera and focus on her work. It was ironic, being unable to focus as a photographer, but she was so worried about her creative block that she couldn't see the humour in it.

Clementine's documentary photography focused on issues related to marginalized women, drug addiction, and homelessness, and had appeared in *TIME* magazine, *Vogue*, and *National Geographic*. For her last project she had spent a year on the streets, getting to know Toronto's female drug addicts and capturing their stories on camera. It had been an incredibly difficult, emotionally draining year where she had witnessed death, despair, violence, and sorrow, but also moments of tenderness, community, and so much raw humanity that she was still reeling. Her project had been made into a book, and ever since its completion Clementine was creatively paralyzed.

While she held great tenderness for the women she'd encountered in her heart, she didn't feel the same about her city. Clementine had been born and raised in Toronto, and despite travelling extensively for her work over the years she'd always been glad to come back. Toronto was home. But lately she had the uneasy sense that the fondness she'd always felt for it was gone, maybe forever. She was sick of the city.

The phone rang, interrupting her reverie. When she saw that it was her best friend Jules, her face brightened. "Bad timing, Jules. I'm busy contemplating throwing myself off the balcony, and you're interrupting this important activity. Call back later."

"I'm told the first eighteen stories are easy. Let me know how it goes," Jules deadpanned. Then she added in a softer voice: "What's going on, Clem? Is it the breakup? Are you still upset about losing Becks?"

Clementine sighed. "No, I don't think so. I don't really know. I think I'm either burnt out or I'm having a midlife crisis."

"Are you still blocked with your photography?"

"Yes! It's been months and I still can't take a decent photo for the life of me, let alone come up with a new project. There's dust and tumbleweeds blowing around where I once had new ideas and motivation. I've been teaching a few yoga classes a week for the last six months and staring at my camera, willing her to be my friend again. So far she hasn't complied. I'm freaking out, Jules."

"That year on the street took a lot out of you. You got really close to some of the women, and seeing them suffer would be tough on anyone, but especially to an empath like you, you old softie. Be patient with yourself."

"You're probably right. I'm working through it in therapy, so I'm having a handle on it. To tell you the truth, I'm just fed up with everything. I'm sick of the city, and I'm sick of feeling sad and guilty all the time since Becks and I broke up. And I miss you! I hate that you moved halfway across the world. How is it? Do you love it?"

"I don't want to be a bitch and gloat while you're feeling so down ..." Jules began.

"No, please, go ahead. At least one of us is happy, and I want to live vicariously through you. Tell me everything!"

Jules had fulfilled her lifelong dream of wanting to live in France and moved to Aix-en-Provence in southern France the previous year. She had spent a semester there as a college student and fallen in love with the city. Twenty-five years later she decided that it was now or never, so she rented out her apartment, took a sabbatical from work, and booked a ticket. Jules had dual citizenship because her parents were French, and she spoke the language fluently. Initially she'd thought that she would only stay for six months or so, but that was over a year ago and she showed no signs of wanting to come back to Canada.

"Clem, I don't think I'm coming back," she told her friend now. "Life is so different here, so much more laid-back and relaxed. I love it! Oh, and I got a job!"

"You did? Where? And what about your job here?"

"I quit my job here. Because guess what: I got hired at an art gallery! It doesn't pay much, but between the rent coming in from my Toronto apartment and my savings, I'm fine. And you know the best part?" Jules paused for a moment.

"What? What's the best part? You met someone?" Clementine guessed.

"No, even better. I've been painting, Clem. I'm painting every day, and I'm not half bad, and that gallery that I've started working at –" she paused again for dramatic effect.

"What?! Spit it out, woman!" Clementine shouted.

"They agreed to feature three of my paintings!" Jules shouted back.

"Oh Jules, that's fantastic. Ohmygod, I'm so excited for you! That's your dream! You are actually living your fucking dream, you crazy, wonderful woman!"

Jules loved art. She had a degree in art history, she had been a prolific painter in college, and she had dreamed of becoming an artist and making a living of it. But after college she couldn't find a job, she was riddled with self-doubt, and then she met Matt.

Matt was a dentist, a self-proclaimed realist, and the asshole who had killed Jules' dream. Shortly after he'd proposed he had convinced her that it was time for her to grow up and "get serious with her life", and according to him that meant to have a "sensible career", a mortgage, and a kid. Jules got all three in that order: she became a dental hygienist; bought a house with Matt, who was now her husband; and then had a daughter, Paula. She stopped painting, became majorly depressed, and was desperately unhappy for years before she finally decided that she needed to leave Matt if she ever wanted to become herself again.

Jules got divorced on her fortieth birthday, "the best birthday present of my life" as she put it. She also received a generous divorce settlement, and to her surprise found that Matt was a much better ex-husband than he'd ever been a husband.

"He isn't a bad man," she'd told Clementine after they met at a yoga class six years ago, hit it off immediately, and went for coffee afterwards.

"He's just incredibly narrow-minded and boring."

"Well, he *is* a dentist," Clementine pointed out. "They are not exactly known for being the adventurous type."

"Matt is boring even for dentists' standards. Living with him was slowly killing me. I felt like I couldn't breathe, like he was suffocating me. I couldn't be myself, and after a while I didn't even know who I was anymore." Jules stared thoughtfully into her chai latte before continuing: "But he's a wonderful father to our daughter Paula. And I'm so grateful that I have her, which I wouldn't without him. So it all worked out in the end! But enough about me. Tell me everything about yourself!"

They had talked until the coffee shop closed and then continued in Clementine's apartment until three in the morning. That night they became best friends.

Jules had slowly started tiptoeing her way back into the art scene, reconnecting with some of her college friends, going to exhibitions and galleries, and spending many Sunday afternoons at the Art Gallery of Ontario. But she didn't paint. The fire she used to have inside her had been extinguished, and Jules was convinced nothing could ever rekindle it.

But then she'd had a health scare two years ago, not knowing for three terrifying weeks if she had breast cancer or not, until the lumpectomy results finally came back negative. During that time she thought about everything she'd never done but wanted to do, and promised herself that if she got through this ordeal alive, she would go for it.

That's how she'd ended up in France, and to her delighted surprise she found that she could paint in her little apartment on the top floor of an old building, with the windows wide open to let the mild breeze in and her head filled with inspiration gathered on her long walks through the charming streets of the provincial town.

34

Clementine was thrilled for her friend. "I'm so proud of you, Jules. You took a huge risk and it's paying off!"

"Thank you, Clem. I miss you and Paula like crazy, of course, but that aside, this is what I've always wanted. I never thought I'd ever be this happy."

"You deserve it." Clementine fell silent then, feeling a wave of misery wash over her. She sighed. "I feel so stuck, Jules. I honestly don't know what's wrong. Sure, I'm still hurting after the breakup and I miss you, but it's more than that. I'm having a serious case of the blahs. I can't work, I'm bored, and I find everything and everyone utterly and completely dull."

"You have ennui," Jules said softly. "You, my friend, need an adventure."

* * *

Clementine took her friend's words to heart. Over the next few weeks she looked inward, searching for her deepest desire. She knew from experience that the answer was only to be found inside of her, not coming from the outside, so she meditated, continued her yoga practice, and went on long walks, waiting to work out what her body was trying to tell her. She was convinced that her artistic block was a sign that something wasn't right in her life, and that her creative spark would come back once she figured out what it was and did something about it.

What slowly emerged was that she felt trapped. She had lived in Toronto her whole life and had never considered moving anywhere else. Now she wondered why. Sure, her family was here, most of her friends lived here, and it was a convenient location for work, but were those the real reasons? Or had she stayed out of convenience? Habit? Fear of the unknown? She had no idea. All she knew was that somewhere along the way she'd stopped living, and that being with Becks had a lot to do with it.

Her ex Becks was an introvert with anxiety issues. They had been together for ten years, and for most of that time her anxiety had been manageable. But once COVID hit it got completely out of control. Becks had been terrified of the disease, locked herself inside her house and refused to come out. When Clementine came over, she had to leave her clothes outside the door and take a shower before Becks would touch her, and she developed a compulsive hand-washing habit, washing her hands up to seventy times a day. Becks had always been uneasy about Clementine's job, but when she started photographing drug addicts and prostitutes it had pushed Becks over the edge. She couldn't handle it and begged Clementine to abandon her project, something she wasn't willing to do. Clementine was passionate about her work, and as much as she loved her girlfriend, she knew that giving up this project wouldn't be enough. Whatever her next project was going to be would also be too much for Becks. The entire outside world was too much for Becks.

Beck's OCD and anxiety disorder destroyed their relationship. Clementine did her best to help her, talked her into getting therapy and tried to coax her outside the house, but despite therapy and giving her as much time and patience as she could muster, Becks didn't get better.

In the end, Clementine couldn't do it anymore. She felt like the worst person on the planet for leaving someone who was clearly sick, but it was making her sick too, and she couldn't continue to live like that. The breakup had been brutal, with lots of tears on both sides, and she would have taken it back and stayed if Becks hadn't urged her to go. "You deserve more than this," she had told her with tears streaming down her face. "I want you to live a bigger life than the one we have together. I won't get better as long as you make it so easy and comfortable for me to stay here, so I need you to leave. Go out into the big, wide world, spread your wings, and fly."

Clementine had protested, but in the end, she had given in. And what had she been doing with her newfound freedom? Nothing. She was still in the same place, still stuck, except without the companionship. No wonder she was depressed.

And then an idea occurred to her. A wild, crazy idea that electrified her and hit her like a triple shot of espresso. What if she sold her place? What if she left Toronto and went out into the big, wide world, honouring Becks' request? What if she travelled west?

Clementine felt a rush of excitement hit her. She jumped up from the couch and did an impromptu dance, yelling into the air "I'm breaking free! I'm breaking free!" She stopped when her hip started aching, which happened alarmingly fast. "You're not thirty anymore," she reminded herself and sat down carefully.

She went over the logistics next. She could do her job from anywhere, assuming she'd feel inspired again at some point. A change of scenery was definitely more likely to make that happen than being stuck in the same old place. Her best friend didn't live here anymore. She had no partner, no kids to consider, and her parents were both gone. Selling her place wouldn't take long; real estate was hot, and she lived in a desirable area. *Nothing is stopping me but fear itself*, she realized. *Time to do it scared.*

The next three months passed in a whirlwind of activity. Clementine listed her apartment for sale and combed the classifieds for a used camper van. After several misses she pulled up one sunny March afternoon in front of a ginormous, turquoise former school bus that had been converted into a home.

An elderly couple greeted her warmly. "Hello, dear, you must be Clementine. I'm Dorothy, and this is my husband Harold."

"Nice to meet you both," Clementine said and shook hands.

Dorothy gestured at the bus behind her. "This is Matilda."

"The bus has a name?" Clementine asked delightedly.

"Oh yes, she's part of the family. It wasn't an easy decision for us to sell her, but Harold is having some health problems and I have a bad back. Our camping days are over, and it would be a shame if Matilda wasn't used anymore. We thought it better to pass her on to someone who will love her as much as we do. Matilda belongs on the road, not banished to a garage." She leaned in conspiratorially and whispered: "To be honest, it's been expensive to store her, and we thought we could put the money that we're spending on the garage to better use."

"She looks amazing from the outside," Clementine said, eager to check out the interior.

"Why don't you take a look inside on your own first? Meet her in private. Come out when you're ready and we'll answer all your questions. How does that sound?" Dorothy offered.

"Perfect! Thank you so much."

Clementine opened the door, stepped inside – and her mouth fell open in amazement. Matilda was *gorgeous*. She had wood floors, benches along one wall decorated with colourful pillows, and polka-dotted curtains in front of the windows. On the other side there was a beautiful kitchen with white cupboards and butcher block countertops, and a real wood-burning stove! Wood was stacked neatly in a little alcove next to the stove, and on the other side of it was a large dog bed on the floor. A hammock was hanging from the ceiling behind the driver's seat next to an empty bookshelf, just waiting to be filled with books and knickknacks.

At the end of the bus was a raised queen bed with storage underneath, and next to it was an adorable little bathroom with concrete floors and walls, a copper shower head, stained wood counters, and the teeniest little ceramic sink Clementine had ever seen.

She sank onto the bench to soak it all in, noticing more details: the little handmade wooden spice rack on the wall with handwritten labels on the spices; the fresh flowers on the table; the industrial-style lights along the walls. She knew that she was going to buy this bus; that Matilda was her ticket to a new life.

* * *

Clementine sold her apartment, all her furniture, and most of her possessions, and learnt as much about Matilda as she could. Dorothy and Harold, upon realizing how little she knew about RVs or living in a converted bus, had made her a detailed manual about how everything worked. The bus was powered by solar panels, a charge controller, 600AH batteries, and a 1,000-watt inverter, and had two propane tanks for the stove, water heater, and fridge. Clementine watched countless YouTube videos to learn how a composting toilet worked, how to refuel the bus, how to fill up the propane tanks, where and how to empty the grey water tank (and what it was), how to check the batteries, and where to get fresh water. She also joined an online forum about van life that taught her where she could park for free at night, and they gave her a checklist of everything that needed to be checked and/or changed regularly: oil filter, air filter, coolant, engine oil, radiator coolant, brake fluid, transmission fluid, windshield fluid, tires, bulbs, battery, brakes – they went on, but Clementine stopped reading to prevent herself from freaking out.

Deciding that she wasn't going to become an expert in bus maintenance any time soon, she drove Matilda to a friend who was a mechanic and let him check everything thoroughly. She upgraded her CAA membership to the highest level and made sure it included coverage for her converted bus – she had a feeling she would need it.

A month later, on a rainy day in mid-April, Clementine started on her journey. She didn't have a specific destination in mind aside from going west, and she also didn't know if she was going to live in Matilda forever or if she wanted to live in a place without wheels at some point.

"Don't try to solve a problem that hasn't happened yet," Jules advised her during one of their frequent phone calls. She was full of excitement and support and kept telling Clementine that she was going to have a life-changing experience. "You don't have to figure everything out just yet. You have your home, your camera, money in the bank, and me just an email or phone call away. All you need to know is how far you want to go today. Keep an open mind, see new places, meet new people, and the answer will present itself when you are ready."

"You are very wise," Clementine told her friend affection- ately. "I'm a bit nervous, but mostly I feel alive! For the first time in years. Who knew you could feel like this in your fifties?"

"Being young is overrated," Jules confirmed. "I wouldn't want to be back in my twenties or thirties for all the tea in China. They're just riddled with uncertainty, insecurities, and money worries."

"And dieting, people pleasing, playing by the rules of the patriarchy, and thinking you have to fit into a category."

Clementine had spent decades in sexual confusion, going from thinking she needed to be straight to believing she was gay to finally coming to the conclusion that she was neither, or both. She had had relationships with both men and women, being drawn to the person, not the gender. For years she had identified herself as bisexual, but that didn't feel quite right either. It wasn't until she was in her forties that she heard the term pansexual, which in its simplest translation means being attracted to all genders. For the first time in her life, she felt seen. "I like the wine, not the label," as David put it in her favourite sitcom *Schitt's Creek*, which summed it up perfectly.

No, Clementine didn't miss her younger years one bit.

"Open road, here we come!" she said loudly as she rolled out of Toronto. She couldn't wait to find out what would happen next.

Chapter 4

The first time Matilda broke down was somewhere in Wisconsin. "Your transmission is toast," the small-town mechanic she had been towed to informed Clementine, and then added, "it's going to take a few days before I can fix it."

"Okay," Clementine replied good-naturedly. This was all part of the experience, right? It gave her time to explore this cute little town she had never been to. She threw a few clothes, toiletries, and her book into a bag, grabbed her camera, and gave Matilda an affectionate pat on her rear when the mechanic wasn't looking before setting off in search of a hotel.

Clementine stayed three nights in a slightly dilapidated motel, exploring the town during the day, eating in diners and coffee shops, and watching trashy TV in her room at night. Once Matilda was fixed she continued on, heading north to Lake Superior, and staying on the scenic route along the shore until she headed west again.

Clementine soon developed a routine. She got up around seven, made coffee, and drank it sitting outside, wrapped up in a blanket against the morning chill, enjoying the view. Whenever she could she'd park in nature, looking for quiet roads with rest areas, free campsites, logging roads, or trail head parking lots. Once she'd finished her morning coffee she'd do yoga, either outside or in Matilda, to keep her body flexible and her mind peaceful and strong.

In June she started looking for sleeping places by a lake or river so she could go for a quick cold dip in the morning – naked when nobody was around. She squealed with the shock of the cold water, but nothing made her feel more alive than submerging herself fully, feeling every fiber of her body vibrating with life.

And Clementine could take photos again. She took photos of the deer, elk, moose, and antelopes she spotted from the perch of her driver's seat, pulling over abruptly whenever she saw them because she wanted to get the shot before the animals were gone.

Just before dusk, she often tracked coyotes trotting across the wide-open fields, looking for prey, through her zoom lens. At night she could sometimes hear them yipping to each other, and once in a while she even heard wolves howling in the distance.

She photographed every sunrise and sunset, how the light reflected off the rivers and lakes she stopped at, and she took thousands of pictures of the open road: of the seemingly endless sky over Saskatchewan, the morning fog just before the sun broke through, of tumbleweeds being blown across the road that made her think of how she'd described to Jules what her brain had felt like back in January. Her mental block was gone, replaced by an insatiable appetite for photographing nature, animals, and landscapes. Clementine had only ever worked in cities and specialized in portrait photography, and the challenge of figuring out something new energized her.

During her drives she listened to music, local radio stations, podcasts, and audiobooks, or spent hours in silence, letting her mind wander freely, thinking of everything and nothing. At night she'd light a fire in Matilda's stove, and either read, talk to friends on the phone, or watch Netflix on her laptop.

Just past Winnipeg she had a flat. Clementine tried to change it herself, but she couldn't loosen the lug nuts, so she had to call CAA again. The guy who arrived changed it for her, full of admiration for her bus, but leaving with this ominous warning: "It's good that you are a premier member, we'll be hearing a lot from you."

Clementine frequently left the highway to drive through small towns, sometimes editing on her laptop from the public library or a coffee shop, sometimes staying in larger camp-grounds if she wanted company. She also started having one meal a day in a restaurant, usually a diner or mom-and-pop place, to have some human interaction. Despite that and talking to Jules regularly on the phone, she felt lonely.

She mentioned that during lunch one day as the grandmoth-erly owner of the diner was asking her about herself. "I sold my place and almost everything I own to go on an adventure," was Clementine's usual line whenever she was asked about who she was, where she was going, and what she was doing. "I was tired of being stuck in a box," she would continue, and then end with, "I love the freedom! This is the best thing I've ever done." Which was the truth – for the most part.

"I miss sharing this with someone," she confided to the kind diner owner, Fran. There was something nurturing and compassionate about her that made Clementine say more than she usually did. "My best friend lives in France, I'm single, and sometimes I'm lonely," she admitted.

"I may have a solution for that," Fran said, looking at

Clementine thoughtfully. "A friend of mine had puppies a few months ago, and she sold all of them except for one. She couldn't find a home for him, so she kept him, but she doesn't need him. Would you want to take a look?"

"A dog?" Clementine wondered aloud. "I've never had a dog."

"It might not be a bad idea to have one with you, travelling alone as a woman," Fran said. "And dogs are wonderful companions. I've had dogs all my life, and I can guarantee you that they are the best friends you could ever ask for. Nobody loves you the way a dog does."

"How old is he? And what breed?"

"He's a mutt, honey. The mother is a Shepherd mix, and nobody knows who the father is. He's six months old, and he has a lovely personality. Do you want to take a look at him?"

"Sure," Clementine decided. Fran called her friend who invited her to come right over, and Fran gave her directions. Half an hour later Clementine pulled up in front of a fenced yard – and a large, black, fluffy *something* catapulted itself towards the fence. For one heart-stopping moment she thought it was a black bear, and she instinctively jumped back into the bus and slammed the door shut behind her. But then she heard the bear bark and realized that this must be a dog. *I sincerely hope that's not the puppy*, she thought, and stayed in Matilda until a woman came up to the fence as well.

"George, calm down," she said, pulling the beast back by its collar. "Are you the lady Fran sent over?" she called, and Clementine carefully opened the door and exited Matilda.

"Yes, I am," she replied, keeping a watchful eye on the animal now sitting next to the woman, tail wagging frantically. "I'm Clementine." She hesitated outside the fence. "Is it safe to come in?"

The woman laughed. "He's a lamb," she assured Clementine. "The worst thing he'll do is lick you to death. Come in, come in. I'm Ruth," she introduced herself. "And this is George," she said, pointing to the big dog beside her.

"Wow," Clementine breathed as she slowly approached the pair and shook Ruth's proffered hand. "He is big."

"Hold out your hand and let him sniff it," Ruth advised.

Clementine reluctantly did as she was told. George sniffed it, and then, just as advertised, started to lick her hand enthusiastically. Clementine's fear melted away. "Who's a good boy?" she cooed, petting the dog who promptly pressed his entire body against her legs. She scratched behind his ears, and he closed his eyes in ecstatic bliss.

"He likes you," Ruth said with a smile.

"The feeling is mutual," Clementine assured her.

The two women spent an hour in the yard with the puppy, watching him play, and Clementine asked her every question under the sun she could think of about dog ownership. How much did he eat? How big would he be fully grown? Was living in a bus suitable for a dog? Was he house-trained? Did he listen well?

Ruth answered patiently, telling her that dogs ate less than people thought, that she had no idea how much more he was going to grow, that dogs simply wanted to be with their owner, so being with her 24/7 in a large bus was heaven for him, yes, he was house trained, and yes, he listened when called, and could sit and lie down on command. Clementine tried it out by calling George's name. He bounded over, pink tongue lolling out of the side of his mouth, and when she said firmly, "George, sit," he promptly sat down. She crouched down until she was at eye level with the dog and looked into his trusting eyes. "What do you think, George? Do you want to come and live with me in Matilda?" In response he wagged his tail and licked her face.

Ruth gave her his bed, leash, toys, bag of dog food, and medical documents, and told her to call anytime should she have more questions. "He's a good boy," she said as they were saying goodbye. "I have a feeling you two will be very happy together."

Clementine had been worried that George might miss his old owner, but he never showed any sign of it. He inspected every inch of his new home, wagging his tail, and then curled up contentedly on his bed that she placed next to the wood stove, just where the previous dog bed had been. When she was driving he sat in the passenger seat next to her, and after she invited him onto her bed on the third night, he never slept anywhere else. Clementine hadn't exactly thought she was in danger before, but she was surprised by how much safer she felt now with George by her side. Early one morning he chased off a bear who sniffed around Matilda, growled loudly when someone knocked on her door late at night at a busy campground which elicited a distinct "holy shit, let's get outta here!", and his presence gave her the courage to go for walks at night in areas she hadn't dared go before.

Fran, the nice diner owner, had been right about the sense of safety a dog gave a single woman traveling alone, and she was right about something else as well: George was the solution to her occasional bouts of loneliness. Clementine started talking to him and soon had lengthy conversations, not feeling embarrassed in the least that she was speaking to a dog. "I've had worse conversationalists than you, Georgie-boy," she told him affectionately, and he looked at her as if he knew exactly what she meant.

Life with George became a lot more fun. Being a woman in her fifties, Clementine had become largely invisible, ignored by catcalling men and sales assistants in stores, and no longer the recipient of the incredibly annoying demand to "smile more". She far preferred it to the harassment she'd had to endure when she was younger, but it was inconvenient when she wanted to be seen as a person. With George by her side the spotlight had been turned back on. But this time it wasn't leering looks and inappropriate comments that came her way – people were smiling, wanting to meet her dog, or keeping a wary eye on him if they were scared. George made Clementine feel powerful, safe, respected, and seen. "If I would have known a dog does that to a woman I would have gotten one years ago," she told George, and then added "but then it wouldn't have been *you* who's my first doggy love, and you are the best boy in the world!"

While her relationship with George was thriving, the one with Matilda was rockier. Matilda turned out to be a cranky old lady, who apparently wasn't thrilled to be working this hard at the ripe old age of thirty. It was August, and either the engine didn't like the hot outside temperature, or something was broken, but it kept overheating. Whenever she saw smoke billowing out from under the hood she panicked. Not wanting to risk the whole thing blowing up, she called CAA whenever she saw smoke, ruefully remembering the tow truck operator's prediction about seeing a lot of them. He had certainly been right about that.

Before entering Banff National Park, Matilda seemed to lose power, and her mileage reclined rapidly. The diagnosis was that the compression on two cylinders was zero, meaning some

48

valve or another needed to be replaced. Clementine couldn't be bothered to listen to the technical details, and simply asked the two questions she had become depressingly familiar with: "How long will it take?" and "how much?"

While she was in yet another motel, waiting for the latest repairs to be done, she considered her options. She had been on the road for four months, driving over 7,000 kilometres, and it looked like Matilda wasn't having it anymore. Who could blame her? Thirty years in bus years was probably the equivalent to about eighty-nine in human years, and most eighty-nine-year-olds didn't do cartwheels anymore either. Clementine had grown very fond of Matilda, thinking of her as the third member of her little family consisting of George and her, and she figured Matilda deserved her retirement. "George, it's time to find a place to settle down," she told her attentively listening dog. He agreed.

She didn't know yet where to move to, but one thing she knew for sure: she didn't want to go back to Toronto. That realization both surprised and pleased her, because it meant that leaving had been the right decision. Clementine had enough of big city living, and besides, she suspected that it would be close to impossible and very expensive to keep Matilda in a large city. Selling her was out of the question, so she was going to look for a place where she could keep her bus in the yard, to be taken out for leisurely drives once in a while. Since spending so much time in small towns, Clementine had fallen in love with them, charmed by the friendliness and helpfulness of the locals, the restaurants and coffee shops where people knew each other, and the prospect of becoming part of a community. She had a new goal: to find a town that could become home.

* * *

On a sunny afternoon in early October they crested a hill, and when Clementine saw the view she gasped, pulled over, and turned off Matilda's ignition. "Look at this, George," she whispered. In the valley below was a picture-perfect village sprawled out in the sunshine. It looked like it came straight out of a children's book: colourful houses nestled between trees, a river that sparkled in the sun wound its way through the little town, and in the distance were mountain peaks already covered in snow. The air coming in through Clementine's open window was fresh and crisp, smelling of pine, leaves, and a hint of wood smoke. "It's so pretty!" she told George, smiling broadly. "Let's drive down and check it out." She started the bus up and pulled back on the road. As they approached the town she saw the name of it for the first time:

Summerfield
Where Dreams Turn into Reality

The town was as charming as Clementine had hoped it would be. Knowing from experience that it could be difficult to find parking for Matilda, she left her at a grocery store's large parking lot at the edge of town, clipped the leash on George's collar, and headed towards downtown with him by her side. They strolled on a sidewalk under a canopy of red, gold, and honey-coloured leaves of maple, birch, and aspen trees, fallen leaves crunching under Clementine's boots. The delicious smells of warm apple cider and pumpkin-spiced hot drinks wafted out of a cozy-looking coffee shop, and she passed by a bookstore, library, antique shop, and a unique

50

gift store with a gorgeous window display filled with candles, home decor, throw pillows, art, knitted scarves, jewellery, and more. The town centre had a park at its heart with a gazebo, several benches, an ice cream parlour, and a diner nearby, which was Clementine's next stop. She was hungry, but more importantly, she wanted to find out more about Summerfield, and diners were the best places for information. She told George to sit and tied him to a bench in front of the diner, making sure she could see him from the window. "You stay and wait for me, okay? I'll bring you a treat when I come back," she told him, and he wagged his tail in response.

A bell cheerfully announced Clementine's arrival as she pushed open the door. There were half a dozen tables scattered around the room, surrounded by wooden chairs painted in bright blue, green, yellow, and purple. About half of them were occupied with people eating an early dinner, drinking coffee, and chatting. Golden sunlight streamed through the lace-curtained windows, and the smell of coffee, toast, and burger grease hung in the air.

"Hello there," the grey-haired lady behind the counter greeted her warmly. "Sit anywhere you like. Coffee?"

"Yes, please," Clementine answered, and pulled up a stool at the counter.

"I saw you with your dog outside," the woman said while pouring coffee. "What a beautiful animal! And look at him now –" They both glanced through the window at George, who was sitting and facing the building, his ears alert. "He's waiting for you so calmly, not pulling on the leash or barking. What a good boy!"

"Yes, he's great," Clementine agreed with a smile. "I got lucky with him."

"You are new in town," the older woman stated, handing Clementine a menu. "Just passing through?"

"Actually," Clementine began, "I've been travelling in a converted school bus for the last six months, and I'm looking for a place to settle down. What can you tell me about Summerfield?"

"Oh, it's a wonderful town. I was born and raised here, and I couldn't imagine living anywhere else. Very strong community spirit, the people are nice, and you have everything you need here."

"Sounds great!" Clementine said. She ordered a burger and fries, and then asked the friendly owner – who introduced herself as Tilly – about access to medical care, local businesses, and the housing market. While they were chatting, the diner filled up, and Tilly greeted all the newcomers by name.

"You have a lot of regulars?" Clementine asked her.

"Oh yes," Tilly replied cheerfully. "I have a lot of old bachelors and widowers who eat here every day. Many of the widowers never learnt to cook, and they would starve if it weren't for me. But it's more about the social aspect than the food. Meeting here gets them out of the house, they have company, and if I've learnt anything in my life it's that men are bigger gossips than women. You should listen to them! Chattier than a bunch of magpies." Tilly leaned in conspiratorially. "A word of advice: only believe half of what they tell you."

Clementine nodded sagely. "The only trouble is: which half?"

Tilly laughed. "I like you! I hope you decide to stay. Call the real-estate-agent I told you about, she'll set you up. We have quite a few houses for sale right now, I'm sure you'll find something."

Clementine promised she would, paid her bill and said goodbye. George went wild with happiness upon her return. "Did you miss me? I was only gone for half an hour, sweet boy," she laughed, hugging him tight.

They took a different route back, passing more stores, a couple of restaurants, a movie theatre, community hall, and an arts centre that offered a variety of creative classes such as pottery, painting, making Christmas cards, and crafting for children.

It really was a delightful little town. Clementine fished the real-estate-agent's business card Tilly had given her out of her pocket, pulled her phone out of her bag, and punched the number in.

The real-estate-agent, Susan, picked Clementine up the next morning from the local Walmart's parking lot where she had stayed overnight. The first three houses she showed her weren't a fit – one was too large, the second too shabby, and the third one didn't have a yard.

"I have a beautiful Craftsman house," Susan told her as they got back into her car. "It's 1,300 square feet, two bedrooms, one bath, with a large yard. The neighbourhood is one of our most sought-after ones, Pleasant Hill, with a gorgeous view over the town." As she was talking they were leaving the town centre behind and driving towards a wooded hill dotted with houses.

"Is it up there?" Clementine asked, admiring the trees in their spectacular fall foliage surrounding the houses.

"Yes, that's it," Susan replied. "It's a well-kept, cherished neighbourhood. Many people have lived there for years or decades, so it's a close-knit community." She continued to praise the virtues of the area and then moved on to the many superb qualities of the house.

The house *was* pretty. It was a one-story bungalow in earth tones with two tapered columns flanking the main entrance. The neat front yard was small, but the backyard was large and shaded, with enough room to park Matilda. As Clementine walked through the house, charmed by the open fireplace, built-in bookcases, exposed ceiling beams, and a reading nook off the living room, a deep sense of peace enveloped her.

She had come home.

Chapter 5

The doorbell rang, making Valerie jump. Oh God, who could that be? She started shaking almost immediately, frozen to her spot on the couch. Should she pretend she wasn't home? But her lights were on, so they probably knew she was. And her car was in the driveway. *Shit.* Not for the first time did Valerie wish that she'd have a large dog who could protect her, who would bark so fiercely that whoever was at the door would run away in fear, being as scared as she was for once. *Give them a taste of their own medicine.*

The doorbell rang again. Valerie lifted her wine glass to her mouth with a trembling hand, taking a fortifying sip. In a spurt of defiance, supported by liquid courage, she jumped up. "If it's *her* I'll give her a piece of my mind," she muttered to herself. "She can't just show up uninvited to harass me. I'll tell her where she can go and how to get there," she continued, psyching herself up. With a flourish she opened the front door.

"Holly, how dare y–" She stopped. It wasn't Holly Kent at her doorstep. A strange woman was standing in front of her, and her appearance rendered Valerie momentarily speechless.

The woman was larger than life. She was tall and big, with waist-length grey hair and a smile that rippled like waves across her tanned, freckled face. She was dressed in colourful, flowing clothes, and sitting next to her was an enormous black dog with his tongue lolling out.

"Hi there," the stranger said with a twinkle in her eyes. "I take it you were expecting someone else? Or not expecting, judging from your fiery greeting?" She waited for a beat, and when Valerie remained silent she continued.

"I'm Clementine, your new neighbour. And this is George," she said, gesturing to the animal next to her. "The third member of our family is Matilda, my temperamental bus. You might have seen her, she's parked in front of my house, hard to miss."

Valerie had seen the bus. Just like the stranger – what was her name? – said, it was impossible to miss. Humongous and a vivid shade of blue-green, it stood out like a sore thumb. So did the woman herself, with her bright-coloured clothes, giant dog, and her overall *otherness*.

Valerie finally found her voice. "Uhm, hi," she said haltingly. "Sorry about that, I thought you were someone else. I'm Valerie." She offered her hand, and the other woman shook it warmly.

"A pleasure to meet you, Valerie," she beamed. "I would have brought something, but I'm faced with the frightening task of furnishing an entire house from scratch, and I need advice on where to go to buy furniture and kitchen things and stuff like that, so I thought I pop over empty-handed, pick your brain, and once I have a functioning kitchen, I'll bake up a storm and show my gratitude by bringing you a selection of everything. I make an excellent apple pie and fabulous lemon bars!"

Valerie was charmed. "Would you like to come in?" She eyed the dog warily. "I have a cat, is your dog okay with cats?"

"Oh yes. All he wants to do is play. He's still a puppy – he's only nine months old. I'll keep him by my side though, in case your cat doesn't like dogs."

"Thanks, I'd appreciate that," Valerie said gratefully. "Come in, both of you!"

She led them both into the living room, picking up glasses, an empty wine bottle, and a pair of dirty socks on the way. "Sorry about the mess," she apologized, blushing. "I didn't expect company."

"Don't apologize," Clementine said firmly. "You can do whatever you want in your own home. It's beautiful! I really appreciate you being so gracious to an unannounced visitor."

Valerie blushed again, this time with pleasure. "You're welcome. I wasn't doing anything special anyway, just watching TV. Sit down! Can I get you a glass of wine?"

"No thanks, I don't drink."

"Oh! Okay." Valerie was taken aback for a moment. Everybody she knew drank. "Can I make you some tea then? Or a glass of water? I don't think I have anything else ..."

"Tea would be lovely. Thank you so much! Let me help you." She jumped up, surprisingly nimble for a woman her size. "George, stay." She pointed at the ground, and the dog obediently laid down, his massive head resting on his front paws.

Valerie led her into the kitchen, heading straight to the kettle. "What tea do you like? I have herbal, green, Earl Grey ..."

"Earl Grey would be great, thank you."

While Valerie busied herself with filling the kettle she asked: "What was your name again? I'm so sorry, I have this terrible habit of forgetting names as soon as someone has introduced themselves to me."

The other woman laughed. "I used to be the same! But I have a trick how to remember them. When someone introduces themselves to you, repeat their name back to them. That's what I did earlier when you first told me your name. 'Nice to meet you, Valerie.' It's not foolproof, but it works at least half the time. I'm Clementine."

Valerie grinned. "Nice to meet you, *Clementine*."

"Another way to remember names is to associate them with something. In my case, I'm wearing orange today, and my butt is as round as a clementine orange. Does that help?"

Valerie burst out laughing. "You're something else! Now I'm certainly not going to forget your name ever again."

"Good."

Valerie filled two mugs with boiling water, put out milk and honey, and told Clementine to help herself. Once they'd both prepared their teas how they liked them they went back into the living room. George was still lying in the same spot, and to Valerie's surprise, Smokey the cat was snuggled up against his side, purring loudly.

"Look at that," she said in amazement. "I had no idea Smokey likes dogs!"

Clementine smiled. "He's a special dog."

They settled onto the couch, facing each other, and chatted for a while, covering their lives in broad strokes. Valerie told her about her job, her late husband, where she grew up, and that she'd lived in Vancouver for most of her adult life.

Clementine told her about her trip across the country, what made her take it in the first place, and how she'd found George. They bonded over both being childless, single, and middle-aged, and exchanged perimenopause war stories. Then Valerie asked: "What made you choose Summerfield?"

Clementine thought for a moment before answering. "It felt right. As soon as I saw it I got a vibe that this is going to be home. It's the first time I've chosen my place, it's so empowering! I've lived in Toronto all my life, not questioning it. I happened to be born there, and I stayed, because why not? I thought everything I needed was there. But I realized last winter that I have never chosen Toronto on purpose. It wasn't my choice; it was an accident. An accident of birth, if you will. And while I didn't know where I wanted to live, I knew that I wanted to be in charge for once. I didn't want to wake up in twenty years noticing for the first time I had lived a life dictated by chance and circumstance. I wanted to be in the driver's seat, you know?

"My best friend Jules upended her life two years ago and moved to France, a lifelong dream of hers. She's an amazing woman, I hope you'll meet her one day! So brave and creative and full of life. Anyway, she took a risk, and it paid off big time. I wanted to take a risk too, because even if it didn't work out, at least *I* made the mistake, and it didn't just happen *to* me. Do you know what I mean?"

"I think so," Valerie said slowly. "I never lived alone until Luke passed away. I went straight from my parents' house to Luke, with the briefest interlude of living in a dorm. But even then I spent most of my time at Luke's." She went quiet, lost in thought. Clementine didn't interrupt her thoughts, waiting patiently.

"You know what?" Valerie asked. "I've just realized something. My entire life has been decided by other people. By Luke, my parents, my friend Hattie. Both Hattie and Luke chose me, and I just went along with it. Moving here was Luke's idea. Our friends were his friends first, and never felt like mine. Not really. I feel closer to you than I feel to them, and I've just met you!" Valerie fell into a shocked silence. Then she said: "I'm forty-four years old, and I have no idea who I am," and she burst into tears.

"Hey, it's okay!" Clementine said soothingly and pulled Valerie into a hug. "Let it all out," she murmured, patting Valerie's back gently. "Have a nice, long cry."

"I've been so lonely," Valerie cried. "I can't function without Luke. How pathetic is that?"

"It's not pathetic at all, it's completely normal," Clementine assured Valerie, still hugging her. "You've lived with him for most of your adult life, of course this is new and scary."

"Can I tell you something terrible?" Valerie lifted her teary face up and looked at Clementine.

"Of course you can. Anything."

"While Luke was alive –" she faltered, searching for words – "sometimes I hated him!" she burst out. "He was such a know-it-all, so domineering, it always had to be his way. He didn't know the meaning of the word compromise. I would fantasize about life without him, sometimes, thinking it would be better. But now I have it, and it's not better, it's awful, and I miss him so much, and I feel so guilty for having those horrible thoughts." She burst into a fresh round of tears that prevented her from speaking.

"Honey, it's normal to have those thoughts. Everybody gets them from time to time. Living with somebody is hard! You see all of them, unfiltered, the good and the bad and the annoying. Of course you get frustrated! It would be weird if you didn't. That doesn't mean you didn't love him. I can tell that you did, that you still do, and that's the reason you are in so much pain. You've been together a long time, right?"

"Twenty-four years, married twenty-two," Valerie hiccuped.

"You've already lived an entire lifetime, and that time has come to an end. You are grieving not only Luke, but the life with him and the woman you have been with him." Clementine leaned in closer. "Can I tell you a secret?"

Valerie nodded.

"There's more than just one version of us. Women are far too complex for that. We will be many different women in our lifetime, and we are always evolving. You are currently in a state of transformation, morphing from one version into another. Growth and transformation are painful, there's no doubt about that. But you know what?" Clementine squeezed Valerie's hand. "The pain is worth it. You are currently growing into a different, more independent woman." She leaned in conspiratorially. "And hopefully into a less well-behaved one."

Valerie calmed down after a while, wiping her eyes and blowing her nose. She looked at Clementine ruefully. "I can't believe I fell apart like this. I don't even know you! You're a stranger, a guest, and I completely lost it. I'm so embarrassed."

"Val, I've been there. I've had my share of breakdowns, believe me. Sometimes it's easier to confide in someone you don't know than in someone who you share a history with. It's absolutely fine; don't feel bad. We women have to be strong all the time, it's healthy to fall apart every so often. Good for the soul."

Valerie gave her an uncertain smile. "This is either the beginning of a wonderful friendship or you'll want nothing to do with me from now on."

Clementine squeezed her shoulder. "It's the first one. I'm honoured you felt safe enough to let your guard down in front of me. I would never betray that trust."

"I appreciate that. Thank you."

Valerie took a deep breath and then let it out slowly. "Okay, now I have to tell you something very unpleasant about your new neighbourhood. I didn't plan on doing it, but you deserve the truth. Forewarned is forearmed, and maybe there's still a way for you to back out of your house?"

"I don't think so, and I have no intention of backing out. What is it? Is my house haunted?"

"Ghosts would be better, trust me," Valerie said darkly.

"Now you've piqued my curiosity," Clementine smiled. "Spit it out, I can hardly wait!"

"Okay," Valerie began. "You know that we have a home-owner's association here, right? It must have been part of your contract."

"Yes, it was. To be honest, I didn't pay too much attention to the covenants. This is the country; how bad can it be?"

"Very bad!" Valerie hissed. "The couple who runs it, Holly and Homer Kent, are evil."

"Holly and Homer?" Clementine burst out laughing. "The Ho Hos? That's funny!"

Valerie didn't crack a smile. "No, listen. They are not your run-of-the-mill president and vice president. Holly and Homer run this neighbourhood with an iron fist. They are drunk with power, out of control. People are scared of them, so they do whatever they say just to stay on their good side."

"Come on," Clementine said doubtfully. "They are not the king and queen of the world, how much power can they have?"

"You don't get it," Valerie said with a real note of desperation in her voice. "They will want you to get rid of your bus. And probably of your dog, too! I think there might be a weight restriction for dogs in the rules. Holly is going to watch you like a hawk because you're new, and trust me, she will find more things you're doing wrong. Maybe there will be too many leaves on your lawn, or your patio furniture is wrong, or, or ..."

"Relax!" Clementine said soothingly. "The Ho Hos sound like classic bullies. You know that all bullies are cowards who are scared little children inside, right?"

"Clementine, listen. You have to take them seriously, please!" Valerie pleaded. "Holly and Homer have been president and vice president since founding the HOA. In fact, *they* were the ones who founded it. There's a board, but it's just for show. There's no democracy here – the Kents do whatever the hell they want. They threaten, torment, abuse, and they have a gift for turning people against each other. They make people spy on their neighbours and report any wrongdoings to them. You can't trust anyone here."

"Are you serious? In my experience, most people are nice and want to get along with each other."

"Not when they live in a dictatorship," Valerie said darkly. "It brings out the worst in people. I've only been here three years, so most of what I know is what other people have told me, but there are a lot of weird stories floating around. If Holly and Homer don't like someone, they tend to move away fairly quickly. And people are saying it's not always voluntarily."

"Let's disregard for a moment what people are saying. Did something bad happen to you? Are they threatening or harassing you?"

Valerie looked defeated. "They're making my life a living hell. They've been doing that almost from the moment we moved here. Holly took one look at us and decided she didn't like us. And Luke, well – he was the kind of guy who pushed back when you pushed him. He hated bullies, and he wasn't scared of them in the slightest. That's a bad combo, hate and fearlessness.

"Maybe the relationship between them and us could have been saved, or at least not deteriorated so horribly, if Holly hadn't reacted the way she did. But she said something really terrible, and that was it for Luke. From that moment on he detested her, and there was no way that he was going to abide by their rules. Luke had been looking forward to getting into gardening when we moved here, and that first winter he spent a lot of time researching different gardening techniques. During his research he came across rewilding." Valerie did a funny little movement of simultaneously sighing, smiling, and shaking her head in exasperation. "Do you know what it is?"

"I do! It's restoring land to its original form and then letting nature take over. This is most beneficial when done on a large scale, but its principles can be applied to backyards as well by planting native plants which support native animals. It's a wonderful way to restore ecosystems and support the environment," Clementine replied enthusiastically.

"Exactly. Unbeknownst to us at the time, unkempt yards and lawns that need mowing are Holly's pet peeve. She's a stickler for all the rules, but yard maintenance is the one she's most finicky about. When she saw that Luke wasn't planning on having a yard like everybody else she declared us enemies number one. I asked Luke if he would consider abandoning his rewilding plans for the sake of trying to fit in and playing by the rules, but he wouldn't hear of it. And then he died, leaving me all alone, and I'm not fearless. I'm scared all the time, so

64

I'm hiding in my house because I'm afraid to go outside. I'm constantly worried that they or one of their henchmen might insult me in my yard or out on the street."

Clementine had been listening attentively, absorbing it all. "You are no longer alone, Val. You have me now. We're going to fix this. Now, tell me exactly what happened."

Chapter 6

Three years earlier

"The Chapman house sold," Holly told Homer over breakfast.

"Do you know who bought it?" he asked.

"A couple from Vancouver, no kids. Middle-aged, I believe. I don't know anything else yet. I'll stop by as soon as they arrive, I heard they're moving in next month."

"Good," Homer grunted, and fell silent. He wasn't much of a morning person.

Holly had kept up her habit of visiting every house in the neighbourhood. What had started purely as means to sussing out allies and foes had proven to be an invaluable tool to know all the people who lived in Pleasant Hill. The notebook she had started thirty years ago had long been replaced by an extensive document on her computer consisting of thousands of pages, carefully backed up every night. It contained detailed folders on every single house with every occupant who'd ever lived there. The notes from the notebook she carried around with her during her daily inspection tour were immediately transferred to the document as soon as she got home.

But that wasn't all. Holly added everything she could find

out about the residents of Pleasant Hill and included it in their files – the more incriminating, the better. Affairs, gambling problems, trouble with the kids, problems at work, a fondness for drugs or alcohol, debt, mental health issues – everybody had something. She knew the political views of her neighbours, how well they complied with the lockdown restrictions, how they felt about wearing masks, if they drank more now than they did before the pandemic.

Her house was placed in a perfect location for keeping an eye on her domain: perched on a hill, overlooking half of the community. She'd bought a telescope years ago, ostensibly for stargazing, but in actuality to spy on the neighbours. For the houses she couldn't see from her place she used a combination of bribes, flattery, or threats to get other people to do it for her. She didn't like having to rely on others – they were never as thorough as her – but it couldn't be helped. Luckily they lived in the age of social media, and it was unbelievable how much people shared online these days.

Out of the forty-four houses in Pleasant Hill, thirty-six were on Facebook or Instagram. Not all of them posted regularly, and some had those annoying privacy settings on, preventing her from seeing their page, but the majority of residents posted at least once in a while, and a lot of them did regularly. She'd caught pet violations, unapproved tenants, illegally built structures, and someone's so-called "art" installation (an absolute eyesore) in their backyard because people posted pictures on their social media accounts. People's stupidity never ceased to amaze and delight Holly.

She'd taken the points system that she used in the beginning to score people's houses and attitudes, and developed it into a sophisticated ranking system. There were four categories:

house, yard, pets, and personal conduct.

The house category pertained to the look and upkeep of the house: it had to be repainted every five years in an approved colour, decorations were to be kept understated and tasteful, and seasonal decor was strictly regulated, prohibiting anything trashy and low-class such as going overboard with Christmas lights, those ghastly inflatable Halloween or Christmas decorations, and keeping seasonal decor up past the season. There were non-negotiable cut-off dates for all of them, and the day after, Holly was out at the crack of dawn to write up every house that hadn't taken their decorations down yet.

The yard category included adhering to an approved plant palette, staying within the acceptable lawn furniture and garden sculpture limits, having standardized picket fences, very strict policies regarding fruit-and vegetable-gardens, and rules against removing trees. The maintenance portion was one of Holly's favourites, because it was extensive with lots of room for failure, and almost impossible to comply with unless you had a gardener or lots of time to devote to the upkeep. It included but was not limited to: mowing the lawn regularly, weeding, watering, pruning, raking, seeding bare patches, keeping leaves off the lawn and sidewalk in the fall, removing snow of the sidewalk in the winter, removal of dead plants, and leaving garbage cans at the curb no longer than one hour after it had been emptied on garbage day.

The pets section of the official CC&Rs was pretty straightforward. No more than two dogs were permitted, and the owners had to clean up after them. Livestock such as chickens, pigs, or goats were prohibited. That was it, and it was woefully inadequate.

Holly's private ranking system went a lot deeper. She

despised large dogs, barking dogs, and those silly little purse dogs. She couldn't stand roaming cats (their habit of using the entire world as their litter box was abhorrent) and any and all birds. In a perfect world there would be no animals where people lived, because they created dirt and noise, they smelled, they were unruly, and they scattered their excrement all over the damn place. Holly would never understand or condone people's absurd obsession with animals.

While she technically couldn't use the HOA to enforce rules that didn't exist, many people were delightfully clueless about the actual rules. With her friend Mary's help she had successfully managed to create the impression that there was a weight limit for dogs, that cats weren't allowed outside their owner's houses or yards, and that there would be dire consequences for dogs who barked excessively. What exactly "barking excessively" meant was open to interpretation – her interpretation. Holly had bamboozled the batty owner of the local animal rescue shelter into believing that Pleasant Hill was rife with bad animal owners who neglected their poor critters and had called her more than once to collect "stray" cats (whose collars she had removed prior to her arrival), and to get her to "rescue" dogs that had been left outside in the yard for too long.

The last category in her system was *personal conduct*, her favourite. The phrasing in the official rules was purposely vague, summarizing personal conduct as "the requirement to maintain a general standard of neatness and attractiveness". She was extraordinarily pleased with that wording, because she had been using it countless times against people, particularly against the ones who annoyed her. Personal conduct included but was by no means limited to: noise restrictions, being

69

dressed appropriately, general disorderly conduct such as public drunkenness or disturbing the peace, how many vehicles should be allowed in front of one's house, the cleanliness and condition of said vehicles, and how long recreational vehicles such as trailers, boats, vans, motor homes, etc. were permitted to be parked on the street.

The highest score to reach on her private ranking system was two hundred – fifty per category – and the only house that consistently stayed at two hundred was her own. What could she say? She had high standards that were difficult to meet, and she refused to lower the bar just because other people weren't as disciplined as her. She had created a spreadsheet for every house, and she updated them regularly.

Nobody had ever seen her ranking system. It was for her eyes only, because she knew that people would think it was too strict, maybe even accuse her of being unreasonable. But she loved it. She loved reading through it, updating it, ranking the residents of Pleasant Hill according to it. It gave her great joy to see her name at the top, and wicked pleasure to think up ways of getting rid of the people on the bottom.

Doing that was an art, not a science. She had to strike the right balance between using the regular tools at her disposal when official HOA rules were violated – warnings, fines, threatening legal action – and getting more creative when it came to violations against her personal standards. It was a fine line, but she had nearly perfected it. Life was good in Pleasant Hill for Holly Kent in September of 2020.

* * *

A week into October, Holly got ready to meet the new people

who had moved into the Chapman house. She still knew annoyingly little about them, since the real-estate-agent who'd sold them the house wasn't one of her cronies. In fact, the woman positively hated her, a sentiment Holly reciprocated completely. "The silly cow thinks she's better than me," Holly muttered to herself, her blood boiling as she remembered how high and mighty the real-estate-agent had reacted to Holly's probing questions about her clients. All she'd wanted to know was their names, profession, and the three Ws: if they were white, western, and wealthy.

"This is private information," the real-estate-agent had said icily. "There are laws protecting clients from insufferably nosy people like yourself, and I'm not risking my licence to satisfy your curiosity. Even if there weren't laws, you'd be the last person on earth I'd tell anything. It's about time you learn to mind your own business and leave other people alone."

Holly had been speechless, and ever since that encounter she'd brooded over how best to pay the other woman back. But never mind that now – it was time to meet the new neighbours.

The Chapman house was one of the nicest houses in Pleasant Hill. It had five bedrooms and three bathrooms, had been fully remodeled only four years ago, and there had never been any problems with the different occupants of the house. It was within telescope distance to Holly, which is why she knew so much about it. Not only had she been inside the house several times, but the Chapman's never installed blinds and rarely closed their curtains, giving Holly an unimpeded view into half of the rooms. It was also one of the most expensive houses, which boded well for the new people's social standing. Money often meant at least a certain amount of class, which hopefully translated into order and neatness.

From the outside it looked promising. The car in the drive-way was a Mercedes, there were no pets in the yard, and everything appeared calm and quiet. Holly rang the doorbell and waited. No dog barking – another excellent sign. She could hear approaching footsteps and pasted a huge, insincere smile on her face. The door opened – and Holly's smile fell from her face like overripe fruit from a tree. She hastily took a step back.

"Hello," the man on the other side of the doorstep said pleasantly.

Holly stared at him with a mixture of fear and indignation.

"Can I help you?" the man inquired warily. He had a knowing look in his eyes.

"Are you from China?" Holly blurted out.

The man's face closed down. He regarded her coolly before answering, seemingly weighing his words carefully.

"No," he said eventually. "I'm from Vancouver. Who are you? Why are you here? What do you want?"

"You know what I mean," Holly said impatiently. "You are Asian. It's you Chinese people who are responsible for the pandemic. What are you doing here in my neighbourhood?"

"I own this house, and I want you to leave. You are incredibly rude. You come to *my* place and start attacking me with false, ignorant accusations. If you don't go I'll call the police."

"How dare you?" Holly shrieked. "You can't call the police on me. Do you know who I am?"

"No I don't, because you lack the common courtesy to introduce yourself. Frankly, I don't give a damn either, because I don't plan on ever speaking to you again. Get off my property!"

A woman had appeared behind him while he was speaking. She was white, with shoulder-length dark blond hair, and a conciliatory manner.

"What's going on?" she asked, looking from the man to Holly.

"I don't know, Val," the man said angrily. "This lady apparently has nothing better to do than ring strangers' doors and start insulting them for no reason. I have no idea who she is or why she's here."

Holly collected herself and addressed the woman. "My name is Holly Kent. I'm the president of the homeowner's association and I wanted to introduce myself. My husband Homer and I live three houses over," she turned and pointed at a house behind her halfway up the hill— "and I wanted to welcome you to the neighbourhood."

She reluctantly turned towards the man. "I was surprised by your appearance. We don't have any—" she grappled for words — "people like you here in Pleasant Hill."

He raised his eyebrows at her. "*People* like me? What do you mean? I was under the impression that this hill is full of middle-aged, middle-class people. Could you be more specific, please?"

Before Holly could spell out that she meant Asians — why was he so touchy about that, for God's sake? — the woman intervened.

"Luke, leave it be. It was a misunderstanding, right?" She turned towards Holly. "My husband has experienced a few very unpleasant incidents of anti-Asian hate since the beginning of COVID. It's part of the reason why we decided to move away from Vancouver. We didn't feel safe there anymore. His heritage is Korean, not Chinese, and he was born and raised in Canada, but that makes no difference to people who are determined to be ignorant."

The man – Luke – gave his wife a significant look. "On this note, let's not keep Mrs. Kent from her no doubt pressing duties. I'm sure there are a few more people whose day she needs to ruin today. It seems to be a favourite pastime of hers. Don't bother coming back."

And with these words he slammed the door in her face.

Holly was outraged. How dare he? Who did he think he was? Excuse her for being taken aback by having an Asian man move in next door. Summerfield had a substantial percentage of First Nations but few other people of colour, and there were none in Pleasant Hill. Most natives were living together in their reservations, and in Holly's opinion it worked best that way. She wasn't racist, but wasn't it best for people to live among their own? Everybody was more comfortable, including the people of colour.

"You can't say anything anymore these days," Holly muttered to herself as she stalked home. She heartily disliked the state of the world. Political correctness, rainbow flags everywhere, people getting offended about everything – the world had gone crazy. You couldn't call a spade a spade, or the coronavirus the Chinese virus, even though that was exactly what it was. They had done it for the Spanish flu and Ebola, named after the country and river of origin respectively, but suddenly it was considered "offensive".

But never mind that. Holly had a more pressing problem on her hands: the Asian man Luke. *Nobody slams a door in my face without consequences*, she swore to herself. *Least of all a foreigner who doesn't belong here.*

From that moment on she watched him like a hawk. Much to her irritation, they didn't break any rules that first fall and winter. As was her custom, she found out as much as possible

74

about the couple: Luke Park was Korean, fifty years old, a retired investment banker, and still in his first marriage. His wife Valerie was nine years younger than him and soon started working at the local hospital as a nurse. They had no children, no obvious vices, and they were well liked by their immediate neighbours. Holly started to worry that she'd have no easy ammunition against him and would have to resort to more underhanded methods to discredit them.

But then spring arrived, and with it a gift. While everybody else started fertilizing their lawns, reseeding bald patches, getting pesticides out to kill weeds and pests, and preparing their flower beds for planting, Luke Park rented a sod cutter and took out his entire lawn over the course of a week.

Holly watched from her house in fascinated horror as Luke was ripping out the lawn, driving truckload after truckload of sod to the local eco-depot, leaving nothing behind but exposed dark soil that looked like an open wound. She expected him to re-turf the whole thing, impatiently waiting for a landscaping company to arrive and to start rolling out fresh, beautiful rolls of emerald grass. When that hadn't happened after two weeks she gave them a call.

"Hello?" It was Luke Park.

"Hi Luke, it's Holly Kent, your neighbour. How are you?"

"I'm doing fine. What do you want?" he asked coolly.

"I've noticed that you're doing some yard work. I'm just wondering when you'll get your new lawn in?"

To Holly's surprise, Luke chuckled. "I'm glad you asked. I've decided to rewild our yard."

"What?" Holly had no idea what he was talking about.

"I'm rewilding, sometimes referred to as ungardening. It means that I'm letting my yard grow untamed and wild. I've

75

removed the previous owner's useless grass that provided neither food nor shelter for bees, butterflies, and birds, and I'm replacing it with native plants. I've planted a wide variety of wildflowers to attract pollinators and reduce watering, and I'm not using any fertilizer or pesticides at all. Very toxic not only for wildlife but also for us."

Holly was stunned. "You can't be serious."

"As serious as a heart attack, dear neighbour," Luke said, and Holly could hear him gloating through the phone.

"You can't do this," Holly hissed. "You are violating covenants and creating an eyesore. The homeowner's association won't let you get away with it."

"Try and stop me, Madame President. I'm going to contact every wildlife and environmental group, every "save the bees" organization, every last climate change activist I can find and have them fight alongside me. Do you really think you and your outdated, corrupt, planet-destroying views stand a chance? Good luck – you're going to need it."

And he slammed the phone down.

"This means war!" Holly screamed over the dial tone before slamming her receiver down, too.

Luke Park had gone too far.

Chapter 7

Now

The sun tickled Clementine's closed eyelids, waking her gently. She opened her eyes to her bedroom flooded with bright sunshine, dust motes dancing in the shafts of light.

"Good morning, George," she mumbled sleepily to the dog stretched out on the bed beside her. He wagged his tail in response but didn't move otherwise. George liked to sleep in.

Clementine stayed in her bed for a while, thinking about everything she'd learnt a few nights ago at Valerie's house. The poor woman had been through the ringer, and it showed. She was jumpy and skittish, with dark circles under her eyes and a haunted look about her. She'd also smelled strongly of wine, and swayed slightly as she opened the door. Clementine had the impression that Valerie wouldn't have confided so much if she hadn't been quite tipsy, because she struck her as a reserved, private woman. But she was glad she had. It looked like she could use a friend, and Clementine had decided that she was going to be that friend.

Clementine hated bullies. She didn't know a single queer person who hadn't experienced prejudice and bullying, and she was no exception. As a bigger kid she had endured relentless ridicule for her weight throughout school, and when a bunch of stupid jocks discovered her and her first girlfriend kissing in a classroom in high school, the bullying had kicked up several notches. She had developed an eating disorder during that stressful time, leading her first to amphetamines, which she used as appetite suppressants, and then to other drugs.

Clementine accidentally overdosed when she was twenty-one, an event she would be forever grateful for. It introduced her to rehab and therapy, and from there she went onto her lifelong journey of self-discovery, sobriety, and healing. She learnt to make peace with her body, going from hating it to feeling neutral about it to loving it. It was a strong, healthy body, capable and reliable and free of disease, and these days she celebrated and cherished it. Nothing taught you appreciation for your body like getting older, especially after witnessing many of her friends and family members getting sick or frail. She'd never had a serious illness, accident, or health scare since her overdose, and she deeply appreciated her body for it.

Clementine had checked out of the diet- and beauty-race a long time ago, and she had been amazed at how much brain space it freed up when she stopped agonizing about the way she looked. She had more energy once she stopped starving herself and a truly unbelievable amount of extra time, and she had tried to get other women to join her in easing up on the relentless pursuit of beauty. It was a game that was rigged against women because of its ever-changing trends and beauty ideals, and she'd come to the conclusion that the reason for this was to keep women insecure and preoccupied, which made them much easier to control. That they had to pay for being sent on a pointless quest that led nowhere just added insult to injury.

She hadn't been very successful in convincing other women of her point of view when they were in their twenties and thirties. Women instinctively knew that beauty was power. It was sadly true that physical attractiveness helped getting ahead in the workplace, attract new people, and give an edge in the dating game. Women were relentlessly judged by their looks, and the confidence required to opt out of that game only came with age, experience, or a near-death experience. Besides, the beauty industry had cleverly convinced women that the pursuit of beauty was all about self-care and self-love, and if you spoke up against it you were met with the accusation that you didn't want women to feel good about themselves.

The opposite was true for Clementine. She wanted more than anything for women to love themselves and to recognize their inherent worth and strength. She knew that you could only get there if you made peace with who you were. The diets, nip and tucks, Botox, and fillers weren't created to make women confident; they were created to keep them in an endless loop of never being satisfied with how they looked.

To Clementine's delight she'd started to get through to more women once they entered their forties and beyond. "Women grow radical with age because they're fed up with the bullshit," Clementine was fond of saying. She adored middle age; at no other time in her life had she felt more empowered and more powerful. With age came wisdom, financial security, and the ability to read people in a way only experience could teach you.

And now here she was, in this cute new town that looked so pretty on the outside but harboured some ugly, dark secrets on the inside. Clementine had the strong sense that the universe had led her here for a reason. There was a wrong to be righted here, and a woman in serious need of help. Valerie was desperate and alone and seemed dangerously close to giving up. She had lost her lifelong partner, and instead of getting the support she needed, she was being hassled by a pair of narrow-minded thugs.

The Ho Hos sounded like classic schoolyard bullies who had gotten away with it because they were hiding behind their homeowner's association.

"Their reign of terror has reached the end of the line," Clementine told George, who continued to snore peacefully. In her experience, all bullies were secretly afraid of people standing up to them. They thrived in an environment of division and conflict, secrecy and animosity. The Ho Hos had successfully isolated Valerie by intimidating her so much that she was afraid to reach out to anyone else in the neighbourhood. She had confided that she was worried that everybody hated her and was on Holly and Homer's side, a view Clementine didn't share. She highly doubted that Valerie was the only victim, and suspected that there were more people who had grievances with the Ho Hos.

It was time to find out.

Valerie had told her that Holly's MO was to show up unannounced and uninvited on people's doorsteps, trying to catch them unawares. *Two can play that game*, Clementine thought to herself as she dressed carefully. She wanted to make sure to give the Ho Hos the correct first impression, so she chose one of her most colourful outfits: an olive-green, wide-leg jumpsuit with a flower print and mustard-yellow blouse with lantern sleeves, paired with her favourite chunky lilac cardigan and wooden clogs that added another three inches to her five-foot-ten frame.

Valerie had also mentioned Holly's daily inspection tour which she started at 8 am every day, so at 7:30 she clipped a leash on George, grabbed the pie she'd bought from Tilly, and set out for the Ho Ho house.

Clementine had decided to drop off a pie as a gesture of neighbourly goodwill, introduce herself and George, and set eyes on the couple that terrorized Pleasant Hill. She was quite curious to meet these people and to see how they'd react to her.

The walk from her house to theirs took less than five minutes. As she was approaching their front door she noticed that they had a perfect view over her house and into her backyard.

"Interesting," she murmured to herself and filed that information away. It might become useful.

Clementine rang the doorbell and waited. After what seemed like only seconds she heard approaching footsteps, and she put on her most gracious smile. The door opened, and two people stood in front of her. The man was large, with a big round belly, red face, and a receding hairline. He was still in a dressing gown and slippers, and he scowled at her, obviously not pleased by the intrusion. The woman next to him was small, trim, with neat blond hair cut in a bob, and immaculately dressed in grey slacks, a cream-coloured blouse, and loafers. But the deep lines extending from the corners of her mouth down towards her chin made her look like an angry puppet, an impression that was emphasized by her cold eyes and overall hostile demeanor.

The woman looked pointedly at the watch on her wrist.

"A bit early for a visit, isn't it? It's 7:38 am."

Clementine beamed at them. "I've seen you out and about

early every morning, so I know you're an early riser. I wanted to introduce myself and George and give you a peach pie. You should have a slice for breakfast, pie for breakfast is the best. I'm Clementine Harrison, your new neighbour." She gestured to George. "And this is George." She held out the pie towards the couple, but neither of them reached for it. Clementine shrugged and placed it on the bench next to the front door.

The woman's facial expression changed to one of revulsion as she took in the large dog. "I'm Holly Kent, the president of the homeowner's association, and this is my husband Homer, the vice president. Having a dog that size is a violation against the CC&Rs."

"Actually, it's not," Clementine replied pleasantly. "I studied the CC&Rs carefully, and you restricted the number of pets allowed, not their size. George is the only pet I own. Even though calling him a pet is doing him a major disservice; he's very wise, and he's my best friend. A much better conversationalist than most people I know."

Holly looked as sour as if she'd just bitten into a lemon. Before she could say anything however, Homer piped up. "Are you the one who drives that hideous green bus?"

Clementine grinned. "Not to split hairs, but the colour is called turquoise. Yes, that bus is mine, her name is Matilda. I've driven her all across Canada and lived in her for over six months! She's a grand old lady, temperamental but with lots of character. I guess you could call her the third member of my family."

Homer didn't look impressed. "That bus is an eyesore. I hope you know that you can't keep it parked in front of your house, it's classified as a recreational vehicle and can only stay on the road or in the driveway for the purpose of loading and unloading."

Clementine stared at the couple with raised eyebrows, her smile gone. "Aren't you two a barrel of laughs. Anyway, it's been fun, but I've gotta go now." She turned and started heading down the garden path but looked back one more time to call out: "I'll see you around!"

* * *

"You went to their house today at the crack of dawn? Why so early? And how did it go?" Valerie looked anxious. They were sitting on a bench outside the hospital during Valerie's lunch break and Clementine had just recounted that morning's events.

"Two reasons. One, I wanted to introduce myself and meet these people face to face. And two – let me tell you a story my dad told me. He grew up on a farm in Saskatchewan, and they had this horse who was a real dick. He had been to seven previous owners in seven years before they got him, and he was a devil. Spoiled and headstrong and wild. They'd gotten him for a song because the last owner was scared of him and just wanted to get rid of him. He had a habit of standing on peoples' feet, which hurt like hell, and my dad was really scared of the horse. You know what my grandpa did?"

"If he beat the hell out of the horse I don't want to know," Valerie interjected.

"No, no, he never did that. He stayed perfectly calm around the horse. But while he was grooming him he suddenly kicked him swiftly in the leg, completely out of the blue. Not enough to hurt him, but to startle him. He did it again a while later while he was leading him around, just turned around and socked him in the front leg, then continued on like nothing had happened."

Clementine paused for a moment and smiled, reminiscing.

"My grandpa would tap his nose at this point of the story and grin conspiratorially. 'From that day forward, he was watching *my* feet, not I his.'"

Valerie looked astonished. "It worked? The horse didn't step on peoples' feet anymore?"

"Never again." Clementine confirmed. "Two swift, unexpected kicks were all it took."

"So, you gave Holly and Homer a kick this morning?" Valerie asked with dawning understanding.

"Not a kick, not yet. But I want them to watch my feet. They're so used to stepping all over people, I thought it would do them some good to meet someone who's not worried about their feet."

"I love it!" Valerie squealed.

"I've been wondering about something," Clementine began. "How many of your interactions with the Ho Hos have been in person?"

"Almost none. Holly came to our house three years ago when we first moved here, which was when she reacted so racist towards Luke that he kicked her out and told her to never come back. They called a couple times after that when we took out the lawn, which drove them nuts, but everything else has been official letters and emails from the HOA. They hired a lawyer who also sent a few letters, but Luke always said that they don't have a legal leg to stand on and ignored them. A bunch of letters were sent as registered mail, but Luke refused to accept them, and they were returned to sender. I haven't talked to Holly since that incident three years ago, and I have never seen Homer up close or spoken to him at all."

"Hmm, interesting," Clementine said thoughtfully. "Not unexpected, and in fact, exactly what I was hoping for."

"Why?" Valerie asked.

"Because it means that they are as afraid of confrontation as you are. They are hiding behind a computer screen, an organization, and lawyers. Having to deal with people face to face makes them uncomfortable. That's excellent news for us!" Clementine grinned at Valerie. "They are in for a rude awakening. I *love* dealing with people face to face, and they'll get to see so much of me from now on that they'll wish they'd never started the HOA."

Chapter 8

"Who does she think she is?" Holly fumed at Homer. "Banging down the door at this time of the morning, she could have woken us up. That woman has no manners. And did you see what she was wearing? She looked like a clown. Those colours at her age, and at her size. She's as big as a house."

Holly took a breath before she continued. "No wonder, if she eats peach pie for breakfast. I hate women who let themselves go, they have no pride or discipline. How hard is it to stop stuffing your face?"

"What did you expect from someone who's driving around in such a monstrosity of a vehicle? That bus of hers belongs on the scrap pile. I can't wait for the day when she leaves it parked in front of the house and we can fine her."

"I wish I could have gotten her for the dog, that beast is a menace. I can't believe that hippie actually read the CC&Rs, wonders never cease. But I'm sure it's only a matter of time before she violates the regulations. Women like her think rules don't apply to them, and that they can do whatever the hell they want. They act like the world revolves around them and everybody exists to please them. I can't stand that attitude."

"We'll get rid of her, don't worry," Homer said. "Do some

digging, we need to know more about her to see what her weak points are. She clearly doesn't belong here, and the sooner she realizes that the sooner she will leave."

He shook his head in disgust. "She didn't mention a husband, I bet you she's a dyke. She has that look about her. Unmarried women are nothing but trouble. A woman needs a man around for common sense."

"No they don't," Holly said icily, scowling at him. "You better get dressed, or you'll be late for work."

As Homer shuffled off, she called after him: "And make sure that you're dressed for breakfast from now on! It didn't look good in front of her that you were still in your robe and slippers."

Homer didn't reply.

Holly cleaned up their breakfast dishes, still mad as hell. She hated women like Clementine Harrison. Women who acted confident and bossy when they had nothing to be confident about. She was overweight, dressed ridiculously, drove that insane bus around, and lived alone. She had bought one of the smallest houses in Pleasant Hill, indicating that she probably didn't have all that much money, and she clearly had no manners. Yet she had appeared self-assured and at peace with herself, even happy. How was that possible?

Holly worked hard for everything she had. She strictly watched what she ate, exercised religiously, had her roots touched up every four weeks, and received discreet Botox injections every few months into the elevenses between her eyes to soften the permanent scowl she had on her face otherwise. When she turned forty she had consulted a stylist to give her an age-appropriate, understated wardrobe and got rid of anything too short, too brash, or too trendy. Trends were a young woman's game in her opinion, and she found it embarrassing when mutton dressed as lamb.

Another area of her life Holly had to work hard on was her marriage to Homer. They had met in college in the pharmacy program in their second year. Holly hadn't been interested, finding Homer arrogant and crude. He was loud and full of himself, with a tendency to drink too much and not take no for an answer. But he was persistent, and one night after a party when she'd had too much to drink he offered to walk her home. She said yes, not wanting to be alone on the street after midnight.

Holly never allowed herself to dwell on what happened next. What was the point? It was what it was, she couldn't change it. She was hardly the first girl who'd gotten pregnant while in college. Abortion was illegal in Canada in the early eighties, and faced with the choice between being a disgraced, struggling single mother or a young wife to a promising pharmacist-to-be, she chose the latter.

She rewrote history, telling herself that he had convinced her to sleep with him instead of that he'd forced her. Holly was too much of a realist to believe that she would stand a chance if she accused him of rape. She'd been drunk, she'd let him walk her home, she was wearing party clothes. She had no doubt that she would be blamed for what happened to her, and Homer would be fine. Holly wasn't going to let him get away that easy.

It had been simple. Homer was into her, he'd been raised Catholic, and when she saw that he was reluctant about marrying her, she'd contacted his parents and told them about the pregnancy. Holly would never forget the looks of disgust on their faces when she told them, making her feel like she was the whore of Babylon. They clearly gave her the full responsibility for what had happened, as if she'd seduced their innocent boy and led him astray. If it wasn't so desperately unfair she would have laughed at the irony of it. Instead she gritted her teeth, listened stonily to their insults and accusations of being a gold digger, and waited for them to reach the conclusion she'd hoped they would: that it was best for them to get married to save face.

Homer wasn't happy about it, but he listened to his parents, and they got married before she started showing. Holly told her family and friends that it was a whirlwind romance, and stayed in school until she couldn't hide the pregnancy any longer. She dropped out with the plan to go back and finish college when the baby was older, but it didn't work out that way.

Christopher had been a colicky, cranky baby. Holly was alone with him while Homer was in school, with no help from either of their parents. She had learnt at a young age not to rely on her mother Bernice. Her father had taken off when Holly was only a year old, and Bernice never recovered from it. She spent large periods of time in bed, spending money she didn't have on stuff she bought from the shopping channel, slowly filling their shabby apartment with thousands of boxes, many of them unpacked. Holly learnt to set an alarm by the age of six, got up on her own, and walked to school. She raised herself while also looking after her mother, and she had promised herself that she would never let her baby alone with her.

Hell would freeze over before she asked her in-laws for help after the way they'd treated her. Even if they offered to help – which they didn't – she wouldn't have accepted it. Holly was too proud.

They'd lived in a small apartment close to the university.

Homer hadn't let a small thing like marriage and fatherhood change his ways, and he still went out with his buddies several times a week. His parents paid for the apartment, but nothing else. Holly needed money for herself and Christopher, so she started cleaning on campus at night. If Homer didn't come home in time to look after the baby before her shift, Holly had to rely on a neighbour to babysit. She hated it, but there was nothing she could do.

Christopher was three when Homer graduated and started working. She'd always thought that she would go back to school once he was done. But Homer had student loans to pay back, and they wanted to buy a house with a yard for Christopher. Holly had been promoted to supervisor at her cleaning job, mortgage rates were sky high, and they needed both incomes. Besides, Holly had realized that she'd need a spouse who was willing to help out with housework and childcare should she ever return to school, and Homer wasn't that kind of husband. In his mind his job was to be the provider, and she'd do everything else. It didn't matter that she also worked, that she was chronically exhausted from working nights and doing everything else during the day, that she had no family support. Homer expected a warm meal and a clean house when he came home, and she sucked it up for Christopher's sake. Homer loved his son, and Christopher adored his father. Holly would never tear the family apart and condemn her only child to a childhood like the one she'd had.

And that was that. Holly kept working nights to be home in the afternoon when Christopher returned from first preschool and then kindergarten, which had the added benefit that she didn't see her husband very much.

She despised Homer. Even though she pretended to herself

that he hadn't raped her that night, deep down she'd never forgiven him. He had taken away her dreams of a career, of independence, of making it on her own. Holly hadn't even known if she wanted to have kids, and he'd taken that choice away from her as well.

But appearances mattered to her more than anything else, and on the outside her life looked great. She had a healthy son who did well in school, a husband with a successful career as a pharmacist, and a beautiful home. By the time Christopher started school Holly had stopped working, and she threw herself into her role as dedicated school mom. She joined the PTA, and in less than a year she'd worked her way from committee member to being the chair. She started going for regular manicures and pedicures instead of doing them herself, lost twenty pounds by hiring a personal trainer and cutting out carbs, and copied the dress style of the professional stay-at-home moms and trophy wives who were in the PTA with her. She befriended other wives who, like her, either detested their husbands or had married for other reasons than love. There was a reassuringly large number of them and surrounding herself with women in unsatisfactory marriages made hers feel more normal. Not that she ever let anyone get close enough to tell them what had happened to her. How could she admit that when she'd married him? No, Holly intended to take that secret to her grave. She doubted that Homer remembered – they never mentioned it, and he'd either forgotten the details or thought she'd slept with him willingly. Homer had always had an overinflated sense of himself and what he considered his irresistibility to women.

* * *

91

When Christopher was twelve Homer had an affair with the neighbour's wife. Holly didn't mind the infidelity – it had been years since they'd had sex, and she couldn't care less if he slept around – but she couldn't stand being laughed at or, even worse, pitied. If he'd been discreet she would have turned a blind eye, but he was as careful as an elephant in a china shop, and too many people in their life knew about it. It was unacceptable. Appearances were everything to Holly, and his affair not only made her look like a fool but also reflected poorly on her life's work, which was her family.

Holly told him that they had to move. She started searching for a smaller town to move to, because she had realized that she would always be a nobody in a big city. Better to be a big fish in a small pond than the other way around. She chose Summerfield because house prices were good, there was an opening for a pharmacist at the local Walmart, and it had everything they'd need while still maintaining small-town charm. It didn't hurt that it was a day's drive away from Homer's parents, who they got along with on the surface, but whom Holly had never forgiven for the way they'd treated her in the beginning.

Homer didn't have a choice. She had given him an ultimatum, saying that she'd only forgive him for the affair and the humiliation if he agreed to move. He meekly agreed, eager to make it up to her.

Moving to Summerfield and starting the homeowner's association were the best decisions Holly had ever made. She loved building something from the ground up, and it made her feel powerful to be in charge. Not having a career was the biggest regret of her life but being the president and trying to transform a mediocre neighbourhood into an exceptional one almost made up for it.

CHAPTER 8

The only problem were the people. For the life of her Holly couldn't understand why not everybody shared her vision. Didn't they see that all of them would benefit if they'd just go along with what she wanted? Who in their right mind would prefer to live in a messy neighbourhood with a bunch of crap in people's front yards instead of a neat, uniform, and beautiful one? Why would anyone settle for staying ordinary if they could become extraordinary?

Holly couldn't think straight in a chaotic environment, and she was convinced that must be true for everyone. She had despised growing up in an apartment that was filled to the brim with stuff, where it was impossible to properly clean because of all the clutter, and where she lay awake at night, terrified of the rats she heard rustling around. She equated mess with fear, loneliness, and abandonment. Being organized meant being in control and being in control meant survival. Her neighbours didn't realize that even the smallest lapse in vigilance could mean the beginning of the end. They might think that letting the lawn grow another week was no big deal, but it was a slippery slope. Before they knew it they could be up to their eyeballs in teetering piles of stuff, threatening to collapse onto a little girl that had to make tunnels through it to get from room to room, and who could never bring anyone home because she was too embarrassed to show anyone how she and her mom lived.

Holly would be damned if she ever lived like that again. It was imperative that she made sure Pleasant Hill was as far removed from the squalor of her childhood as possible, and the key to that was to keep raising the tone of the neighbourhood, keep raising house prices, and to keep riffraff like her mother out of it. Clementine Harrison with her bohemian clothes, disregard for social conventions, and airy-fairy attitude was *not* going to undo all the years of Holly's hard work.

She wouldn't let her.

Chapter 9

Valerie headed back into the hospital after her lunch outside with Clementine. She was deep in thought, feeling equally scared and hopeful about Clementine's plan to provoke Holly and Homer. *The Ho Hos,* she reminded herself with a smile. How come her and Luke had never thought of that nickname? They had always referred to them as *Dumb and Dumber,* which was satisfying every time they said it. She'd have to tell Clementine that.

It felt amazing to have made a friend and not feel so alone in the neighbourhood anymore. In the three years she'd lived in Pleasant Hill she hadn't made friends with any of the neighbours. She and Luke had been on good terms with the people on one side, but they'd moved away. The people on the other side had disapproved of their yard, complaining several times about the rewilding, and pleading with them to reconsider and get a regular lawn installed. When Luke refused they'd complained to Holly and Homer, and that's when it all went downhill. They ended up moving as well, shortly before Luke's death, but by then the damage was done. Valerie felt like she had a target on her back and was convinced everybody in Pleasant Hill hated her. She went out of her way to avoid all of them, never stopping at the community mailboxes when someone else was there, checking the street before she left the house to make sure it was empty, and never making eye contact on the rare occasion she bumped into one of the few neighbours she knew in town.

Luke had gone to a few of the regular neighbourhood meetings, but she never went, afraid they'd either talk about them or attack them. It had gotten so bad that Valerie was too scared to spend any time in her yard, feeling too conspicuous, and as a result it was wilder than ever. Shortly after Luke's death they'd had the audacity to send her another letter, demanding that she immediately change her yard back to a "neat, clean" lawn.

"We suspect that your husband was the one insisting on turning this property into an eyesore, and we appeal on your female sensibility and sense of propriety to follow the rules and regulations of the Pleasant Hill Homeowner's Association," the letter read. If she didn't comply, she would face fines or worse.

At first she'd been too grief-stricken to care, throwing the letter in a drawer and giving herself fully over to her bereavement. For weeks she barely left her bed, crying until no tears were left, and then staring numbly at the TV, not taking anything in. Her friend Hattie had come to stay with her for a while, but Hattie kept trying to coax her to return to the land of the living, and Valerie had no interest in that. She sent her back to her own family after a week, insisting that she felt better, and that Hattie was more needed at home than here.

After three months Valerie had returned to work. She'd been an ICU nurse in Vancouver but retrained as an emergency nurse in Summerfield. Despite Luke's promise that she'd never have to work again after the sale of their Vancouver house,

Valerie had looked for a job almost immediately upon moving to Summerfield. Not only did she feel much too young at forty-one to retire – the thought to be financially dependent on her husband had scared her. Sure, she loved Luke – but how certain could one ever be of another one's love? It was best to be self-sufficient.

Working in the emergency department of a smaller hospital had been a revelation. Valerie loved the pace, the unpredictability of it, the close bond between the staff. She felt more at home in this hospital than she ever had anywhere else, and many of the nurses and a couple of the doctors had become friends. Despite the drama in her neighbourhood, Valerie never regretted the move thanks to how much she loved her work.

During slow night shifts they'd do chair races through the hospital, exercise challenges in the trauma room, and play pranks on each other. Once they dressed up the department skeleton, Mr. Bones, in scrubs, took the doctor's keys to his truck, and put Mr. Bones in the doctor's back seat. Another time they used a pumpkin and folded blankets to create the illusion of a patient in bed, added a phone playing a recording of snoring, and covered it all with a blanket. Then they turned off the light and called the lab and x-ray technologists for urgent blood work and x-rays, laughing their heads off when they both got spooked by a pumpkin greeting them instead of a person.

Valerie also appreciated that she got to know many of the patients that came in and was eager to learn more about their backgrounds and families. When she returned to work after Luke's death she found it comforting to be surrounded by all that raw humanness. In one shift she could encounter someone who'd chopped off their finger and brought it along in a mayonnaise jar, a lonely widower who craved human touch, a hypochondriac who was a frequent flier and needed reassurance that they weren't going to die today, a cowboy walking in on a broken ankle asking if "the doc can set it and let me go, I have to fix a fence before my cattle is all over the goddamn road", an addict who was so high they had to sedate him because he was a danger to himself and others, someone panicking because they had a tick, a woman in excruciating pain because of an ectopic pregnancy, and a homeless man looking for a warm bed and a sandwich. Being surrounded by humans at all stages of the human experience – from their happiest days when they gave birth to a healthy baby to their worst ones, when they lost a loved one, and everything in between – put her own grief into perspective. It made her feel less alone, because it showed her that every single person in the world had to experience grief and sorrow along with joy and happiness. One couldn't exist without the other, and the daily reminder helped.

What it didn't help with was the situation in Pleasant Hill. While Valerie was competent and authoritative at work, in her own neighbourhood she felt as small and insignificant as a child. There had been several more letters after she ignored the cease-and-desist letter demanding she put in a lawn, and her only way of dealing with it so far had been to throw them all into the same drawer. She had stopped opening them despite knowing that ignoring them wasn't a solution, but she simply couldn't muster the courage to read them.

Valerie was paralyzed with indecision. The easiest way out of this mess would be to give in and install that damn lawn they were so keen on, but giving in felt like a betrayal to Luke. Besides, he'd always said that giving them what they wanted wouldn't be the end of it. "They are not going to be satisfied no matter what we do," he liked to say. There was no point arguing with him since it was only speculation – they hadn't done a single thing the HOA had demanded of them.

Hattie knew about her problems with Holly and Homer, and she kept saying that Valerie should sell and move. "That's the easiest way to fix everything," she pointed out, slightly exasperated by what she considered Valerie's stubbornness. But Hattie, who was unsentimental to a fault and hadn't lost anyone important to her yet, didn't get it. She didn't understand that Valerie used up every ounce of energy she had at work, and that she was as limp as an overcooked spaghetti by the time the workday was over. She had no energy left to paint her nails, let alone for something as strenuous as packing up a house and moving. Hattie also didn't get that Valerie couldn't bear the thought of leaving the house that held her memories of Luke, that it was a comfort to feel the floor under her feet that had been touched by his feet, sit in the room they'd sat in together, stare at the same ceiling at night that he'd looked at. Besides, she had never sold and bought anything by herself, and she wouldn't even know where to start. Valerie had spent her entire adult life with a take-charge person by her side, and she felt utterly lost and directionless without him. She had no idea who she was or what she wanted without Luke.

"Val, can you give me a hand?" Valerie's co-worker Sima called to her as she came back into the department, pulling her out of her reverie.

"Sure, I'm right there." Valerie grabbed a pair of gloves and joined Sima at a patient's bedside. Sima was one of her favourite co-workers – a gentle, hardworking nurse who truly cared about her patients. She was one of the people who helped

Valerie the most when she first started and didn't know much about how things worked in an emergency department. Valerie hoped she'd one day become as good an emergency nurse as Sima was.

Sima introduced the elderly grey-haired lady lying in the bed. "This is Marjorie, she had a fall and injured her right hip. She's just come back from x-ray, but the doctor hasn't seen her yet." Sima gave her a meaningful look across the bed, indicating that the hip was broken. Nurses weren't allowed to give a diagnosis to the patient; Marjorie had to wait for Dr. Pierce to deliver the bad news.

"Can you help me turn her? I want to clean her up and put a catheter in."

"No problem," Valerie replied.

Marjorie's bladder had emptied, so they needed to take out the wet sheets and replace them with dry ones. Sima was standing behind Marjorie, Valerie in front of her as they carefully turned her away from her injured hip. Marjorie winced but didn't complain. Once the sheets had been replaced Sima expertly inserted a urinary catheter into Marjorie's bladder, since she wouldn't be able to go to the bathroom until after the surgery. While Sima worked, Valerie put a blood pressure cuff on Marjorie's arm, stuck a pulse oximeter on her finger to measure her blood oxygen levels, and attached leads for the bedside heart monitor to her chest.

"I know you," Marjorie said suddenly. She had been staring intently at Valerie.

"Oh?" Valerie asked. She didn't know her, but that didn't mean anything. They saw so many patients in a day, it happened frequently that one of them recognized her and she couldn't remember them. "Maybe I've looked after you before?" she offered.

"No, not that. You live in my neighbourhood!" Marjorie exclaimed enthusiastically. "I've just realized that you are the girl that lives two houses down from my friend Edna's place." She grew serious. "I'm so sorry about your husband. He was way too young. How are you holding up, dear?"

"I'm fine," Valerie said automatically, an answer she'd given what felt like a thousand times since Luke's death. "It's been a year, so—" She trailed off. She didn't know how to continue. People seemed to expect her to have gotten over it by now, that a year's grief was more than enough self-indulgence and that it was time to get on with living. A few of her co-workers had tentatively asked her about dating, a suggestion that Valerie found ludicrous. She was nowhere near ready to get involved with another man.

"A year is nothing," Marjorie said dismissively. "My Bill passed away fifteen years ago, and I still miss him every day." She reached for Valerie's hand. "You never really get over it. You learn to live with it, and you will find happiness and joy again. But the grief stays with you forever. It gets smaller, but it doesn't go away."

Valerie's eyes filled with tears. "Everybody always says that time heals all wounds. They make me feel like I'm behind, like I should be over it by now."

"Pish posh," Marjorie said contemptuously. "What do people know? Nothing, my dear. Loss and grief don't have a timeline. It takes as long as it takes."

Dr. Pierce chose this moment to come into the room. "Hello, Mrs. Burns, I'm Patrick Pierce, the doctor on duty. I'm afraid I have some bad news."

"I'll come back later, Marjorie," Valerie said hastily and

bolted out of the room. She was full-on crying now, something that hadn't happened at work in months. She headed straight to the bathroom, locked the door behind her, and sank onto the floor with her back to the wall. She sobbed and sobbed, but it wasn't all out of sorrow. Valerie sobbed with relief, because Marjorie had given her an unexpected gift: she had made her feel normal.

It may sound stupid, but Valerie hadn't been able to shake the feeling that she was doing grief wrong. Well-meaning friends and family had recommended all sorts of things that she was supposed to do after Luke's death: go to grief counselling, join a bereavement support group, lean on friends, go easy on the alcohol, find a new hobby. And after a few months they started telling her to "get out there", start dating, exercising, get a new haircut, get rid of all his clothes, "start over".

Valerie hadn't done any of those things. After the whirlwind of activity that follows death – telling people, organizing the funeral, the phone calls and condolence cards and offers of "call me if you need anything" – Valerie retreated from the world. She stayed in bed for the first month, unable to function. She could barely remember what she did that month, the memory lost in a haze of grief and tears and too much wine.

The second month she spent on the couch, staring at the TV for hours without taking much in, replaying all their favourites. She'd remember his laugh or the comment he made at a scene, and for a split second it would feel as if he was in the room with her. But then the reality of his absence would hit her anew, dropping another truckload of pain onto her, burying her in it until she felt like she was drowning.

In the third month Valerie got angry. She roamed the house, wine glass in hand, and held long, angry monologues. "How dare you leave me alone with the mess *you* created," she'd yell, kicking his shoes she hadn't been able to put away across the room. "You started this fucking fight with Dumb and Dumber, and then you just up and die. You *asshole*!" Valerie had never sworn in her life, but now she couldn't stop. It felt liberating. "I didn't want your idiotic wild yard!" She paused for a swig of wine, considering. "Okay, that's not fair. I thought it was a good idea too, at first. It's good for the environment, it's not wasting water, and it's great for insects and animals. And it looked sooo good last summer. All the hummingbirds and bees and butterflies coming to us, it was amazing." Valerie smiled at the memory. "Those purple flowers with the yellow in the middle are so pretty. What are they called again? You know I'm hopeless with plants, I can never remember their names." A sob escaped Valerie's throat. "But is a stupid yard worth the stress and fighting? Is it? I told you I wanted to do what they asked and put the stupid lawn back in. I *told* you and you wouldn't listen."

A howl rose up inside her, powerful as a tsunami. All her life Valerie had held back anger, swallowed it, and buried it, bit her tongue until it bled because being angry wasn't appropriate for a woman. It was unladylike, shameful, not right. And Valerie had always tried to do the right thing, to follow the rules and fit in, to stay small. A lifetime of anger was inside her, bursting to get out, and for once Valerie wasn't stopping it. She exploded in the middle of her empty living room, shouting so loud that the cat fled into the kitchen.

"ALL I WANTED WAS A PEACEFUL LIFE, LUKE! GO TO WORK, HANG OUT WITH YOU, HAVE A BARBECUE IN THE SUMMER WITH THE NEIGHBOURS. WAS THAT TOO MUCH TO ASK? NO IT WASN'T, YOU JACKASS. IT WAS *NOT*."

She threw the empty wine glass against the wall, watching it shatter and fall in countless glittering shards onto the hardwood floor. Galvanized by how satisfying that had felt, Valerie stormed to the cabinet where she stored her good china and threw open the doors. Without stopping and considering what she was about to do she grabbed four plates at once, spun around, and flung them like discs into the air, aiming for the opposite wall. After she'd tossed the four plates she grabbed more, not stopping until the stack of plates had vanished, leaving a pile of broken pieces, a dent in the wall, and a ringing silence in its wake.

Going back to work in month four had been a relief. While Valerie had needed alone time and couldn't stand company in the beginning, she craved normalcy and human contact after three months of solitude. Busy days were the best antidote for the depression that had replaced her anger, and being around other people's tragedies soothed her. She felt terribly guilty for feeling that way, but she couldn't help it. Nobody knew about it, and she intended to keep it that way. She had sometimes thought that it would be nice to confide in someone, but she'd been too ashamed to open up to a friend, and too indecisive to make up her mind about finding a counsellor.

But now, sitting on the cold bathroom floor of the hospital, wiping the tears that had finally stopped flowing from her cheeks, she felt hope and excitement sprout inside her. Marjorie was the first widow she'd met since becoming one herself, and she would need some help over the next few weeks. Valerie was going to offer it to her.

She sprang to her feet, splashed cold water into her face, dried it, and unlocked the door. Before returning to Marjorie's room she checked with the doctor about next steps for her.

"We're keeping her here overnight and then get her transferred to Grace Memorial tomorrow morning for surgery. I've spoken to ortho, they're putting a plate and screws in to stabilize the fracture. Sima has just given her some pain meds and she's resting comfortably. Nice lady," he added, before moving on to the next patient.

Valerie collected herself for a moment before going in. She was nervous about what she wanted to do, even though it was a nice thing and shouldn't be scary at all. *Forty-four years old and I still don't know how to make friends*, she chastised herself. Hopefully that was about to change.

"Hi, Marjorie, I'm back," she greeted the older woman upon entering her room. "I hear Dr. Pierce explained your injury to you?"

"He did, dear, I broke my hip. I'm not surprised, it hurt like heck."

"Are you comfortable now? Do you need anything?"

"I'm fine, thank you. Forgive me, but I've forgotten your name."

"It's Valerie, Valerie Park." Valerie hesitated for a moment, then added, "My husband was Luke."

Marjorie took Valerie's hand in hers. The skin was dry and papery, the fingers gnarled with arthritis. "If you ever want to talk, come and visit me. I know how it feels to lose a husband, and I expect not many of your friends do, seeing how young you are."

"None of them do," Valerie admitted. "And none of them mention him to me, probably because they think it will make me sad to talk about him. But I *want* to talk about him! I still think about him all the time, and it's exhausting to pretend I don't."

Marjorie nodded. "Talking about them and reminiscing makes them come alive again, doesn't it."

"Yes, exactly. And never mentioning him makes it feel like he never existed in the first place."

A sense of complete understanding passed between them. Valerie smiled at Marjorie, and a sudden impulse made her blurt out: "I'd love to help you when you come home after your surgery. You know, get groceries, cook, clean your house, help you shower. What do you say?"

The older woman beamed at her. "I know it's considered polite to decline, but I'm too old to care about what's polite. This is a wonderfully generous offer, and I happily accept."

They exchanged phone numbers and Marjorie gave Valerie her address. Valerie insisted to pick up her new friend from the hospital in a few days when she was discharged. Before she left to return to work she spontaneously bent down and gave Marjorie a hug. "I'm so glad we've met," she whispered. "Even though I'm sorry you had to break a hip for it."

Marjorie hugged her back. "I have a feeling that it was worth it."

Chapter 10

"Don't go looking for trouble," Clementine's mother used to tell her repeatedly as a child.

"I'm not, trouble is finding me," she'd retort, nettled. Clementine was born with a strong sense of right and wrong, and a fearlessness to fight for what she believed in. She was the kid that stood up to bullies, defended the outcasts, and tried to help everybody who needed help. It was one of life's cruel jokes that when the bullies targeted her, there was nobody helping her. It had been a bitter pill to swallow and was one of the myriad of reasons why she had turned to drugs during what she referred to now as her "lost years". Clementine had been so disappointed by people that her initial reaction had been to heed her mother's advice and stay out of other people's problems.

But she couldn't help it. She learnt in therapy that she was fighting a losing battle trying to suppress her nature, and that the reward was in the act itself, not in other people's reaction.

"You can't control other people's actions," her therapist in rehab had told her. "The only thing you can control is your own actions, and how much power you are willing to give other people by letting them affect you." She had smiled. "I'm not saying it's easy. I still struggle with it as well. We are herd animals, and it's in our DNA that we want to be accepted and liked. And you are – you are beloved by both patients and staff here. But wanting to be liked by others should never be the goal. It's setting yourself up for disappointment. What should matter most to you is how *you* feel about yourself. Everything else is a nice bonus, not the goal. If you've made yourself proud, you've won."

Clementine had taken the therapist's words to heart. She stopped fighting her instincts and started acting according to what felt right to her, regardless of it being popular or not. To her surprise she found that once she stopped worrying so much about pleasing other people, she got more respect than she had before. People seemed to gravitate towards her, seeking *her* out instead of the other way around. "Isn't that interesting," she mused to a friend. "Once you stop chasing something it will come to you." It was a life lesson she didn't forget.

Clementine was thinking of that as she headed to her back-yard towards Matilda. She had parked her there after moving in because she took up so much room on the road and Clementine didn't want her to be in anyone's way. But it was time to poke the bully and provoke them to come to her.

As Homer had said, the HOA's guidelines stated that "RVs and other recreational vehicles are only permitted to be parked at the street for the purpose of loading and unloading". Clementine smiled to herself. The Ho Hos were in for an unpleasant surprise about how slowly a person could unload a vehicle.

She drove into town to buy some things at the grocery store, then stopped by the hardware store, dollar store, and feed store to get more dog food for George. Clementine whistled as she added bag after bag to the growing pile on Matilda's floor.

"That's a lot of stuff to unload, Georgie-boy, don't you agree? This will take a looong time. Days and days, I think," she told him, and he wagged his tail in agreement.

Back at home Clementine parked Matilda in front of her house, careful not to block the sidewalk. She wanted to provoke the Ho Hos, not inconvenience the neighbours. Then she took a single item – the carton of ice cream – out of the grocery bag and carried it inside the house. She deposited it in the freezer and then sat down in her office to do some work while she waited. It was only a matter of time before someone was going to get in touch.

Every half hour or so she would go outside to Matilda and get another single item from the bags, carrying it ceremoniously into the house: one apple, one loaf of bread, a box of laundry detergent. She'd just gone out again and was rummaging around for the chocolate she'd bought when she heard someone call.

"Hello? Uhm, excuse me?"

The voice was so quiet that Clementine could barely make it out. She stuck her head out of Matilda's open door. "Did someone say something?" Her gaze fell on an older woman who stood nervously outside the door, hands clasped in front of her. She looked uncomfortable.

"Hi there!" Clementine said pleasantly. "Can I help you?"

"Oh, uh, hello. Are you Clementine Harrison?" the woman asked haltingly.

"I sure am. And who are you?"

"My name is Mary Potter. Holly Kent sent me."

Clementine raised her eyebrows. "Sent you? What do you mean?"

A pale flush spread across Mary's narrow face. "I mean, she asked me to come and talk to you. I, uh–" Mary seemed lost for words and Clementine took pity on her.

"I was just going to make myself a cup of tea. Why don't you come in and tell me why Holly is too cowardly to face me and sent someone else to do her dirty work?"

"D-dirty work? What do you mean? No, it's not like that—"

Clementine didn't let her finish. "Come on, Mary, let's break open these delicious chocolates, sit down, and have a little chat." She gave the other woman an encouraging smile. "What do you say? I promise I won't bite."

Mary hesitated, but then nodded. "Alright."

Clementine led her inside the house. "This is George, he's a sweetheart. You are not afraid of dogs, are you?"

Mary's face lit up. "Not at all, I love them! I grew up with a Saint Bernard. Oh, you are a handsome boy, aren't you." She bent down and nuzzled George's head while scratching behind his ears. George lapped it up, pressing himself against her and wagging his tail happily. Mary's entire demeanor changed while she was interacting with the dog: her hunched shoulders dropped, her body seemed to unclench, and the worried look on her face was gone, making her look ten years younger.

"I'm going to boil water for the tea, make yourself at home!" Clementine called to Mary as she headed into the kitchen. Mary straightened up right away and followed her with George by her side, keeping her hand on his back as if drawing strength from him. The ease that she had displayed a moment earlier was gone, replaced by a tenseness that Clementine sensed rarely left the older woman.

"Mary, I don't know what Holly has told you about me, but there's no reason to look so worried," Clementine said. She gestured towards the kitchen table. "Have a seat, the tea is almost ready." Mary sat down, and George put his big head on her lap. *Good boy*, Clementine thought. "Why don't you tell me why you're here? Get it out and over with." She smiled at her encouragingly.

Mary took a deep breath. "I'm here in an official capacity, as the secretary of the homeowner's association. I'm supposed to issue you an official warning for having your bus parked on the road for too long."

Clementine nodded. "I figured it was about Matilda."

"Matilda?" Mary looked confused. "Who's Matilda?"

Clementine laughed. "That's the name of my bus. And you will be pleased to know that I'm not breaking any rules by having Matilda parked out there. I read the rules and regulations carefully, and it clearly states that 'RVs and other recreational vehicles are permitted to be parked at the street for the purpose of loading and unloading'." She beamed. "I went shopping this morning and I'm currently unloading my vehicle. You can take a look if you want, the shopping bags are in there. I was a big trip, so I'm still unloading. According to your rules I'm perfectly within my rights to have her parked in front of my house."

"But you've had your bus parked on the street all day!"

Clementine grinned. "I'm a *very* slow unloader. The rules don't give a time limit for how long the loading and unloading are supposed to take, and I don't do anything rushed. I'll move Matilda when I'm done." She paused for effect. "Which will only be another few days."

"Another few *days*?" Mary looked stressed. "Holly is not going to like that."

"Let me tell you a secret, Mary." Clementine leaned in conspiratorially. "I don't care one bit about what Holly Kent likes or doesn't like. In fact, Holly is about to get a taste of her

111

own medicine, and I have a feeling she's not going to like that at all."

"What do you mean?"

"Holly is a bully. From what I've heard she's been abusing her role as president to harass the good people of Pleasant Hill, and I'm not joining the long line of her victims. I don't like bullies, and I especially don't like it when they pick on vulnerable people, which is the only people they are brave enough to pick on. They seem to have a particular liking for kicking someone who's down, and I'm planning to stop the Ho Hos from continuing their reign of terror."

"The Ho Hos?"

"It's my nickname for Holly and Homer, Ho Hos. Even though they're not exactly as jolly as Santa, are they?" Clementine winked and Mary giggled.

"I got you to laugh! That makes me happy, you have a beautiful laugh." Clementine poured them both tea and offered Mary a chocolate. "Tell me, how did you get tangled up with those two? And what's the history of the HOA?"

Mary nibbled at her chocolate for a moment. Clementine had noticed that she liked to think before she spoke, an admirable quality that was in danger of becoming extinct.

"My husband and I have lived here since we got married forty-five years ago. When we bought our house the neighbourhood was different. It wasn't as highly regarded as it is now; the houses were old and some not in great shape, and because it was cheap it was mostly a blue-collar neighbourhood. We didn't mind, because that's what we are. Albert – that's my husband – worked at the sawmill until he retired last year, and I've been a homemaker all my life. Anyway, Holly and Homer moved here thirty years ago, in 1993."

"You have a good memory," Clementine said, impressed.

"I remember it because the year after was the year the homeowner's association was founded. I will never forget it." Mary smiled at the memory. "They were different. Homer is an educated man, a pharmacist. He works at the Walmart pharmacy. And Holly came in like a whirlwind. She was full of energy and big plans for Pleasant Hill, wanting to make it better. She didn't know a soul, but that didn't stop her. Holly went from house to house with freshly baked muffins and introduced herself to people. Then she threw a party and invited most of the neighbourhood."

"Most?" Clementine interjected. "Not all?"

Mary's smile faded. "No, not all. I can't believe that you picked up on that right away. Holly can be great if she likes you, but a scary enemy if she doesn't." She sighed heavily. "I don't want to say anything bad behind her back. She's my friend."

Clementine waited for Mary to go on, but she stayed silent, true to her word.

Devoted friend or scared of her? Clementine wondered. Out loud she said: "I respect that. I hope Holly appreciates your loyalty. Why don't you tell me more about the homeowner's association then?"

"Well, it was started because of the state some of the properties were in. Older houses are one thing, but some of the yards looked like junkyards. You know the kind, with broken-down cars, empty beer cans, and all sorts of garbage lying around. It was bad for property values, and Holly and some other people thought that it attracted–" she hesitated, searching for the right words– "well, they called it 'the wrong kind of people'." Mary blushed.

113

"That's alright, I know you're just repeating what they said. Go on," Clementine said encouragingly.

"We also had a lady here who ran a halfway house for addicts. She was wonderful, really passionate about helping the less fortunate. She took in people fresh out of rehab who needed support to get back on their feet. You know, when they get out of rehab and go back to their old home and friends and whatnot, they don't stand a chance. They might have the best intentions, but their old life pulls them right back in, and before they know it they are back on drugs. Having a place like hers with other people in the same situation is a real godsend. But people around here didn't like her running that place, they were worried about safety and drug dealers coming in." Mary paused for a moment and took a sip of tea. Clementine didn't say a word, not wanting to interrupt her flow.

"When we set up the homeowner's association it was voluntary for people to join. We couldn't force them if they didn't want to, because when they bought their house the association didn't exist. Most folks joined willingly, because they were excited about making Pleasant Hill better and see the value of their home go up. But some didn't. Not everybody is a joiner, and some people just want to be left alone. Taylor, the lady with the halfway house, didn't join either, for obvious reasons. According to the rules we created she would have had to close it down, and she wasn't going to do that. Helping those poor people was her life's work." Mary stopped talking and stared into space, lost in the past. She seemed to have momentarily forgotten where she was.

"What happened to Taylor?" Clementine asked softly.

Mary closed her eyes for a moment. She seemed to debate how much to tell, torn between her loyalty to her friend and her obvious fondness for Taylor. With her eyes still closed and her hand buried in George's soft fur, Mary continued: "Holly and Homer became obsessed with wanting Taylor to move. She became all they talked about during meetings. I wasn't allowed to take minutes whenever her name came up, because what they said about her was too nasty to put in writing." She opened her eyes and looked at Clementine. "Please don't ask me to repeat it, I won't. But it was nasty. I was truly shocked and tried to make them stop, but there's no stopping Holly once she sinks her teeth into something. She won't let go. Still, I kept hoping that they would get over it at some point and move on." She fell silent.

"But they didn't?" Clementine asked.

Mary shook her head. "It got so bad that I didn't want to go to meetings, but Holly told me that I had to because I'm the secretary. A few times I stayed home anyway, pretending I was sick. Well, not so much pretending, because I did get sick with all the worry. I have a nervous stomach, and it was acting up all the time back then."

"Sounds terrible," Clementine said sympathetically.

"One night after supper the doorbell rang. It was Taylor. At first she seemed her normal spunky self. She asked me and Albert to get Holly and Homer to lay off of her. 'I'm doing something good here,' she said. 'Can't you appeal to their humanity? Or do they not have any?' I told her that I'd try, but she must have seen right through me and known that Holly wouldn't listen to me. 'Look what they've been sending me,' she said, and pulled a bunch of letters out of her purse. 'I've been getting these for over a year now. They're anonymous, but obviously they're from them.' I didn't read them, but Taylor said they were full of threats and nastiness, saying things like 'nobody wants you here', 'if you don't leave something terrible is going to happen', 'we are watching you', 'make sure your doors are locked at night'. She was getting upset while she was telling me this and started to cry. 'I just want them to leave me alone. Is that too much to ask? I haven't done anything to them.' I promised again that I'd try, and I did. But they didn't listen."

"What happened then?" Clementine asked, guessing the answer.

"Three months later, Taylor sold and moved away. I have no idea where she went or what happened to her recovering addicts."

They sat in silence for a long moment.

"How come you stayed on the board? Why didn't you resign?" Clementine asked at last.

Mary looked at her in disbelief. "Haven't you been listening? Holly and Homer are not the kind of people you want as your enemies. I'd rather have them on my side than against me." She stood up abruptly. "I have to go. You have been officially warned about your bus. Move it immediately or you'll hear from us again."

And without another word she grabbed her coat and left, closing the front door softly behind her.

Chapter 11

"She said *what?*" Holly couldn't believe her ears. "Could you repeat it, please?"

Mary looked uncomfortable. "She said that she did a big shopping trip and was still unloading her bus, and that she's perfectly within her rights to have her vehicle parked on the street for the purpose of loading and unloading."

"And what did she say about how long it would take?" Holly snapped.

"Well, she said that there's no time limit for it – which is technically correct, we never put one in – and that she doesn't like to be rushed."

"How long?" Holly asked through gritted teeth.

"She said a few more days."

"That woman is unbelievable," Holly spat, pacing her living room. Mary had come straight to her house after leaving Clementine's to report back on how she had reacted to their request. Holly hadn't expected her to comply right away, but using her own regulations against her? That was unacceptable.

"You know, Holly," Mary began hesitantly, "she's really nice. I think if we'd just ignore her little stunt with the bus and don't react–"

"Out of the question," Holly interrupted. "I won't let her

THE HOMEOWNER'S ASSOCIATION

get away with it. The rules exist for a reason, and if we let her break them without consequences then we'll soon have anarchy on our hands! Absolutely not. You gave her a warning that she intends to ignore, so it's a written warning next. Hmm, I wonder if I could get that monstrosity towed away? I mean, parking isn't illegal there, but if I call Stevie he might do it anyway. But then I'll owe him a favour, and I don't know if I want to be in his debt–"

"Holly, I have to go," Mary interjected. "I have to get supper on the table. Maybe sleep on it before you do anything drastic? I hate all that confrontation with neighbours, and I'm not sure you should pick a fight with Clementine."

"What do you mean by that?" Holly exploded. "Do you think I'm afraid of her? Or that I can't take her?"

"I mean that she doesn't seem the type that's easily intimidated. I don't want you to pick a fight that you might not win."

Holly's face clouded over with fury. "It's time for you to leave before I say something I'll regret. Goodbye, Mary."

* * *

Clementine ended up moving her grotesque vehicle two days later, after Holly had sent off the letter with the written warning but before Clementine had received it. Clementine called them and left a cheerful message that was like a slap in the face: "Hi there Holly and Homer, my dear Ho Hos from the Ho-A. It's Clementine, your new neighbour. Have you ever had anyone anticipate your heart's desire like I have? It's like I read your mind, and I fulfilled your dearest wish before you even had to say it. You are welcome. Your letter was unnecessary, but it's nice to receive snail mail in the age of email and text messages. Also, there was a spelling error in it, 'accessibility' is spelled with two c's, not one. Just thought you'd want to know. Anyway, I'm sure we'll run into each other again soon! I for one can't wait. See ya!"

Ten days after that message the snow came, and that ridiculous bus was once again parked in front of the house. This time Clementine preempted Holly's reaction by cornering one of the board members, Don Blake, at the grocery store.

It was impressive that she even knew who he was after just having moved to Pleasant Hill, let alone find the one member of the board who was a thorn in Holly's side, not following her lead at all. Old Don did whatever the hell he wanted, and he was a sucker for charming younger women. At eighty years old, most women were younger than him, and as much as it galled Holly to admit it, Clementine did have a certain charm about her. She'd sweet-talked the old fool into appealing to the board on her behalf by playing the damsel in distress, telling him that she had no choice but to park her only mode of transportation at the street because it would get stuck in the snow in her backyard, and then she would be stranded.

Don showed up at Holly's house one day, ostensibly to tell her about his conversation with Clementine, but in reality to gloat. "The poor gal is all alone, and she promised that she's getting a section of her yard paved next spring, so she won't have a problem driving her bus behind the house next winter. She didn't have time to do it before the snow came because she moved here so late in the year. I told her that I'd talk to the board, but that I didn't anticipate anyone having a problem with helping a neighbour out." Don looked at her beadily. "I've already talked to the other board members. They're all willing to overlook the infraction. You and Homer are outvoted, my dear."

Holly could feel the familiar rage rise inside her but forced a smile. "I didn't know you're such a humanitarian, Don. Where was that side of you when Chris McDermott had his speedboat parked out front last summer?"

Don chuckled. "I must be getting soft in my old age. Besides, I don't like lawyers, and he's so full of himself they call him 'Walking Eagle'. You know why?"

Holly had heard him make this joke before. "Too full of shit to fly," she said exasperatedly.

Don chortled. "That's right. Besides, snooty Chris wouldn't give you the dirt under his fingernails, and Clementine invited me for tea and served me some scones that were as good as my Annie used to make. And then she insisted that I take a tin of cookies home that are better than sex." He looked at her sideways, waiting for a reaction. She didn't give him the satisfaction and moved right past that comment as if she hadn't heard.

"Well, since you've already told her that she can keep that blasted bus in front of the house I can't very well tell her otherwise. It's imperative that we as the homeowner's association present a united front." Holly leaned in close and looked Don straight in the eye. "But listen carefully, Donald Blake. Undermine me like that again, and you're off the board. And one more thing: don't get too attached to that woman's baking. She might not be around very long for you to enjoy it."

Over the next few months Holly became obsessed with watching Clementine. In December she put up a rainbow Christmas tree in her front yard, the ugliest tree Holly had ever seen. It wasn't exactly against regulations though, since it was neither too big nor violated the light or noise restrictions, so Holly had to content herself with gritting her teeth every time she drove past it. She also tried to do something about the bear-sized dog Clementine had, but to her annoyance it had become something of a celebrity in Pleasant Hill. People loved that stupid animal, stopping at the fence to greet him when he was out in the yard and petting him when Clementine was taking him for walks. Since Clementine cleaned up his dinner-plate-sized piles of shit and the dog hadn't harmed anyone so far, Holly wasn't stupid enough to bring up his removal to the board and have them outvote her again. Besides, she wouldn't put it past the woman to claim that he was her emotional support dog or some such nonsense. She was the type to buy into all that new-age, politically correct stuff that claimed that everybody was a victim. Holly couldn't stand the navel-gazing that people engaged in these days. Not everything needed to be dragged to the surface and talked to death. Some things were meant to be buried and never spoken of again.

In mid-January, Holly and Homer went to Tilly's diner for lunch. "I haven't seen you two in a while. Had a good Christmas?" Tilly asked while she poured them water and handed out menus.

"Yes, it was nice. Christopher came home with his new girlfriend. Not sure about that one, she spent most of her time in front of a mirror, touching up her make-up."

Tilly laughed. "She was probably just nervous about meeting you and wanted to make sure she looked nice. It's pretty scary meeting the parents of the boy you like for the first time."

A memory flashed through Holly's mind of two faces contorted with anger, shouting at her. She shoved it away. "Well, I think he could do better. What's your special today?"

They ordered, and while they waited Holly chatted with the couple at the next table. Homer was reading the local newspaper, not participating in the conversation. At home they had the TV on during mealtimes since they didn't have much to say to each other, but in public Holly made sure they never sat in silence. What would people think?

When Tilly came with the food she said: "I went to my first yoga class last night at the community centre. It was great!"

"Oh? I didn't know that they offer yoga there."

"They just started this month. You probably know the yoga teacher, she moved to Pleasant Hill. Her name is Clementine Harrison. I just love her, she's wonderful!"

"Yes, we know her. We're actually having some problems with her," Holly replied, annoyed.

Tilly looked surprised. "With Clementine? How can that be? She's the most easygoing person I've met in my life."

Homer piped up. "She's one of those people who thinks the rules don't apply to her."

"Are you sure? I find her to be very considerate and kind. She's been coming to the diner regularly since last fall, and when old Hank sprained his ankle in November and couldn't drive she picked him up and drove him here five times a week for two weeks. We're all rather fond of her."

"Did she pick him up in that blasted bus of hers?" Homer asked sourly.

"Of course, that's the only vehicle she has. She calls it Matilda, isn't it a hoot? Hank got a kick out of it; he said sitting in it made him feel like the king of the road. She lived in it for six months last year, it looks amazing inside."

"I had no idea that she teaches yoga," Holly wondered aloud. "She doesn't exactly look like the yoga type."

"Clementine says yoga is for every body, age, and fitness level. She explained that it's more about finding your breath and stilling your mind than contorting your body. Not that she can't do that, she's amazingly strong and flexible! That woman can do crow pose like nobody's business. But she doesn't expect her students to do that and has modifications for every pose. She's really encouraging and supportive and says that it's much more about showing up for yourself than doing the poses perfectly."

Tilly noticed Holly's water glass being empty and walked away to grab the pitcher of water. As she was refilling the glass she said: "You should come to one of her classes, Holly! She teaches three times a week, Monday, Thursday, and Sunday. Mondays and Thursdays at seven o'clock at night, and Sunday at ten in the morning. You might like it!" She smiled and walked away to look after her other guests.

"You're not actually going, are you?" Homer scoffed when Tilly was gone. "You would have to pay me to see that elephant stomp around in leggings."

"Of course I'm not going," Holly snapped. For a fleeting moment she had been tempted, seduced by the image of having a supportive, kind teacher instead of the bootcamp-style instructor who yelled insults at her to "motivate" her to push herself harder. It sounded nice – peaceful. Holly shook the image off. You didn't get results by being mollycoddled, just look at Clementine herself. She was as big as a house, while Holly herself was slimmer and fitter now than she had been at twenty. No, she was doing the right thing by sticking with her gorilla of a trainer.

Even if he did slap her ass.

* * *

In February, Clementine had a six-foot barrel delivered and set up sideways in her backyard. Holly was mystified as to what it was supposed to be, until she saw her go out there late one afternoon in the freezing cold, only wearing a bathrobe and slippers. Holly watched through her telescope as Clementine disappeared inside. Nothing happened for fifteen minutes. Just when Holly was about to give up, Clementine emerged – butt naked. Holly gasped. "Oh no! What in the world is she doing?" She watched in stunned disbelief as Clementine danced through the snow, arms spread wide, her head thrown back. Night had fallen and she was only illuminated by the golden glow of the string lights attached around the front of the barrel and the dim light shining from the inside of what Holly realized must be a sauna. Even though she wanted to, she couldn't look away. There was something strangely mesmerizing about the gracefulness in which the large woman moved in the darkness.

Clementine was everything that Holly hated: overweight, age-inappropriate, loud, nonconformist. She didn't follow the visible and invisible rules set for women: she didn't dye and cut her long grey hair, she didn't seem to feel ashamed of the size of her body, she didn't wear the clothes that were appropriate for a woman in her fifties and of her stature. Instead of feeling inhibited by these shortcomings, Clementine truly didn't seem to care. As Holly watched her twirl and sway under the moon, she looked happy and at peace with herself. Holly couldn't help but experience a twinge of envy. What would it feel like to be so free?

Clementine didn't even try to fit in. She bulldozed through

life doing whatever she wanted, and to Holly's disbelief she got away with it. She couldn't understand it. Holly had done everything right: she married the father of her child and stayed with him to provide Christopher with a stable home. She had supported Homer through university by working a job she didn't want to work and given up her own dreams for the benefit of the family. She had made sacrifices, because that's what women did. They put their families first. But here was Clementine, not playing by the rules, and nothing bad was happening to her. Everything about her was large: her stupid bus, her immense dog, her body, her clothes, her opinions, even her laugh. Despite all that, men liked her – as did everybody else, judging from the amount of friends she seemed to have made in the few months she'd lived here.

Holly had been keeping herself small all her life. As a child it was a necessity, to stay under the radar of nosy neighbours and concerned teachers, and to literally fit into a house that was drowning in her mother's stuff. Holly couldn't afford to be loud and to draw attention to herself. She was her mother's good girl, the one who looked after them and didn't cause any problems. She was desperate to be liked, which at home meant to acquiesce and not criticize her mother's bizarre need to accumulate more and more things, and at school to be pretty and easygoing. Being pretty meant being thin, so Holly had been on one diet after another since she was thirteen. She had eaten nothing but cottage cheese, lived on cabbage soup for a week, drank a shot of apple cider vinegar before each meal, and still counted calories to this day. It was a habit so ingrained that she was resigned to doing this until the day she died. When she looked at a food she didn't ask herself if she felt like eating it or see its possibilities for a tasty meal – she

125

saw calorie count, fat and protein content, good food or bad.

Being easygoing meant going along with whatever the other kids wanted, laughing at even the most offensive jokes to prove that she had a sense of humour, and doing the homework for every kid that asked when word got around that she was smart as hell.

And where had it left her? At a college party she didn't want to go to, drinking alcohol even though she didn't like the taste or how it made her feel, and getting knocked up by a boy she couldn't stand.

A thought occurred to Holly that she didn't want to have, but just for a moment she allowed it to unfold. How would her life have turned out if she'd been a bit more like Clementine?

Chapter 12

As promised, Valerie picked up Marjorie from the hospital two days after her surgery and drove her home. The surgery had been a success, and the dreaded postoperative delirium that some elderly patients experienced – confusion and memory problems caused by the anesthesia – fortunately hadn't materialized in her. She was as sharp as she had been when Valerie met her, and eager to go home.

"Those girls that looked after me were fantastic," Marjorie said in the car. "They are doing such a difficult job so admirably. But to tell you the truth, I'm glad I got outta there. I don't like hospitals."

"Is it because your husband spent a lot of time in the hospital before he died?" Valerie asked sympathetically.

"No, he died at home in his sleep, that lucky man. I don't like them because of all the sick people." She grinned. "I'm kidding, sort of."

"Oh, I completely understand," Valerie said, straight faced. "I'm the same. You have to pay me to go into one of those places."

Marjorie laughed. "You are funny, my dear girl. I'm so glad I met you."

"I feel the same way about you. But it's weird that you say that," Valerie mused.

"What is?"

"That I'm funny. Out of the two of us, Luke was always the funny one."

"Oh? Was there only room for one comedian in your marriage?"

Valerie didn't answer right away, and Marjorie didn't interrupt her thoughts.

"I'm trying to find the right words," Valerie said eventually. "It's difficult because I never even realized it when he was alive. There are so many things I didn't see that I'm questioning now, it sometimes makes me feel as if I'm going crazy." She took a deep breath. "Luke was not mean or unsupportive, not at all. But he was an alpha male, I guess you could say. He needed to be in control, and he wanted to be on top, at least in the areas he considered to be his expertise. That included anything financial – which makes sense since he was an investment banker, and I certainly didn't fight him for that role – being the funny one, anything outside the home. Some Iranian guy had told him once how he and his wife divided their responsibilities: 'she's the minister of the interior, I'm the minister of the exterior'. Luke loved that, and he would say it whenever I questioned something in 'his' area. 'You can do whatever you want with the inside of the house, choose the furniture and colours and design it however you want. You are completely in charge. But leave the outside up to me.' Him thinking that he was the king of our yard led to all the problems we ended up having."

They had arrived at Marjorie's house. It was an elegant little bungalow, painted a cheery yellow with white accents. Valerie frowned at the five steps leading up to the front porch. "I didn't know that there are steps. This is not going to be easy for you to get up there. Is there another way in?"

Marjorie nodded. "Yes, there's a door in the back that has no stairs. If you go in through the front you can open the door from the inside."

"Okay. Just wait here; I leave the car running so you don't get cold. I'll be back in a minute." Valerie took Marjorie's house keys, grabbed her bag from the back seat and got out of the car.

Stepping into Marjorie's house was like stepping into an-other world. The walls were painted in rich jewel tones; the floor was covered in a variety of Persian rugs with intricate patterns; and there were plants, patterned pillows, little poufs, and unique trinkets everywhere. "Wow," Valerie breathed, taking it all in. She felt like she'd entered a bazaar in Morocco, and she couldn't stop gazing at the vibrant colours, delicate wicker baskets, soft leather couches, and – was that a mural? Valerie moved closer. An entire wall in the living room was covered floor to ceiling with a tiled mosaic made from tens of thousands of little shards of glass, pottery, tiny rocks, and colourful pebbles, creating several elaborate swirls and circles like colourful suns. It was breathtaking.

The kitchen cabinets were white which set off the radiant Moorish tile and copper sink beautifully. A variety of different-sized metal light fixtures with complicated patterns hung over the island, creating unique patterns on the walls when Valerie turned them on. She couldn't resist peeking into Marjorie's bedroom, and she wasn't disappointed. Large, billowy pieces of fabric in deep red and burnt orange hung under the ceiling from wall to wall, giving the room the illusion of being a tent in the Sahara Desert. The walls were painted a deep purple, and the intricately carved bed was covered in satin bed sheets and a furry throw. There were macrame hangings on the walls, cacti scattered on the bookshelf and window sills, and a mosaic glass chandelier bathed the room in a soft golden light.

"Okay, I *have* to see the bathroom, and then I'm really going to get Marjorie," Valerie muttered to herself.

It was exquisite. The floor was tiled with vintage-inspired Moroccan tile in blue and yellow, and the room contained a large blue clawfoot bathtub, a round porcelain sink with a blue pattern, and a shower stall tiled in turquoise with gold grout and a gold shower head. The walls and ceiling were wallpapered with two different patterned wallpapers, which should have looked crazy but somehow worked.

Valerie finally tore herself away to rescue her friend from the car.

"What took you so long?" Marjorie asked.

Valerie just looked at her, searching for words. "Your house! It's, it's – honestly, I'm speechless. It's spectacular! I've never seen anything like it. Sorry for letting you wait; I was too stunned to move any faster. You better give me a proper tour once we're inside! There's so much I haven't seen yet. Did you have an interior decorator, or did you do it all yourself?"

"I'll answer all your questions, dear, once I've used the restroom and can lie down. My hip is killing me."

"Oh gosh, of course, I'm sorry! I'm a terrible nurse. Let me grab your walker from the trunk and then I'll help you."

Valerie assisted Marjorie in turning on the seat towards the open door, lifting her legs carefully out of the car. Once her feet were firmly planted on the ground, Valerie crouched down and put her arms around Marjorie's waist, giving her a boost up. She made sure Marjorie was holding on to her walker securely before she grabbed Marjorie's purse from the floor and shut the door. Together they made their way slowly around the house and in through the back door into the laundry room. Valerie took Marjorie's shoes and coat off, unable to resist looking around. Even this utilitarian room was beautiful. The walls were painted terracotta, the floor was tiled in yet another beautiful Moroccan tile, this time a star pattern in warm earth tones, and on the open shelves above the washer and dryer were neatly folded towels and more plants in woven pots. Wicker baskets held the laundry soap, dryer sheets, cleaning rags, and other laundry paraphernalia. A sign hung on the wall that said: "As I do more laundry, nudists seems less crazy". Valerie laughed out loud when she read it.

Marjorie had shuffled off towards the bathroom, and Valerie decided to make tea. "Do you mind if I open your cabinets and drawers on the hunt for tea stuff?" she called out.

"Go ahead!" Marjorie called back.

On the stove sat a pink aluminum tea kettle with an intricate flower pattern hand painted on it. The wooden handle was painted forest green, with more tiny flowers entwined with light green vines on it. Valerie filled it with water and turned it on, then went searching for mugs and tea bags. Everything was neat and tidy, and without exception, beautiful. Nothing Marjorie owned looked like it came from Amazon or Walmart. Her dishes were made from colourful stoneware, the glasses looked hand blown, and the mugs were hand-crafted pottery in jewel tones. Valerie found vintage gold cutlery in one drawer and a selection of exquisite teas in another.

"There are some cookies in that cookie jar," Marjorie said as she slowly came into the kitchen with her walker, pointing to a ceramic cookie jar on the counter that was shaped like a tall hamburger. It look incongruously kitschy compared to everything else, and Valerie stared at it.

"How—" she began, and then closed her mouth. She didn't know how to ask the question that was on her mind without being rude.

"How come I have this ugly cookie jar?" Marjorie laughed. "It was a gift from a friend and colleague. It's very special to me. Why don't you bring everything into the living room where I can stretch out on the couch, and I tell you about it."

Valerie put everything on a gorgeous hand-painted wooden tray and carried it into the living room, setting it down on a carved coffee table that held a large book of Annie Leibovitz portraits, a vase with dried flowers, a scented candle, and a few newspapers. Marjorie had followed behind, and with a groan she lowered herself onto the brocade couch. "This broken hip business isn't anything to write home about," she sighed as she settled herself on the sofa, trying to get comfortable. "If I were you I wouldn't do it."

"Thanks for the tip," Valerie replied, and covered Marjorie with a soft blanket. "Lucky for you it's time for your pain killer. Let me get your pills, we'll put them right here on the table so you have them within reach." She got the paper bag of medication they had picked up on the way home and gave one of the pills to Marjorie with a glass of water.

"Okay, story time!" she said gleefully, sitting down in a comfortable arm chair across from Marjorie. "I'm dying to hear about the cookie jar."

Marjorie, who had nibbled on a ginger cookie, put it down on a plate and looked thoughtful. "I used to be a foreign correspondent," she began.

"Really? Wow!" Valerie exclaimed, impressed.

"I wasn't always old, you know," Marjorie smiled. "Young people sometimes forget that before we had wrinkles, grey hair, and hearing aids, we used to be young and had lives as well. Anyway, I traveled wherever there were wars, extremism, and social justice issues to report on. One time, in the early 80s, I was in a small village in Guatemala to write about the civil war and the widespread killing of the Mayan people. While I was there, the village was attacked." Marjorie paused for a sip of tea, a faraway look on her face. Valerie waited patiently for her to continue.

"I was sure I was about to die. I had seen terrible atrocities, most committed by the government, even though they tried to blame the guerrillas for everything. My cameraman Richard was with me when it happened. We had fled into the jungle and were hiding in a hollow tree we'd stumbled across. I was out of my mind with fear, whimpering and shaking all over. To distract me he started bombarding me with questions. 'What's your favourite colour? Your favourite movie? Favourite book?' It sounds crazy, but it helped. It took my mind off what was happening. But when he asked, 'What are we going to eat once we get outta here?' I lost it.

"'I don't know!' I whisper-screamed. 'How can you think of food at a time like this?'

"'Have you never heard of a last meal?' he whispered back. 'Food is one of life's great pleasures. I want to know what your last meal would be.' I stared at him in disbelief.

"'Mine would be a medium-rare steak with baked potatoes, lots of sour cream and chives and bacon bits, and a Caesar salad. And crème brûlée for dessert. Your turn.'

I thought about it. I had been in Guatemala for weeks by then, and I was craving a burger and fries. So I told him: 'What I

133

really want if we get out of here is a greasy hamburger, French fries, and a chocolate milkshake.'

"'Okay, that's what we will have then. I promise,' and he squeezed my hand."

"Did you get your burger?" Valerie asked curiously.

Marjorie was silent for a long moment. "I've never eaten a burger since that day," she said quietly. "We stayed in that tree all day and night. When we finally dared to go back to the village, they were all dead. Bodies were everywhere. By some kind of miracle our jeep had survived, and after Richard took photos we hightailed it out of there to Belize, from where we flew back to Canada. I was really messed up after that. Bill, my husband, tried to help me, but how could he? He was a commercial pilot; he'd never experienced anything like it. Richard was the only one who understood. He talked me into getting therapy, and that helped. Writing about it helped too. I wrote a piece about the genocide of the Mayan people and won an award for it. That's when Richard gave me that cookie jar." She smiled. "Bill thought it was insensitive, but I don't. I know why he did it. It's a memorial to all the people that died that day and a symbol of our survival. Every time I look at it I remember that I not only survived the attack, but the aftermath as well. I could have become a drinker like so many of my colleagues, destroyed my marriage, or become cynical or even suicidal. I've seen it all happen. That job takes its toll. But I learnt to work through it and come out the other side. Life has always been precious to me, and beautiful, too. I'm proud that I've kept that appreciation alive despite all the ugliness I've seen."

Valerie looked at her wide-eyed. "When I listen to everything you've seen and been through, my own problems seem so insignificant in comparison."

"They are not," Marjorie said firmly. "There's no hierarchy when it comes to tragedy. Your problems aren't any less important just because there are wars and injustice in the world. Comparing one's suffering with all the suffering in the world isn't helpful. Earlier in the car you mentioned problems that your husband caused. Why don't you tell me about it."

"Are you sure?" Valerie asked.

"Absolutely."

"Okay." Valerie took a deep breath. "Can I ask you something first?"

"Anything, dear girl."

"I feel paranoid even thinking it, but I need to know. Have you heard anything about us? Have the neighbours been talking about us?"

"You mean about your noncompliance with the yard covenants?"

"So they *have* been talking about us?!" Valerie cried out, burying her face in her hands.

"They have been talking about you, yes. They've also been talking about me, my friend Edna who has five cats, and everybody else around here. People gossip, there's nothing you can do about it. I wouldn't worry about it."

"I can't stand it," Valerie murmured, her face still in her hands. "I feel like everybody hates me."

"What?" Marjorie asked in surprise. "Why in the world would you think that? Nobody hates you."

"Holly and Homer Kent do," Valerie said, lifting up her teary face. "And I can't handle it."

"Come here." Marjorie held her arms out and Valerie walked right into them, sinking onto her knees next to the couch. She rested her head on the other woman's frail shoulder and let the tears flow freely. Marjorie rubbed her back and said soothingly, "There, there, let it all out."

Eventually the tears subsided, and Valerie looked up. "I've been falling apart all over the place lately," she confessed, smiling weakly. "I did the same when Clementine came over for the first time a couple of months ago. I'm sorry."

"You don't have to apologize, dear. You've been through the ringer with losing your husband just last year. Is Clementine the new lady that moved here last fall?"

"Yes, she lives next door. She's amazing, you'd really like her. And she would adore you, I'm sure of it. Clem's a free spirit and would love hearing about your life and seeing your gorgeous place. She's still decorating, so maybe she could get some inspiration from you? We should all get together."

"I'd like that very much. But why don't you tell me what exactly is going on with you and the homeowner's association?"

Valerie told her the story of Holly's remarks when she first met Luke, and his reaction to it. "Luke had been looking forward to spending lots of time gardening, and when he learnt about rewilding he was really excited about it. But when we bought the place here in Pleasant Hill with all its covenants, I thought he'd change his plans and abide by the rules. Maybe he would have, but not after the way Holly had treated him. Luke was a proud man, and stubborn. COVID was bad for people of Asian heritage. He encountered more racism in the two years before he died than he had in his entire adult life, and it was hard on him."

"On you, too," Marjorie said softly.

"Yeah, it was. And you know what's been making me so angry? He *knew* how bad it feels to be victimized. But here he chose to do something that would make us outsiders again, set us up to be criticized and attacked. He knew that I have a hard time dealing with conflict. It makes me feel like I'm a bad person, and I can't stand that feeling. I want to go along with the flow and be a team player, fit in and not stand out. I begged him not to go against them. But he didn't listen."

"Why do you think he didn't?"

"He said that you should never give in to bullies. That they are the sort of people who will never be satisfied, no matter how much you try to do what they want. Luke was convinced that they would pester us even if we did put a lawn in. And he really believed in the philosophy of rewilding, and the good it does to the fauna and flora and the planet. Besides, he said he wouldn't let a pair of narrow-minded bigots tell him how to live his life. He wasn't hurting anyone, so he wasn't going to give in."

"Sounds reasonable," Marjorie ventured.

"Oh, and then he also said that I had to get tougher and grow a thicker skin. 'You don't have a problem giving me a hard time; why don't you do the same to them?'" Valerie frowned at the memory. "God, that really annoyed me. He had no idea how it feels to be scared of people. Did he really think that I *wanted* to be like that?"

"Like what, dear?"

"Scared. I'm scared all the time, Marjorie. Scared of what people think of me, what they might say or do to me, scared that nobody likes me. I feel like I have the emotional maturity of a six-year-old."

"Listen to me. I think you are way too hard on yourself. You are a lovely, kind, thoughtful, caring, funny woman who has gone through significant stress over the last few years. Give yourself time and grace. Have you ever talked to someone?"

"You mean a shrink?"

"Yes, a psychiatrist or psychologist. I went to therapy for two years after Guatemala, and it helped me tremendously."

"No, I haven't," Valerie said doubtfully. "I'm not sure it's for me."

"Why not?"

"Because nothing really bad has happened to me. I mean, sure, my husband died, but it's not like I'm destitute or my life is in danger. I'm doing fine financially, I live in a safe country, and I had a normal childhood."

"You are doing it again," Marjorie smiled.

"Doing what?"

"Downplaying your trauma. But even if we forget about trauma for a moment, therapy is useful in other ways, too. How about if I tell you that a good therapist will be able to help you get over your fear of people?"

Valerie sat up. "I'm listening."

"You're talking to a reformed people pleaser. I used to be like you: worried about not being liked, eager to please, giving other people power over me by letting their judgment make or break my day. Being a female reporter wasn't easy in the 70s and 80s. Well, being female has never been easy, period. But it was especially tricky in such a competitive environment. There was so much male chauvinism in the work place, I figured the best way to navigate it was by being everybody's best buddy, the fast-talking, unflappable, can-take-a-joke Margie." Marjorie shuddered. "I can't tell you how much crap I had to take. I got my butt slapped so often, if I'd have charged a nickel each time, I could have retired ten years sooner. Guys were always trying to take credit for my scoops, leave my name off bylines, steal my stories. That was part of the reason why I started taking foreign assignments; at least nobody else could take credit for my work when they hadn't been there.

"Therapy was a game changer. It made me find self-confidence I never had. You see, I'd been faking it, acted like I was tough, but in reality I cared deeply about the approval of the guys. And the approval of my parents, my husband, my friends – you name it."

Valerie nodded. "Sounds familiar."

"Therapy taught me to forgive myself. I faced my demons, worked through them, and I learnt to like myself. Once you like yourself, the approval of others loses its importance."

"Just like that?" Valerie asked doubtfully.

"Don't be fooled, therapy is hard work. But yes, the secret to confidence is simple: find peace and acceptance within yourself, and everything else becomes secondary. The opinion of others loses its power to destroy. It may sting, but you know that you've survived far worse than a few stings."

Valerie looked the older woman in the eyes, and then nodded. "You've convinced me. I want to learn to be less afraid."

Marjorie squeezed her hand. "Atta girl. You're going to love it."

Chapter 13

C lementine stood in the paint section of the local hardware store, looking at paint swatches. She was trying to decide what shade of green to paint her living room.

Over the last few weeks she'd devoured interior design magazines, spent countless hours on Pinterest looking at home interiors, and ordered half a dozen design books with gorgeous photography. Clementine had always played it safe when it came to decorating her apartment, and she was done with that. She had bold taste in clothes, and she wanted to extend that to her house. Meeting Valerie's new friend Marjorie had been a revelation. Clementine was mesmerized by the old lady's magical home, and hugely inspired to create something creative and daring herself. She gravitated towards lots of colour, mixing patterns and textures, and using natural and vintage materials whenever possible. She'd seen a photo of a living room in *Architectural Digest* that she'd fallen in love with and wanted to recreate. It was painted in this amazing shade of forest green, and she was struggling to find the exact colour.

"Hey, Clementine!"

She turned around. A middle-aged woman approached her with a big smile on her face. "I don't know if you remember me. I'm Justina, from your yoga class. How are you?"

"Of course I remember you! You've been to every one of my classes, haven't you? Thanks for the support, I appreciate it."

"Trust me, it's no hardship to attend, I love your classes. You are a magnificent teacher."

Clementine smiled at the woman, pleased. "Thank you. That's so nice of you to come over and tell me that. What are you doing here?"

"This store is practically my living room, I'm here all the time. I'm an interior designer, and I'm looking for hardware for a client. What about you?"

"You're an interior designer? That's fantastic! I'm searching for the right green for my living room and I'm having trouble. Would you mind lending me your skilled eye for a moment?"

"Not at all. What are you looking for?"

Clementine showed her the photo from *Architectural Digest* on her phone.

"Oh, I remember when emerald was Pantone's colour of the year! Must have been about ten years ago. I used it a lot that year in people's homes, it was really popular as accent colour for curtains or pillows. I also found this fabulous velvet sofa in emerald for a client, it was to die for. I wanted to keep it for myself, it was so decadent. That's the danger of being in my field, I'm constantly shopping for other people and falling in love with the pieces I find for them. I'm *that* good." Justina laughed. "Anyway, it's a fantastic colour, I'm happy to help you find it. You want to use it on your walls?"

"Yes, absolutely. I've been an eggshell-person when it comes to my wall colours until now, and I'm done with it. No matter what they call it – off-white, almond, oatmeal, sand, beige, greige – they're all just fancy names for fifty shades of boring. I want colour!"

Justina laughed again. "You certainly don't strike me as a beige person. Okay, let's take a look here. I forget what the exact shade of green is called in this paint brand, but I'll know it when I see it." Justina's practiced eye travelled down the rows of colour samples, pulling out one strip, then another. As soon as she laid eyes on the third one she turned to Clementine triumphantly. "Ta-da, I found it! *Isle of Pines* is the one you want."

Clementine held the swatch next to her phone to compare. Then she looked up and grinned. "You did it! That's the one. I could have stood here all day and wouldn't have managed to find the correct shade. Thanks so much, Justina, I couldn't have done it without you. Your next yoga class is on me."

"I won't say no to that. If you need any help with painting or selecting colours, give me a call. I'm one of those weird people who enjoys painting walls."

Clementine's eyes widened. "Do you really mean it? Because I will take you up on your offer, I'm shameless. If you'd rather not spend your free time painting a near-stranger's walls, now's the time to back out."

Justina smiled. "Thanks for the escape route, but it's not necessary. I mean it. To me, painting is fun!"

"I'd love your help! If you have time, do you wanna grab a coffee?"

"Sure! While you get your paint mixed I'll just get the hardware I need and meet you back here. Deal?"

"Sounds good."

Fifteen minutes later they walked out together to the parking lot. "I'm parked over there," Clementine said and gestured towards Matilda.

"Are you saying that bus is yours?" Justina exclaimed.

"Sure is," Clementine beamed.

"You live in my neighbourhood!" Justina squealed. "Ohmygod, I can't believe you are the lady with the bus! Boy, do I have a story to tell you. Can I take a look inside? I've been dying to see the interior."

"Sure, come right in. I'll just grab my dog before you go." Clementine unlocked the door, called for George, and let him jump out.

"I've seen you too! You're so handsome." Justina went right up to George and petted him without hesitation. "I'd love to get to know you, my boy, but I *have* to see the bus first. I hope you don't mind." Without waiting for a reply she climbed on board.

"Let's follow her back inside, shall we, George? She clearly doesn't have a problem with you." Clementine flopped herself down in the hammock with George beside her. Together they watched in amusement as Justina exclaimed enthusiastically about everything: the wood-burning stove, butcher block countertops, colourful pillows, and the tiny sink in the bathroom.

"Did you design this?" she asked eventually.

"No, the previous owners did. I can't take any credit, they did it all. I didn't change a thing except for adding George's bed and a rug."

"But this is your style? You want your house to look like this?"

"Yes, I love this. I want my house even bolder though. More colour, more texture."

"Boho-chic," Justina nodded. "Yes, that's perfect for you.

Lots of natural wood, plants, vivid colours and patterns. You know what, how about we have coffee at your house? I know I'm impossible for inviting myself over, but I'd love to see your place. We can pick something up on the way if you want?"

"No, I have everything at home. I'm a baker and a coffee lover; I have an excellent espresso machine at home and some lemon bars in the freezer. That's a great idea, let's go to my house! Feeding you is the least I can do for helping me. You can follow me, but I guess you already know where I live." She laughed. "I'm very curious about the story you're going to tell me. Does it by any chance have something to do with the homeowner's association?"

Justina grinned. "You got it in one. Let's get to your place and I'll tell you the whole sordid tale."

"It's sordid? Even better. Hey, do you mind if I invite my friend Valerie along? She's my neighbour. I know that she's off today, and I also know that she needs to meet some nice people in Pleasant Hill."

"Is she the one whose husband died?"

"Yes. She's had a rough time. You're okay if I invite her?"

"Absolutely. I wanted to reach out after he passed but didn't know if it would be welcome. She seems like a very private person."

"Let me call her on the way. Let's go! We'll meet at my house."

Fifteen minutes later Clementine pulled up in front of her house. Justina was already there, chatting animatedly to Valerie. Clementine had thought that it might take some convincing to get her friend to come over, but to her surprise she'd agreed right away. She was coming out of her shell, and Clementine was thrilled. She got out of Matilda and called out:

"Hey, ladies, since I have you here, could you help me carry those paint cans into the house?"

"So that's why you invited us over, for free labour," Valerie joked.

"Obviously," Clementine deadpanned. "Once everything's inside, bugger off."

The three women laughed. Together they carried in Clementine's purchases, George trotting happily beside them. He loved people. Once inside, Clementine took their coffee orders and told them to make themselves at home. Justina took her by her word. "You don't mind if I roam around, do you? I want to see what we're working with."

"Go right ahead!" Clementine called over her shoulder on her way into the kitchen. Valerie followed her.

"Justina seems great."

"Doesn't she? I met her in front of the paint wall at the hardware store. She's an interior designer – isn't that a stroke of luck? She offered to help me with painting and decorating. I'm a newbie at that stuff, so I need all the help I can get."

"I don't know how you do it."

"Do what?"

"Meet people so easily. She told me that she wanted to reach out after Luke died but didn't know if I'd want her to. I seem to have a *Do Not Approach* sign hanging around my neck."

Clementine gave her a friend a compassionate smile and a quick hug. "Don't be so hard on yourself. You've gone through two traumatic events recently. It's normal to feel skittish around people you don't know, especially when there's a chance they might be one of the Ho Ho's cronies."

"Justina isn't though, right?"

"We haven't talked about them yet, but I doubt it. She seems way too open and fun to enjoy hanging out with those two humourless fools. Can you help me carry the plates and lemon bars into the living room? Our coffees are ready."

They were setting everything out on the coffee table when Justina came back. "I've shamelessly inspected your entire house, Clementine, I hope you don't mind. It's for a good cause – the bohemification of Clementine Harrison's beautiful, but currently blah digs."

Clementine laughed. "What's the verdict of your inspection?"

"Oh, it's good news!" Justina enthused. "The house has great features: the open fireplace, built-in bookcases, exposed ceiling beams, and the reading nook are fabulous! All we need is more colour, texture, patterns, plants, and curtains. You have no curtains anywhere! Why no curtains? It's tragic!"

"You see why I need your help?" Clementine said gravely. "I'm lost without you."

"You certainly are. Good thing you met me. Your house is crying out for help, and I'm answering its desperate plea. How do you feel about wallpaper?"

The three women chatted for a while about textiles, furnishings, and the pros and cons of installing wallpaper on the ceiling. Eventually Clementine said: "You mentioned earlier that you have a story to tell us, and that it's sordid. Spill!"

Justina grew serious. "Do I ever. It's very disturbing."

"It usually is when the Ho Hos are involved," Valerie said quietly.

"Ho Hos?"

"Holly and Homer. Clementine came up with that nickname."

"I like it." Justina grinned, but then grew serious. "I want

146

to tell you, Valerie, that I've heard some stories about how they've been treating you, and it's absolutely disgusting. Is it true that they had your guys' car towed while you were away because it had a flat tire?"

Valerie nodded. "Yup. We came back from vacation and the car we'd left parked in the driveway was gone. We obviously thought that it had been stolen and reported it to the police. But then a neighbour told us that it had been towed while we were away. We called the local towing company and sure enough, they'd towed it to their impound yard two weeks before. We had to pay almost $1,000 to get it back. Luke called Holly and Homer right away, and they told him that the car had had a flat tire which was a violation against the regulations. He was livid."

Clementine looked appalled. "That's insane. You never told me that."

Valerie laughed bitterly. "You want to hear insane? They left a message on my answering machine last summer when I hung up laundry outside to dry. Apparently it's 'inappropriate' for the world to see my undies. That's when I stopped going outside at all, because it was giving me the creeps. I feel like I'm always being watched."

"Wow." Justina seemed lost for words.

Valerie was silent for a moment before continuing: "I must have received at least a dozen letters from them since Luke died, but I haven't opened their mail in months. I just can't bring myself to do it. When Luke was still alive they sent cease-and-desist letters, fined us, and threatened to sue us if we didn't get rid of our wild yard and put a lawn back in. It started a few months after Luke ripped the lawn out. He dealt with it while he was alive and tried to shield me from the worst because he knew how upset it made me. Since his death I've put my head in the sand and ignored it all. I honestly don't know where I'm at with them – if I'll wake up one day and have the police stand at my door to arrest me."

Both women stared at her in horror. "I didn't know it was that bad," Clementine said.

"I heard rumours, but you know how stories like that are usually wildly exaggerated. Looks like in this case they aren't," Justina muttered.

"The letters have stopped coming for the winter. The same happened last year, I guess because there's nothing you can do with a yard in the middle of winter. But they resumed full force in the spring and I'm expecting it to happen again in a couple of months. I don't know what to do."

They were all quiet, mulling it over.

"I don't know yet how, but we are going to stop them," Clementine stated fervently.

"I'll help, too," Justina put in.

"Thank you guys, that means more than you know," Valerie told them. "I've felt so alone with this since Luke's death."

"You're not alone anymore," Clementine promised and squeezed her friend's hand. Then she turned to Justina. "What was it that you wanted to tell us?"

Justina sighed. "I thought it was nothing more than sensationalized gossip, but now I'm not so sure. I'm part of a book club. Most of the women live in Pleasant Hill, and a couple live in town. We meet once a month, drink wine and talk a lot, and sometimes we'll even get to the book, but not always. You know how it is. Well, one of the gals, Louise, is a bit of a gossip. Great girl, but she sure likes to talk. She's friendly with everybody, because she's genuinely curious about people.

Louise says, and I quote, that she 'finds the human condition fascinating'. Anyway, it's useful to have her around if you want to find out what's going on. You just have to remember that whatever you tell her will make the rounds, so be careful what you say in front of her. At our last book club meeting she told us something about Homer."

Both Valerie and Clementine sat up straighter.

"Louise met someone who's friends with a lady who lived here thirty years ago. She's a recovering addict, sober for decades, but when she lived here she had just come out of rehab. There used to be someone named Taylor here who ran an unofficial halfway house."

"Unofficial?" Valerie asked.

"From what I heard it wasn't government-funded. Taylor paid for all of it herself. Her clients found her through word-of-mouth, and they loved her. She treated them like people, not addicts, and she helped them with finding a job, getting their own place, making sure they continued their therapy. She was passionate about supporting them and destigmatizing addiction."

"We could use ten of those houses here," Valerie said seriously. "We have a big problem with addiction in this town."

"I've heard of Taylor before. Something bad happened that made her leave. Do you know what it is?" Clementine asked Justina.

"Louise said that the woman she met told her that her friend had never talked about her time in Summerfield. But one time they were having one of those deep conversations you sometimes have with a friend about being young and stupid, and she'd told her about her drug addiction in her youth and her time in rehab. Then she got really upset when she tried to tell her about the halfway house. 'That maniac almost killed me,' is all she would say. Oh, and she was vehement about never wanting to come back here. 'He's evil,' she kept muttering. 'He's evil.' Justina fell silent.

"That's all?" Clementine asked finally.

"Yes, that's all Louise knew, and trust me, she would have drilled for as much information as she could."

"Did she say that the maniac the lady was talking about was Homer?"

"Yes, she did. She mentioned his name several times. It's definitely him."

Clementine asked the question that was on everybody's mind. "What now?"

Chapter 14

"We have to find her," Valerie stated firmly.

"Yes, we do," Clementine agreed.

"I think so, too," Justina added.

"Can you call your friend Louise and find out more about this woman?" Valerie asked.

"Sure, let me do it right now." Justina pulled her phone out of her bag and dialled a number.

"Hi Louise, it's Justina. How are you?" She listened for a while. The woman on the other end seemed to have a lot to say. "I'm sitting here with a few friends, and I just told them about the woman you met who knows someone who lived here thirty years ago." She listened again.

"Yes, exactly. Do you have a phone number for the woman you met? We'd like to talk to her." Justina glanced at the other two and shook her head. "How about her name then?" She frowned. "You don't even know her name?"

Clementine and Valerie looked at each other, disappointed.

"Where did you meet her? Maybe she goes there regularly?" Justina asked. As she listened, her face turned to bewilderment. She covered the phone with her hand and whispered: "She won't tell me where she met that woman. Clementine, is it okay with you if I ask her to come over? I think we might get more out of her in person." Clementine nodded vigorously and gestured for Justina to invite her.

"Louise, why don't you come to my friend's house so we can talk about it some more? I have someone here who is also being terrorized by the Kents." Another torrent of words erupted on the other end of the line. "I'm at Clementine's house in Pleasant Hill. Yes, the new woman with the bus and the dog." Justina smiled and gave them the thumbs up. "She's coming," she mouthed. "You need the address? Oh, you know where she lives?" She rolled her eyes good-naturedly. "I should have known. Yes, come right over. No, don't bring anything. Okay, see you soon."

Justina hung up and grinned. "I knew she wouldn't be able to resist meeting you, Clementine."

Clementine laughed. "I didn't realize I'm so interesting to people."

"Are you kidding? A famous photographer who happens to be single comes to town with a bear for a dog, teaching yoga and wearing hippie clothes? Tongues are a-wagging, my friend. Also, I should probably tell you what they're calling your bus, because if I don't, Louise certainly will."

"What are they calling Matilda?"

"The clown-mobile."

Clementine burst out laughing. "The clown-mobile? That's hilarious!"

"You don't mind?" Valerie asked in amazement. "It's kinda mean."

"Naw, it doesn't bother me. I can't change it anyway, so why worry about it? And it's cute, I might start calling her that myself from now on."

Justina cut in. "I want to tell you about the conversation

with Louise before she comes. Something was really weird. She's usually extremely forthcoming and shares everything – I mean, *everything*. More than you want to know sometimes. But when I asked her where she met the woman she clammed up. Wouldn't tell me, was very evasive. It's strange. She's told me in great detail about her bathroom habits and periods, but won't tell me where she met someone? I can't even think of an occasion or place that would embarrass her. I thought Louise was beyond embarrassment."

"Maybe a sex shop?" Valerie suggested.

"Nope, she would be delighted to tell the world about that. She's very pro-sex."

"Church?" Clementine asked, half joking.

Justina chuckled. "No, she's no stranger to the church. She goes occasionally if she has nothing better to do."

They fell silent, thinking.

"Maybe a lawyer's office?" Valerie offered.

"Hmm, maybe," Justina mused. "It's just very unlike her to be so reticent."

A thought occurred to Valerie, but she kept it to herself for the moment. She had a feeling she may know where Louise had met the woman.

Twenty minutes later the doorbell rang. Clementine got up to answer it and came back a moment later with a blond woman talking at top speed.

"I've been dying to meet you, Clementine, I don't mind telling you. We need more strong women in this town, for the sisterhood, you know? And I knew right away that you are a strong woman. Do you like to read? You should join our book club, it's a blast! Justina, did you invite her to the book club? We each take turns choosing a book, anything from chick lit to thrillers to serious literature. The other women are great, they're all accomplished women with careers and brains. Well, almost all of them, Anne can be a bit ditzy, but she's great fun. She's the one who always chooses chick lit, the pinker the cover the better. But some of them are actually well written and quite enjoyable as a palate cleanser in between more esteemed books, you know?"

Valerie stared at the woman in amazement. *If you look up verbal diarrhea in the dictionary, you'll find her picture next to it*, she thought. While Louise continued her monologue, Valerie took a closer look at her. Louise had that sort of shoulder-length blond hair that she privately called 'real-estate-agent hair' – it was perfectly highlighted and styled but would be stiff to the touch because of all the styling products and hairspray in it. Her face was suspiciously smooth, but despite that, it was obvious that she was a woman in her fifties. She was dressed in bedazzled boot cut jeans and a plaid blouse, and Valerie would have bet a month's salary that the shoes she'd taken off in the entryway were cowboy boots. Louise clearly identified as a horse woman, which meant that she had horses, not necessarily that she rode them. Valerie had learnt since moving here that identifying as a horse woman was a lifestyle choice, a way to fit in and make friends, and as far as she could tell it didn't require being an accomplished rider or even needing to know a lot about horses.

Clementine finally managed to politely interrupt the torrent of words. "It's a pleasure to meet you, Louise. Thanks for being so spontaneous and coming with no notice at all! Let me introduce my friend to you. This is Valerie, my neighbour and dear friend."

Louise's head swivelled in Valerie's direction, and the once-over she gave her felt like getting x-rayed. "Valerie, it's wonderful to meet you!" Her face took on a somber expression.

Oh no, she knows, Valerie realized, dreading what was about to come.

"I heard about your husband's passing. I am terribly sorry."

"Thanks," Valerie managed, willing someone in the room to change the subject. She didn't have the energy for the condolence dance. As if Justina had heard her silent plea, she interjected.

"Louise, I want you to tell them about the woman you met whose friend lived here thirty years ago. We need to talk to her to find the friend."

"Why do you need to talk to them so urgently?" Louise asked keenly. Justina, Clementine, and Valerie looked at each other. At last Valerie spoke up.

"Holly and Homer Kent are harassing me. They're trying to get me to move, and until now I haven't done anything to fight them. I thought I was the only one they hate, and I didn't have the courage to stand up to them. But now I'm finding out that they have a history of bullying people in Pleasant Hill, and I need to find out more about it. If they have done anything illegal in the past I can use it against them. I need to contact the lady who used to live here and find out what happened. Victim to victim, you know?" Valerie looked beseechingly at Louise.

Louise sighed. "I wish I could help you; I really do. But I don't know anything about the woman I met. We just chatted briefly before each going our separate ways."

"But where did you meet her? We could go there and wait for her to show up again—" Justina interjected.

Louise looked uncomfortable. "Look, it doesn't matter. I'm

sure she wouldn't go back there, so there's no point in talking about it."

Staring at the floor, Valerie said: "I'm so afraid of Holly and Homer that I don't go out. I don't spend any time in my own yard or walk through my own neighbourhood. I don't stop at the mailboxes if anyone else is there, because I'm terrified that they are friends of theirs and might attack me. I'm also scared of finding another letter from them, fining me, or threatening me with legal action, which makes getting the mail extremely stressful. I can't sleep, and when I do I have nightmares. Every time the phone or the doorbell rings, a jolt of panic hits me like I'm being electrocuted. My nervous system is constantly in fight, flight, or freeze mode. I drink one to two bottles of wine a night just to numb the fear and escape my reality. My friends tell me to move, but I can't bear leaving this house with Luke's memories. Besides, I've been so depressed that I don't have the energy to do anything but the bare minimum. I need all my strength to get through a day at work and have nothing left when I'm done. Life has been so dark that—" Valerie stopped abruptly.

"Are you seeing someone?" Louise asked quietly.

"No, not yet. I know I have to, but trying to find someone is so overwhelming, I don't know where to start. Do you like yours?"

The two women locked eyes with each other, Louise hesitated, and then she gave a small, almost imperceptible nod while simultaneously shrugging her shoulders as if to say, *so be it.*

"I met the woman at my shrink's office." She stared them all down defiantly. "Yes, I see a shrink, and I'm not ashamed to admit it."

"You have a funny way of showing it," Justina muttered under her breath.

Clementine looked at Louise in astonishment. "*That's* where you met her? Why in the world wouldn't you just say it?"

"I don't want people to think that I'm crazy. Besides, it's nobody's business what I do." She addressed Valerie. "She's excellent, I'll give you her details. I highly recommend her. If you don't want to see her in person you can also do it online, that may be easier to start with."

"Thank you, I appreciate it," Valerie replied.

"I've been doing therapy for *years*," Clementine said. "Best thing I've ever done for myself. It saved me from my drug addiction."

"You were addicted to drugs?" Valerie blurted out, and then understanding dawned on her. "Is that why you did your photography project about drug addicts?"

Clementine smiled. "Yes, it is. I believe that drug addiction is grossly misunderstood. People like to think that there are two kinds of people, the reckless or stupid ones that end up doing drugs or becoming criminals, and then them, the upstanding citizens this could never happen to. They don't realize that we're all on a sliding scale, and that most of us are much closer to catastrophe than we think. Most of us live from paycheck to paycheck, with mortgages and credit card debt and car loans. What would happen to us if we lose our job today? Or if we became sick?

"People also don't want to see drug addiction as a way to escape profound pain and trauma. Doing that would humanize the addicts too much. When I was in high school I started taking amphetamines to stop eating. You know high school kids, so very inclusive and kind to people who look or behave differently. I was bullied for how I looked and for having a girlfriend, and for a few years I was on a very dangerous path. I almost died when I was twenty-one, which ended up being the wake-up call I needed. I went to rehab and therapy, and it saved me. I've been in therapy on and off ever since."

Valerie knew about Clementine's relationship history with both men and women but had never known about the rest. "I can't picture you insecure and so desperate that you resort to drugs," she said quietly. "I know that I'm weak, and that my nightly wine habit is a sign of my weakness. But you? You are the strongest woman I know. If you were so down you needed an escape there's no hope for me."

Clementine got up and squeezed herself next to Valerie onto the couch, putting her arm around her and pulling her close. "Don't limit yourself by putting a label on you, me, or anyone else. We are much more than a few words assigned to ourselves. Humans are complex, multifaceted, ever-evolving creatures. We live and mess up, and if we're lucky we learn from it and don't mess up quite the same the next time. Some of us go through harsher hardships than others, and that fucking sucks. It's unfair, and there's no rhyme or reason to it. But every person in this world goes through shit, and we all mess up. It's part of being human. I'm no stronger than you, Louise, or Justina." She looked at the other women in turn, acknowledging them.

"I think the only difference between us is that I had more help. I didn't ask for it either – it was given to me after I almost died, whether I wanted it or not. Believe me, I was not receptive at first, either. I knew that I would gain the weight back once I stopped using drugs, and I was terrified of that. At first I thought risking my life to stay skinny was worth it. Better die young and slim than old and fat, you know? My priorities were seriously messed up, not that it wasn't understandable. That's the message that was shouted at me from every magazine cover, that I got from my parents, even from my doctor. He'd known me since I was a kid and told my parents since I was six years old that I needed to lose weight. He was thrilled at first when he saw me after I'd lost eighty pounds on Adderall. 'Whatever you are doing, keep it up, it's clearly working, Clementine,' he told me. Didn't ask how I'd done it, or showed any concern that it could be dangerous to drop such a large amount of weight at seventeen." Clementine paused, lost in thought.

"I OD'd on speed when I was twenty-one. I'd been on drugs for five years at that point, and I couldn't have become sober without therapy. You see, drug addiction is not exactly a disease in itself; it's the symptom of an underlying problem that needs addressing. My problem was that I had zero self-esteem. I thought I was a failure, stupid, worthless. I hated myself. In therapy I slowly, painstakingly, learnt my inherent value as a person. It wasn't an easy process; it took years. But it created the foundation I rebuilt my life on."

Clementine turned and faced Valentine, grabbing her gently by the shoulders.

"You are still standing after everything that's happened to you: your husband's untimely death, the harassment, living in a new town, doing your challenging work as a nurse. You *are* strong, Valerie. With a little bit of help you will become a force to be reckoned with. And you have help now: you have me, and Marjorie."

"And me," Justina said. "I just met you, but I like you, and I want to help, too."

THE HOMEOWNER'S ASSOCIATION

Valerie was moved. "Thank you guys so much, I can't tell you how much that means to me."

Louise spoke up, bringing them back on track. "I've seen the woman more than once, but I'd never spoken to her before that one time when she told me about her friend who once lived here. I used to go twice a month on Tuesday afternoons, and sometimes she would be there, waiting to pick up her daughter from her session. I changed my schedule recently, so I don't seen her anymore, but maybe her daughter still goes on Tuesday afternoons?"

"I assume there's no point in asking your therapist to give you her name?" Justina asked.

"No," Louise and Clementine said together.

"That would be grossly unethical," Clementine added. "A breach of therapist-patient confidentiality is serious. No ethical therapist would do that."

"Okay, tell you what," Valerie said determinedly. "I'll contact her and make an appointment. I've been meaning to do that anyway, and I guess this is the universe telling me that it's time. At what time did you see her, Louise?"

"My appointment was always at three o'clock, her daughter was in before me. Sessions last an hour."

"It's a good thing that your spot opened up recently, isn't it," Valerie said with a nervous grin. "Let's hope nobody else has taken it yet."

Chapter 15

Clementine used the grey, bleak days of winter to transform her house into a whimsical wonderland. After initially saying that boho-chic was her design style, Justina amended it to the design aesthetic *cottagecore*, a term Clementine had never heard before. "The kids call everything *core* these days," Justina had said with a shrug. "Any trend has the word *core* added to it, and there are thousands: Barbiecore, fairycore, gothcore, you name it. I believe the term was first used in fashion, but it's come into design as well. Cottagecore celebrates simple living in the country: think flowing long dresses, hand-knit cardigans, baking bread, collecting fresh eggs from your own chickens, picking wildflowers and putting them into mason jars on your rustic vintage table. The aesthetic is all about using what you already have, sustainable living, vintage, going back to basics. Cottagecore interior design includes dainty florals, pastels, wood, braided rugs, greenery. I think it suits you to a T."

"Cottagecore, huh?" Clementine laughed. "The name is insane, but the concept is gorgeous. Let's do it!"

With Justina's help, Clementine painted, stenciled, and wallpapered every wall of her house. She added lace curtains to the windows, bronze wall sconces to the hallway, and an abundance of throw pillows, plush blankets, and candles to her reading nook. For weeks Clementine was on the hunt for ornately carved picture frames in gold and bronze, going to every vintage store, flea market, and garage sale she could find. She used those frames for the portraits of the drug addicts she had taken. The raw, intimate black-and-white photos surrounded by the gilded, over-the-top frames created a stark contrast that stopped you in your tracks. Clementine loved the symbolism of it: flawed humanity surrounded by beauty; the ache of being alive juxtaposed with the soothing tonic that was art.

When she wasn't painting, designing, or decorating, she took pictures. Clementine still hadn't gotten over the novelty of photographing nature and animals as opposed to humans, and she could spend hours waiting by the window, her camera trained on the bird feeder. Sitting like that lent itself to thinking, and Clementine did a lot of that while she waited for the birds to appear. She was intensely curious about Holly. If all the years of therapy, yoga, and meditation had taught her anything, it was that everybody was hurting. The degrees of hurt varied from person to person and season to season, but pain was a constant of the human experience. The ones who were in the greatest denial about it usually hurt the worst, and Clementine suspected that Holly was one of those cases. Her bristly, highly efficient exterior was hiding something, and Clementine couldn't stop wondering what that was.

Holly projected her pain onto others, spreading the misery around, and Clementine was determined to stop that. Valerie had told her more about what life in Pleasant Hill was like under the Ho Ho's reign of terror, and it wasn't pretty. In addition to the warning she had received for her laundry hanging on a line outside to dry (outdoor laundry lines were against the rules), her and Luke also got fined the first winter they lived there when their basement flooded. A pipe had burst, and they needed to remove the contents of the basement to have it professionally dried and the flooring replaced. They brought everything into the garage, but to do that they had to temporarily park Luke's boat in the driveway. Less than twenty-four hours later they received a warning with the demand to move the boat immediately, and when Luke explained that the garage would be full for at least a week and the boat had to stay in the driveway, they got fined.

"We debated fighting it but decided that it would be easier to just pay the fine. At that point we still thought that this was an isolated incident, and that we'd get them off our backs and move on if we paid," Valerie had explained. "Ahh, to be that young and innocent again," she'd joked, and Clementine's heart swelled with pride. Who would have thought that the twitchy, scared-of-her-own-shadow bundle of nerves she'd met six months ago would be able to joke about her situation like this?

"You know what's amazing?" Valerie had told her another time. "I always thought we were the only ones they're going after. But once I befriended Marjorie I found out that they're like this to everyone! I know I shouldn't be happy about it, but it feels so good to know that I'm not singled out. I really thought everybody in Pleasant Hill hated me and wanted me gone, and now I hear that other people are also having problems with the Ho Hos. I haven't found the courage to talk to them yet, but just knowing they exist means the world to me."

The list of horror stories about the HOA's rigidness and

absurd behaviour kept growing. Marjorie was a wealth of information, since she'd lived in Pleasant Hill forever and knew a lot of the neighbours. She'd also never lost her journalistic instincts when it came to gathering facts, and she kept a file of transgressions she'd labeled "Infractions and reactions".

The reactions were predictably unimaginative – warnings, fines, threats of lawsuits, cease-and-desist letters. Interestingly, as far as Marjorie knew, the HOA had never filed a lawsuit against anybody. "That's strange, isn't it?" Clementine mused during tea one afternoon.

"I'm not complaining," Valerie said darkly. "If they decide to start suing people they'll probably start with me. I can do without that, thank you very much."

"I don't want them to start lawsuits either. But there must be a reason that they haven't gone there, and I doubt that it's out of the goodness of their hearts. I wonder if they're hiding something."

"Wouldn't surprise me," Marjorie said. "Reading through the infraction section of my file is like taking a lesson in pettiness 101. People like that are not rational, and irrational people do irrational things."

The incidents that were considered infractions were a study in narrow-mindedness; a seemingly endless list of yard violations, appearance-related transgressions, and improper seasonal decorations. Among the many items on the list were violations related to lawn length, lawn appearance, unacceptable landscaping, weeds, leaves in the fall, snow removal in the winter; the "wrong" house colour, style of front door, or garbage cans not moved quickly enough from the curb back into the designated garbage can spot; and seasonal decorations deemed inappropriate, such as Skelly, the twelve-foot Home

Depot skeleton that had become the bane of the homeowner's association's existence since it became hugely popular in 2020.

"Some so-called infractions are less petty and more abusive or downright crazy," Marjorie told Clementine and Valerie. "The Larsons installed a children's play set a few years ago, one of those fantastic wooden structures with a playhouse, slide, swings, and climbing wall. Their daughter Violet was obsessed with pink, so they painted it pink. It was professionally done and looked beautiful. Well, you would have thought the Larsons had announced World War III based on the reaction of the homeowner's association. They sent an escalating series of fines and letters threatening legal action, and in the end the Larsons gave in and had it repainted in 'approved' colours. Little Violet was devastated. She never played on the play set again, and eventually they sold it."

"Wow," Valerie breathed. "I had no idea. Do the Larsons still live here?"

Marjorie shook her head. "No, they ended up moving. They're still in Summerfield, but they moved to the other side of town." She leafed through the sheets of printed "Infractions and reactions" in front of her. "Oh, this one is terrible. Just terrible." She sighed. "This incident goes back ten years. Molly Peterson was an elderly lady who lived alone in a house at the end of the cul-de-sac. Well, one fine spring day she was puttering around in her driveway when her leg gave out and she fell. She couldn't get up because, as it would later turn out, she'd broken her hip. Poor Molly lay in her driveway, calling for help. None of the immediate neighbours were home in the middle of the day, and with her house being at a dead-end, it took a few hours before someone found her and called an ambulance. By that time Molly was hypothermic, because spring in Summerfield is as cold as a witch's thorax."

At that phrasing Clementine and Valerie grinned at each other but didn't interrupt.

"They kept her in the hospital for a few days, fixed her hip and got her stable again. When she came home, a letter was waiting for her." Marjorie paused dramatically.

"Who in the world could it have been from?" Clementine asked, wide-eyed, feigning ignorance.

Valerie said: "I'm at the edge of my seat with nervous anticipation."

Marjorie played along. "Patience, children, patience. It's a virtue, you know." She smiled for a moment, but then her smile faded. "It was a letter from – you guessed it – the HOA. It was a fine, and I dare you to guess what it was for. You never will."

"Slippery driveway conditions?" Valerie ventured.

"Leaving her house without asking the Ho Hos for permission?" Clementine joked.

"You're both way off. No, the violation was 'sleeping in the driveway in the middle of the day'."

Clementine and Valerie both stared at her with their mouths open.

"You are kidding," Valerie said, appalled.

"You can't be serious," Clementine added weakly.

"I'm as serious as a heart attack," Marjorie assured them. "I saw the letter with my own two eyes. You realize what that means, don't you?"

"That the Ho Hos are even more insane than we thought?" Valerie said angrily.

Clementine got it first. "They saw her lying on the ground and didn't check if she needed help."

"Exactly. There have been rumours for years that the Kents have a telescope in their house that they use to spy on neighbours. It must be true, because there's no way that they could have seen her without one. Either that, or someone else saw Molly and reported her to the HOA instead of helping her."

The three women sat in silence for a long moment, digesting this. "I can't believe that. I don't want to believe it," Valerie murmured at last. "These are our neighbours! We are supposed to be a community. How can people be so callous?"

Clementine looked thoughtful. "How many people know about this?"

Marjorie shrugged. "Not many, I don't think. Molly was a very private person. I only know about it because we were friends, and she was so distraught by the letter that she needed to confide in someone."

"What did she do? She didn't pay the fine, did she?"

Marjorie sighed. "She never got the chance. Molly had a stroke, probably caused by a blood clot from the surgery. She went back to the hospital less than a week after she'd left it, and she never came home."

"That's just awful." Valerie looked upset. "Everybody is so alienated from each other in this neighbourhood, so suspicious. I assumed Luke and I were the only ones they hated, because of the yard and everything. When I found out that they treat lots of people like me I was relieved at first, because I didn't feel so isolated anymore. But now I can't stand it. They're like a contagious disease that infects everything around them and makes all of us sick."

"That's a perfect analogy, Val," Clementine said appreciatively. "And you being a nurse know better than any of us what happens to diseases."

"Yes I do," Valerie said grimly. "We cure them – or we fight them with all we've got."

* * *

In March, Clementine invited Valerie, Justina, and Marjorie over to celebrate being finished with the renovations to her home.

"It looks fantastic, Clem," Valerie told her as she gazed around the completely transformed space.

What had been a pleasant, but nondescript home was now a quirky cross between a Hobbit house, a fairy cottage, and a bo-hemian farmhouse. The living room was painted in earth tones and had plants everywhere. Clementine had hired builders to install rustic wooden ceiling beams and added vintage metal barn lights that cast a warm, golden glow. Large, comfortable couches and a plush velvet-covered armchair were grouped around the open stone fireplace. A wooden shelf above the fireplace held thick pillar candles, framed photographs, and an assortment of nature treasures Clementine had found on her walks: pine cones, an empty bird's nest, a heart-shaped rock, an eagle feather. George's large dog bed was placed between the armchair and the fireplace, currently empty as he was excitedly weaving between everybody's legs.

Marjorie had wandered off into the kitchen, and her excited voice floated out to the rest of them still standing in the living room. "Clementine, dear, it's gorgeous! I love what you've done with the floor, it's exquisite!" She was referring to the white ceramic tiles with an intricate black star pattern that gave the kitchen an old-world feel. Paired with the robins-egg-blue cabinets, butcher block counters, and open shelving, the kitchen looked homey and cozy.

"Thanks, guys!" Clementine beamed. "I couldn't have done it without Justina's help. She really has an extraordinary eye and vision."

Justina took a bow and then laughed. "It was my pleasure, Clem. Most of the time I have to restrain my vision because clients want to play it safe and tell me not to go 'too crazy'. Worst phrase in any creative's life. Thanks for trusting me and letting me go all the way!"

"You sound like a football player who got lucky on prom night," Valerie deadpanned, and they all laughed.

Clementine had prepared spaghetti puttanesca and served it with a mixed green salad dressed with olive oil and freshly squeezed lemon juice. They ate at the large farmhouse table in the kitchen, washing the delicious meal down with iced tea and sparkling water. She'd told her friends to bring their own wine if they wanted any, because she never bought alcohol on principle, refusing to support the alcohol industry.

"I can't stand how unethical big corporations such a Big Booze are. They sell a highly addictive product and then blame the consumer when they get addicted. They know that alcohol is a known carcinogen but market it as healthy. It's the tobacco industry all over again. I don't mind if you want to have a drink, but I won't provide it. You're more than welcome to bring your own." None of them had. Marjorie had never been a big drinker and didn't like to mix her medication with alcohol; Justina said she drank too much anyway and was glad for the break; and Valerie was too self-conscious to be the only one drinking.

While they ate, they chatted companionably about Clementine's successful renovation, Marjorie's ongoing recovery from her hip surgery, Justina's next project, and Valerie's upcoming first session with the therapist Louise had recommended. Once they were done, Clementine led them all into the living room for tea and coffee, and lit a fire in the open fireplace.

"I've had an idea about the Ho Ho situation," she said when everybody had settled in.

Justina sat up straighter. "You have? Let's hear it! It's about time we're doing something about them. They're completely out of control."

"Hear hear," Valerie muttered, nodding vigorously.

"From everything I've learnt – thanks to your detailed and well put-together list, Marjorie, it's awesome – by far the biggest offense has to do with landscaping. Sure, there are some infractions about paint colours or decorations, but they only take up a small percentage of the transgressions. The vast majority is lawn maintenance, weeding, watering restrictions, leaves on the ground, the kind of plant pots that are permitted, and more petty little details than I ever thought someone could possibly come up with and would want to waste time on. It's mind blowing, and it has taught me a lot about the human capacity to put cages around themselves in the name of 'progress' and 'civilization'. In my opinion it has backfired when it turns free people into prisoners of small minds, but not everybody shares this point of view."

"I do," Justina and Valerie said together, and then laughed.

"Same here," Marjorie put in.

"What if," Clementine asked slowly, leaning forward and looking at each woman in turn, "the four of us are not the only ones? What if there are more – maybe a lot more – residents of this neighbourhood who are also getting just a little bit tired of the constant surveillance and micro-management?"

"As you all know, I have no idea how other people feel since I successfully hid from everyone for the last three years," Valerie said.

"Oh, my book club ladies are pretty annoyed with the HOA. Every single one of them has received warnings or worse. Of course, they're mostly bark and no bite, so I'm not sure how much they'd be willing to actually do about the HOA."

"I know what you mean. Most people are happy to complain about work or politics or other people, but are too passive to do anything about it," Marjorie agreed.

"Or too scared," Valerie added.

"Bingo! That's exactly what I thought. What we need is something that doesn't require a lot of action from people," Clementine said excitedly. "If you ask people to go against the status quo, most will be very hesitant. They prefer the evil they know to the potentially great thing they don't. Rocking the boat is scary. But what if we offer them something that will require *less* work of them, costs less money, and will make them feel good about themselves since it's good for the environment?"

"If you can pull that off, my dear," Marjorie said with a grin, "you have found the perfect revolution."

"Ladies," Clementine opened her arms wide in invitation, "who would like to join me in starting a little rebellion?"

Chapter 16

I t was the first warm day of the year, but instead of enjoying it as she set out on her morning inspection in early April, Holly was scowling.

It had been a long winter. If Holly believed in seasonal depression she would blame that for her feeling so down the past few months. But she didn't believe in it, because it was nonsense. They didn't live in medieval times anymore, shivering in drafty huts, eating gruel, and sitting by the flickering light of one dying candle. People had warm, comfortable houses with good food, entertainment, and all the light their spoiled little hearts desired. Seasonal depression was just an excuse for people to be lazy, another one of those snowflake inventions to analyze everything to death. Yes, winter was dark and cold. Get over it.

Since Holly didn't think that seasonal depression was a thing she blamed Clementine Harrison, Valerie Park, and the ungrateful residents of Pleasant Hill for her bad mood. They'd had their annual general meeting two days ago, an event she usually looked forward to all winter. To her, the AGM signalled the beginning of another exciting season where she felt full of energy and alive with purpose. She was almost giddy with anticipation of seeing her neighbours out and about again, working on their yards and showing pride in their neighbourhood by making their properties look as flawless as possible. Nothing made her feel more alive than chatting with them, complimenting their efforts, and giving them helpful advice on how to do it better.

Holly's goal was simple: every year she wanted to make Pleasant Hill better than it had been the year before. There was no limit to excellence, no "good enough". Things and people could always be better, and what was wrong with that? A lot, apparently, as she'd found out at last Saturday's meeting. It had not gone as planned.

It started out with Clementine, Valerie, and, inexplicably, Justina Denbow and Marjorie Burns standing by the door, handing out flyers. Well, Clementine, Valerie, and Justina were standing, while Marjorie was sitting on the seat of her walker, looking pleased as punch to be in the company of the two women Holly liked least. Holly knew Justina, a confident interior designer who was popular in the neighbourhood but had luckily never given her any trouble. She was also aware of Marjorie's existence, obviously, since the old lady had lived in Pleasant Hill for decades, but she had never paid much attention to her. Old people didn't interest Holly. At her age, Marjorie should really be thinking of selling her house and going to an old folks' home, especially since she lived alone. But since she had no children there was nobody to make her see reason, so she was still living by herself. Her yard was always in good shape, so Holly didn't have a reason to put pressure on Marjorie. But she had heard that the old lady had broken her hip not too long ago, which could mean that she wouldn't be able to keep up with the yard work. Holly made a mental note to keep a closer eye on her from now on.

"Good morning, Holly!" Clementine called out cheerily as soon as she saw her. "Here, take a flyer, there's some important information on it regarding saving the environment and reversing climate change." She pressed a glossy sheet of paper into Holly's hand and gave her a radiant smile. "Together we can be the change we want to see in the world," she added, winking at her. Winking at her! Maybe the rumours were true, and Clementine really was a lesbian. Holly shuddered. To avoid Clementine's eyes she looked down at the piece of paper in her hand.

The headline read:

> *Do you want to live healthier, have more time, save money, and help the environment? Great news: you can! Bring some colour, wildness, and wilderness into your life by ditching your lawn and rewilding your yard.*

Holly gasped. The audacity! What were these crazy bitches thinking? Rewilding went against the rules and regulations of the homeowner's association!

Below the headline was a photo of an – admittedly– pretty spectacular yard filled with wildflowers, a bird bathing in a picturesque bird bath, and neatly kept walkways making it all look symmetrical and pleasing to the eye. *They are good*, Holly thought sourly. Under the picture it continued:

> *Lawns are ecological dead zones that cost us too much water, effort, and peace of mind. They destroy wildlife, bird and insect populations, our health (use of herbicides is toxic), our marriages (who hasn't fought with their spouse about mowing the lawn?), and our community.*

174

Not to mention that they look boring while also being high maintenance, which is a double insult to our intelligence and sense of style.

Sustainable landscaping is about creating a harmonious balance between humans and nature, an environment where plants, animals, and people can flourish. Not only does it support local ecosystems, but it also contributes to the overall health of the planet − our home.

Here are some of the profound environmental and personal benefits of rewilding:

1. Biodiversity. Many species face extinction due to the loss of their habitats. Rewilding your yard will play a vital role in preserving and enhancing local biodiversity.

2. Saves the bees. Pollinators such as bees, butterflies, and birds are essential for the reproduction of many plants, including those we use for food. Without pollinators nearly 90% of plants on earth would disappear.

3. Better air. Natural ecosystems are efficient at removing carbon dioxide from the atmosphere and storing it in natural vegetation such as your rewilded yard.

4. Conservation of water. Native plants are naturally adapted to local rainfall and soil types, reducing the need for irrigation and fertilization.

5. Fewer nature calamities. Rewilded areas provide ecosystem services such as air and water purification, flood control, and erosion prevention.

6. Adapting to climate change. Diverse ecosystems such as rewilded yards are more resilient in the face of environmental changes, including climate change.

175

   7. ***Living in harmony with nature.*** *In our fast-paced, technologically burnt-out world it's becoming more essential than ever to (re-)connect with nature to relax, recharge, and ground ourselves. The high-maintenance, useless green carpet we have around our houses isn't nature. Nature is a colourful, natural yard created from native plants that produces clean air, a home to countless animals, and a tranquil oasis for the senses.*

   Join us in replacing your lawn with an easier, water-saving, low-maintenance rewilded yard!

"I knew she was a do-gooder and a shit disturber from the moment I saw her," Holly muttered furiously under her breath, resisting the urge to crumple the paper into a ball and throw it at that obnoxious Clementine's fat head. How dare she do this before *her* meeting!

People were watching her, so Holly couldn't let on how she was feeling. She took a deep breath, hitched a smile onto her face, and hoped like hell that nobody had noticed her initial enraged reaction.

At first the meeting had gone as planned. Holly had almost started to relax, thinking that maybe nobody would bring up the stupid flyer. She should have known that she wasn't that lucky.

Don Blake, the oldest board member who had gone behind her back about Clementine once before, spoke up as she was taking a sip of water before moving on to the next item on the agenda.

"Before Holly continues, I'd like to take a moment and find out more about this." He picked up the flyer lying on the table in front of him and held it out to the room. "I've only heard of rewilding when Luke and Valerie Park did it to their yard a couple of years ago." He looked down the table to where Holly still stood, a glint in his eye. "You didn't tell us any of that good stuff that's written on this paper when you convinced us that allowing the Parks to rewild their yard would destroy the neighbourhood," the old coot said with an unmistakable air of mischief in his voice.

"I don't think now is the time to talk about this–" Homer began, but he was interrupted by Clementine, who addressed Don.

"I'd be delighted to tell you more. What would you like to know?"

"Well, where did you get any of that stuff? Did you just sit down and make it all up?"

Clementine laughed. "No, Don, we didn't make anything up. Everything that's written on this paper is scientifically proven. Valerie's late husband Luke did a lot of research before he converted his yard, and we read it all and verified it before creating this list."

"If it saves water we should definitely talk about it," someone in the audience piped up. "Water is a precious commodity, and anything that preserves it is worth considering."

"Hear, hear," someone else said heartily.

"But what about resale value?" one man asked worriedly. "Won't it hurt our property values if we have wild, untidy yards?"

"That's just like you, Todd, thinking more about money than the environment," a woman fired back, shooting daggers at the man.

"I wouldn't mind not having to mow my lawn every week

for months on end," another man announced. "I like the idea of doing something good by doing less work. Sign me up!" He received a few appreciative chuckles for that.

"People, people!" Holly shouted. Everybody shut up and looked at her. "There's no point talking about this. You know that it goes against the CC&Rs we have in this community."

"Rules can be changed, Holly," Don, the traitor, put forward. "I for one think this is something that ought to be discussed properly." He looked around at the rest of the board, but nobody would make eye contact with him.

Holly was furious, but she hid it. "Alright, here's what we will do. The board will meet separately and discuss this. We will then announce our decision about any possible changes to the landscaping regulations. Let's continue with our agenda, shall we?" *Hell will freeze over before I'll allow them to turn my beautiful Pleasant Hill into a hippie commune*, she thought to herself before continuing the meeting.

Now, two days later, Holly was still fuming. As she walked down the street she brooded on how to handle the situation.

While she had managed to get through the rest of the items on the agenda, she had lost their attention. There was an unrest in the crowd with a lot of shifting in seats, people whispering to each other, and a general sense of dissent in the air. Holly had been worrying about it ever since. What if she was losing her grip on the neighbourhood? It didn't bear thinking about.

Holly was pretty sure that the board would support her – but she wasn't 100 percent sure. She couldn't walk into the next board meeting blindly without knowing the outcome with absolute certainty. Don Blake obviously was a problem. Holly often wondered if the only reason he made trouble was to amuse himself, because she didn't believe for a second that he gave a shit about the environment. But even if he only did it because he got a kick out of stirring the pot, it still put her and her position at risk. Holly had managed to get away with having no regular elections, mostly because none of the other board members wanted the job or the trouble of aggravating her and Homer. But old Don had always fancied himself as the biggest rooster on the manure pile, and it rankled him that he didn't get a chance to go for the top job.

Holly had reached the upper level of Pleasant Hill and was approaching Marjorie Burns' house. Marjorie was sitting in a rocking chair on her front porch, her face tilted up to the sun and her eyes closed. She looked utterly blissful. Seeing the old woman so contented made something in Holly snap.

"Hey, Marjorie" she bellowed over the fence, making Marjorie jump in her seat. Her eyes flew open.

"What? Oh, it's you, Holly. You startled me."

That was my intention, Holly thought but didn't say. "I'm sorry," she lied. "I'm glad to see you, I want to talk to you."

"Sure," Marjorie replied. "Come on in and sit on the porch with me. It's such a beautiful day."

"Uh-huh," Holly replied distractedly, her mind racing while she unlatched the gate. She hadn't planned on talking to Marjorie, so she had no idea what she was going to say. Holly was moving slowly up the walkway, collecting her thoughts. She didn't want to mess this up.

Marjorie watched her patiently. "That's nice of you to stop by," she said once Holly had taken a seat in the rocking chair opposite. "You've never done that before."

"Well, I'm very busy," Holly retorted defensively.

"It wasn't an accusation, just an observation," Marjorie said mildly. "I didn't mean it as a rebuke. I appreciate you making the time today, that's all I'm saying."

"Oh." Holly didn't know what else to say.

"How can I help you?" Marjorie asked.

"Uhm, well," Holly faltered, trying to find the right words. Why was the old lady getting her so discombobulated? Something about her calm, clear eyes made her feel flustered, as if they were looking straight into her soul. Holly had the sudden gut feeling that this wasn't a woman who could be fooled easily.

Seeing that Holly seemed at a loss for words, Marjorie spoke up. "Have you had a chance to read through the pamphlet we distributed last Saturday?"

That got Holly going. "That's what I wanted to talk to you about. How could you do this? You know that it goes against the CC&Rs of the homeowner's association. Do you have any idea what it would do to the neighbourhood if everybody started letting their yards go to seed? How untidy and ugly it would look?"

"Have you seen rewilded yards?" Marjorie asked gently. "They actually look stunning. Clementine and Valerie have spoken to the Summerfield nursery about bringing in more native plants, and they've agreed. They also offered a free consultation to anyone who wants to get started on rewilding and doesn't know where to begin."

"What?!" Holly sputtered, appalled. "They can't do that! IT'S AGAINST THE REGULATIONS."

"Holly, dear," Marjorie said soothingly. "Nobody wants to harm Pleasant Hill. We all care about this neighbourhood and are proud of it. Can't you see that there are more than one kind of beauty? You may think a green lawn is the only way, but a lush, colourful yard filled with life and wildflowers is gorgeous! They are not doing this to antagonize you. Valerie wants to keep her yard the way it is in memory of her husband. Justina has dedicated her life's work to creating beauty – she wouldn't support this if it wasn't aesthetically pleasing. And Clementine is passionate about the environment. She wants to live in harmony with nature, not against it. You've gotta admit that the upkeep of lawns is time consuming, expensive, toxic with using fertilizer and pesticides, and a terrible waste of water. And when we are on water restrictions as we have been every summer for the last few years, they turn brown and really don't look good. Wouldn't it be nice to have another option? Most people won't change their yards anyways, but why couldn't you give the ones who want to the opportunity?"

"Absolutely not," Holly replied stiffly. "We created the regulations for a reason. If I give them an inch they'll take a mile. I'll either get Valerie to fix her disgrace of a yard or I'll get her out, and the same goes for Clementine."

Marjorie shook her head. "Holly, you're making a mistake. Times are changing. I know you've been in charge around here for a long time, but if you go against them you might lose. Are you willing to risk that?"

"Is that a threat?" Holly asked with raised eyebrows.

"No, it's not. Just the opinion of someone who's seen a few power struggles in her time."

"You don't know what you're talking about," Holly said dismissively. "No offense, but why would I listen to an old woman who's out of touch with the world?"

"You know, Holly," Marjorie said thoughtfully but with a steely undertone, "whenever people use the phrase 'no offense', they are planning to be offensive. I wonder why you feel the need to say it when you intend to be hurtful anyway?"

Holly stared at her for a moment, taken aback. "Do you

always just say what you think?" she asked eventually.

Marjorie grinned. "I usually do; it's a privilege of old age. You stop giving a damn about what other people think. Besides, it saves time, and time is in short supply at my age."

"Well, be that as it may, you better tell your hippie friends to say goodbye to their idea of rewilded yards. It's not happening in Pleasant Hill."

"That's your last word?" Marjorie asked.

"That's my last word," Holly confirmed.

"What if the board outvotes you?"

"They won't," Holly said, feigning a confidence she didn't feel. "If they know what's good for them, they won't."

* * *

Holly's problem with the board were the three Ds – Don Blake, Doug Bowen, and Dick Wilson, three of the seven board members. When Holly and Homer had first started the homeowner's association the board had consisted of only three members: the two of them and Mary. Holly would have loved to keep it that way indefinitely, but some of the residents had grumbled that the board was biased since it was run by a married couple and their friend who did whatever Holly told her to. There was too much truth in that to ignore it, and to avoid an election they'd added two more members. That had worked for a few years until Don finagled his way onto the board. It had taken him all of five minutes to see that Holly had the other four members firmly under her control, and he convinced the rest of Pleasant Hill that they would be served much better if two more members were added to the board to ensure that "everybody's interests are represented, not just

Holly's".

Old Don was sly as a fox, and he had managed to get two of his buddies onto the board: Doug and Dick. They usually went along with whatever Don wanted, and the three of them had been a thorn in her side ever since they joined the board. Holly, Homer, and Mary were on one side, the three Ds on the other, and the deciding vote belonged to Wendy O'Reilly, their treasurer, who was nuttier than a fruitcake.

Wendy was unpredictable. One moment she agreed heartily with whatever Holly said, the next she was completely on Don's side. Wendy was fond of her wine and Botox, and putting two toxins into her head, so close to her brain, wasn't doing her mental faculties any favours.

But Holly was stuck. She couldn't call for elections because then she'd risk getting booted off the board herself, and Don knew that. Her only saving grace had been that he'd been fairly uninterested in the running of the homeowner's association and had mostly left her alone. Sparring with her had been nothing more than a way to pass the time when he was bored.

Until now. The arrival of that damn Clementine had changed that, and Don was suddenly highly invested in the management of Pleasant Hill. There was a real risk that she might lose this battle, which was unthinkable. If she lost, her legacy as president of the homeowner's association would be ruined. How could she keep her head high if Pleasant Hill went to the dogs in front of her very eyes? She'd have to resign in protest.

But her position as president meant everything to her; without it, what else did she have? Nothing. She would have nothing left to work for, nothing to strive towards. She couldn't let that happen. There was only one option: fight. Fight with everything she had, using every trick in the book. If she had to fight dirty, she'd fight dirty.

It was time to get Homer involved.

Chapter 17

"I can't believe we're doing this," Valerie muttered, looking nervously around.

"What's the worst that can happen?" Clementine asked.

"I don't know – someone calls the cops and we get arrested?"

"Getting arrested for putting up a couple of posters? I doubt it," Justina said soothingly. "Besides, I don't think I ever mentioned it, but my husband is a cop with the Summerfield police. Nobody is going to arrest us."

"You didn't mention it. Is he really? Oh, that makes me feel better." Valerie breathed a sigh of relief. "Still, I'm pretty sure it's illegal to post something on community mailboxes. They are the property of Canada Post."

"Tell that to the knitting group," Justina said and pointed to the flyer posted on the mailboxes inviting people to join their weekly knitting circle.

"You are allowed to take up space in the world," Clementine told Valerie encouragingly. "And you can't follow every rule in the world, or you'd go nuts. Besides, some rules are bad and need to be broken. This one isn't bad, but I'd put it in the category of being optional. Who does it hurt if we put up a notice? Nobody, and it has the potential of helping a lot of people. The good far outweighs the bad. We're doing something positive here, remember? Righting a big fat wrong."

"Yes," Valerie exhaled. She smiled shakily. "I'm just not used to the lawless life."

"*Yet*," Clementine said. "Stick with us, kid, and you will."

Valerie, Clementine, and Justina had designed posters inviting anybody who was interested to attend a free session about the benefits of rewilding. It was open to anybody in town, not just the residents of Pleasant Hill, and they were advertising it under the catchy name *Born to Rewild* in the local newspaper, on social media, and on posters and flyers they distributed into people's mailboxes.

At first they'd considered hosting it in Clementine's backyard, but Marjorie had advised against it. "Let's do it properly, and not right under Holly's nose," she'd suggested. "This is something the entire town can benefit from, not just Pleasant Hill, and the more support we get, the better for us. Host it at the community hall and get a few experts who can educate people about the benefits of a rewilding. Offer refreshments, get the plant nursery involved, see if the mayor is willing to say a few words. Make it so big that the HOA can't ignore it and sweep it under the rug, which is no doubt what their current plan is."

They had taken Marjorie's advice to heart. In an effort to hold the event before the gardening season, they'd set the date for the last Saturday in April, and in the two weeks that left them they'd managed to get the mayor involved, mobilized the elementary school to have the second graders perform a *save the bees* dance, and secured three speakers for the event: a bee keeper, an entomologist, and a gardener with a spectacular rewilded yard. The three of them were going to talk about the positive ecological impact that even small changes to people's yards could have for wildlife and the environment.

"Most people are good and want to do good," Marjorie had said. "Sometimes you just have to point them in the right direction and show them how." Justina had mobilized her book club into contributing to the snacks they were planning to serve, and the mayor had given them a small budget that they had set aside to pay the speakers. Clementine had put up posters in the community centre and mentioned the event before and after each yoga class; Justina sent out an invite to all current and past clients that lived in the area; and Valerie had let herself be talked into putting up flyers at the hospital. However, she had balked at the idea of putting up invites around Pleasant Hill.

"There's no need for it," she'd tried to convince the others. "I'm sure the whole town knows by now that this thing is happening. Isn't that just rubbing it in?"

"Nonsense. We've plastered the whole town with these posters; it would be odd if we didn't put them up in our own neighbourhood. We are not hiding anything, because we are not doing anything wrong," Clementine reminded her friend. "Besides, you are with us and George. Holly doesn't know that George won't hurt a fly; if she comes too close I tell her I'll sic my dog on her."

Valerie looked doubtfully at George, tongue lolling from the side of his smiling mouth and tail wagging enthusiastically. "No offense, George, but you better behave a lot more intimi-dating should it come to that. Nobody in their right mind will believe for a second that you are a threat to them if you greet them like this." He licked her face in response.

* * *

On the morning of the event Valerie felt sick to her stomach. She was touched by the support of her new friends and over-whelmed by the lengths they went to support her, but the thought of doing something this public terrified her. Part of her still wished that Luke had never done this, that the HOA wouldn't have paid any attention to them, and that she'd never have ended up in a situation where she had to be braver than she was.

"I hate confrontation," she'd confided to the therapist she had seen for the first time the week before. "I just want to get along with everybody and not fight. Knowing that people hate me makes me sick."

The therapist – a bubbly, curly-haired middle-aged woman named Gwen with a cheerful demeanor and brilliant smile – had nodded understandingly. "Most people don't like confrontation. But unfortunately, it's unavoidable sometimes. Where people live close together, there will be conflict. We all have our needs, and they aren't always compatible with the needs of the other members of our group. Are you usually the one who gives in if there's a disagreement?"

"Yes, pretty much always. That's what worked best in my marriage, and I just find it easier to avoid a battle. Why fight if you could get along?"

"What about your needs?"Gwen asked.

"Well, most of the time it's not important," Valerie said tentatively. "If it's smaller stuff like which restaurant to go to or what movie to watch, I just go with what the majority wants.

It's not that important to me."

"But what about the things that are important to you? How do you feel when they're being dismissed or ignored?"

"I feel hurt. Because I'm always giving in and always going along, so why can't they do this one thing for me that's really important to me?"

"How do you communicate that something is really important to you?"

Valerie thought about it before answering. Her face changed as realization dawned on her. "You know what? I don't think I do. I suggest it, and when they're not receptive I shut up. I think I've always sort of expected them to read my mind and just *know* that this is different, that this is something I really want or need."

"Not everything you call confrontation is conflict. Disagreeing with someone is healthy and normal. Having a conversation with someone who has a different opinion than you is not conflict; it's a discussion. Maybe the discussion is lively or gets loud, but that's okay. You deserve to be heard, Valerie. You have a voice, a point of view, you have opinions and insights that are valuable. If people don't listen, make them. Speak up, demand their attention. You are worth it."

"I don't think I can," Valerie whispered with tears in her eyes. "I'm not a brave person."

Gwen handed her a tissue and then held on to Valerie's hand for a moment. "Few people are born brave. We are all scared, even the people who don't look like they are. They've simply learnt to hide it better. But I tell you a secret: courage can be learned. And I'll teach you how."

Now it was the day of the event, and while fear and panic threatened to overwhelm Valerie, she did the practice her ther-

THE HOMEOWNER'S ASSOCIATION

apist had suggested to her. First, she told her cat everything she was grateful for. "I'm grateful for Clementine, Marjorie, and Justina. I'm grateful for being healthy and having a job I like. I'm grateful for having no financial problems. I'm grateful for you, Smokey, the best cat companion anyone could wish for. I'm grateful for this comfortable bed, for coffee, for having started therapy, for doing things that scare me." More and more items popped into Valerie's head, and she spent another five minutes reeling off things she was grateful for. It was astonishing how many there were. How come she never focused on that?

The second part of Gwen's practice was to imagine the worst outcome that could happen and to follow it as far as she could. "Okay, what's the worst that could happen today? Well, one possibility is that nobody shows up. It would be embarrassing, but nothing else. What else? Holly and Homer could show up and somehow boycott the event. I'm not sure how, since nothing about it is illegal and the mayor is involved ..." Valerie thought hard. Was there anything her two enemies could do? They could loudly complain that rewilding was against Pleasant Hill's HOA rules, but that behaviour at a public event would look embarrassing for the Ho Hos, not her. All they were doing was hosting an info session about how to be a little bit kinder to the environment, and there was absolutely nothing wrong with that. Valerie grinned at her cat. "Hot diggity, Smokey. I believe there's really nothing to fear but fear itself. Time to practice courage."

She jumped out of bed, had a shower, and then picked up Marjorie. The night before they had dropped off a dozen platters of baked goods at the community hall and put them on a long table at the back. This morning they were going to set up the chairs for the audience; put out plates, cups, and cutlery; and display the stunning photographs of rewilded yards Clementine had found online. She had gotten them enlarged and wanted to put them up on easels all around the room for people to be able to get up close and see them properly. Nobody had seen them yet, and Valerie couldn't help but be excited. Luke had shown her hundreds of photos of rewilded yards when they changed theirs, and Valerie loved them. Nature was so beautiful when it was wild and untamed. *Just like Clementine,* Valerie thought, and then a thrilling idea popped into her head: what would it feel like if she became a bit more wild and untamed?

At the community hall they met with Clementine, who had brought a few of her yoga ladies along, and Justina, who had brought her entire book club.

"Tilly from the diner is coming by later to drop off coffee and tea," Clementine told them. "I asked her where to get coffee urns, and she offered to lend us hers, already filled! Her coffee is the best, so that's awesome."

Valerie looked at the group of chatting, laughing women in amazement. She did a quick count. "There are ten women here, not including you and me. A dozen women, and it's only nine o'clock in the morning!"

Clementine laughed her infectious belly laugh. "That's right, the Dirty Dozen is present and accounted for!"

"I can't believe this. I was worried that nobody would show up. How did you do it?"

"*We* did it," Clementine said firmly. "And just you wait, you haven't seen anything yet. From what the women have told me, there are a ton of people coming this afternoon. It's going to be great!"

The next few hours flew by. They set up the chairs, podium, and easels with the extraordinary photos Clementine had brought. Justina surprised them all by unloading a dozen potted native flowers that she'd either gotten from the nursery or dug out from wild meadows in the hills around town: sunshine-yellow sagebrush buttercups, delicate spring beau-ties, glacier lilies, purple shooting stars, the first budding larkspur, glorious bluebells, the sunflower-like arrowleaf balsamroot, and half a dozen more. They put them along the edge of the stage with labels stating the name and flowering time.

At lunchtime they ordered pizzas, and while they were eating Tilly came by to drop off the coffee and tea along with fresh donuts and yet another surprise: a gorgeous cake decorated with flowers, grasses, and bees that spelled out in large, loopy letters *Save the earth – rewild your yard.* Valerie stood next to Clementine when Tilly handed the cake over with a conspiratorial smile and the words "my contribution to the revolution." At Valerie's confused look, Tilly smiled at her kindly and said: "I know what that homeowner's association has put you through. I'm glad you're fighting back; they need to be stopped. No neighbourhood should behave like that towards each other. Change is needed, and it's starting today."

"Thank you," was all Valerie could think of to say. She would have liked to express more eloquently how much these words meant to her; how she hadn't even known that Tilly knew or cared; and that the reason she never went to the diner was her fear of running into Holly and Homer. She wanted to tell her that she was determined to be braver, determined not to let other people run her life anymore. But even though Valerie didn't say any of this, she had a feeling Tilly understood anyway. Before leaving she gave her shoulder a squeeze and said quietly, "You got this, kiddo. Don't forget that you have friends in this town; you're not alone."

An hour before start time, people began to arrive. At first they trickled in, but then they came in a steady stream, talking animatedly, descending on the food and drinks, wandering around the room, and looking at the photographs. In the beginning Valerie kept count, but once they reached one hundred she gave up. They were too busy adding more chairs to the floor, making more coffee, welcoming the guest speakers, and making sure that the equipment worked properly. By the time they were ready to start, the room was packed, with some people who hadn't gotten a seat leaning against the wall. An expectant hum was in the air.

Clementine stepped up to the podium. "Good afternoon everybody! Welcome to *Born to Rewild,* an information session about rewilding. I'm thrilled that so many people are here today! My name is Clementine Harrison, I'm one of the organizers of this event. My friend Valerie's late husband Luke became interested in rewilding when they moved here almost four years ago, and they transformed their neat, culturally acceptable lawn into a wild meadow that has provided food and shelter for insects, butterflies, bees, and birds. Unfortunately, our neighbourhood is having some trouble adjusting to a yard that looks different from what they are used to, which is part of the reason why we're doing this event today. The other part is that we want to educate, entertain, and most importantly, invite you to ask yourself why you have a lawn. Let me give you a brief history of lawns: the need for short grass originated in Europe in the Middle Ages, when the areas surrounding castles were mowed with scythes to better see approaching intruders. It was later adopted by the rich and powerful as a status symbol, who used their manicured lawns as play areas for bowling, croquet, or lawn parties. Colonialism brought lawns to North America, a previously unchanged land that had been used for hunting and gathering by Indigenous peoples. It remained a status symbol for the rich and privileged until after World War II, when a pristine lawn became an aspirational symbol for middle-class homeownership."

Clementine paused for a moment and let her eyes roam the room,searching for someone. Valerie, who was sitting in the first row turned around to see who she was looking for. Then she saw it – or rather, them. Holly and Homer must have slipped in once they'd started, because they were now standing stiffly right next to the door, with matching scowls on their faces. Valerie turned back to the front just in time to see Clementine give an almost imperceptible nod. A tiny smile played around her lips for a second, easily missed if you didn't pay full attention. Valerie smiled to herself. She knew that Clementine had hoped that they would show up, and even though most people in the audience wouldn't know it, what was coming next was aimed directly at the Ho Hos.

Chapter 18

"Alusciously green lawn may look like nature, but that's an illusion. It's a monoculture of usually non-native grass that requires an enormous amount of water, pesticides to keep pests and weeds away, and fertilizer to replenish the nutrients you take away when your clippings aren't allowed to stay on the cut grass. We've dramatically decreased the food supply for insects, which in turn has led to a worrying decrease in their numbers. Birds and fish can't eat if there are no bugs, and if we have declining numbers in fish and unpollinated portions of our food supply, we can't eat. Entire ecosystems are at risk without biodiversity. The Monarch butterfly, one of the most recognizable butterflies, has been added to the list of endangered species at risk for extinction. This is due to us destroying milkweed, its main food source and shelter. What has the poor milkweed done to us? It has committed the unforgivable sin of being deemed a 'weed', unsightly and unwanted. To paraphrase the Queen of Hearts in *Alice's Adventures in Wonderland*: 'Off with its head!'

"I won't go into more detail about of how little ecological benefit our lawns are; our lovely experts are going to do that for us in just a minute. But I would like to take a moment and talk about something else that I'm concerned with: how keeping a perfectly maintained lawn has been turned into a weapon. Homeowner's associations and overzealous neighbours are policing each other's lawns as if someone's life depends on it. The length of grass has taken on more importance than our own health, sanity, or community spirit. Instead of being sanctuaries of tranquility and rejuvenation, our yards have been turned into battlefields. We are competing with each other instead of supporting each other, using toxins in our outdoor living spaces to destroy anything that has been declared unacceptable, and turning toxic against each other, to boot. We are slaves to our lawns, imprisoned by the rules our society – or friendly neighbourhood HOA – have created around what's expected. We have to give up time, money, and peace of mind to cater to our lawns, because if we don't do that we will be penalized.

"Take a moment and think about the absurdity of it. We live in one of the freest countries in the world – and we think up ways of making ourselves less free. We live in peace times – and we wage war on our neighbours. We spend thousands of dollars on lawn maintenance – which contributes to the destruction of our planet – while simultaneously worrying ourselves sick over climate change, dwindling food sources, and the helplessness we feel in the face of it all.

"I'm not here to tell you that you all have to change your yards. I believe that every person has the right to live their life the way they want to, as long as it doesn't hurt others. I would like to invite each one of you to ask yourself if your yard is in its current state because that's how *you* like it, or if you conformed to the status quo out of fear to be judged or criticized. Do you have a lawn because everybody else does? Do you think it's expected or even required of you to show the world your prosperity? Do you feel trapped by it, the endless maintenance that's required, the money and time it sucks up as greedily as the vast amounts of water that could be conserved?

"Our goal for today is to show you that there are more than one way of living, more than one way of beauty, and most importantly: that our yards can be more than just another chore that needs to be checked off our endless to-do lists. They can become spaces that host and encourage living; not only for animals and plants, but also for us. Our outdoor living spaces can and should be more than yet another area to be judged in – they should be places of community, friendship, and fun."

There was a moment of stunned silence – and then applause broke out, hesitant at first, but quickly growing stronger. Some people were whistling and stomping their feet, others called out "you go, Clementine!" Clementine smiled and bowed her head in appreciation, and when she looked up she glanced towards the back of the room where Holly and Homer had been at the beginning of her speech. They were gone.

The event was a huge success. The kids from the elementary school kicked it off by performing an adorably clumsy dance dressed as bugs, flowers, and bees. While the entomologist had a monotone, flat voice that made people drowsy, the bee keeper was a bubbly lady whose passion for her bees was infectious, and the gardener proved to be a gifted speaker who had the audience roaring with laughter.

"I really got into it because I'm lazy," he said affably. "I hated mowing my lawn every week, and my wife and I would bicker all summer about whose turn it was to cut the grass. One day I came across an article online that described how mowing less is actually beneficial for the grass because it offers more heat and drought tolerance and gives flowers a chance to bloom

197

and seed. Well, that was just music to my ears! Initially I waited two to three weeks between mowings, but I knew I could do better. Once you stop fertilizing your lawn, it will thin out, so I started sowing native grasses and flowers, because I'd read that they don't need to be mowed at all. It all just went from there. When my mom said that my yard looked somewhat unkempt I tried to ignore it, but it niggled at the back of my mind. You know how moms are, right? Always getting into your head, whether you want them in there or not. Then I had an idea. I thought to myself, *what I need is business in the front, party in the back – where have I seen that before? A mullet!* I took a leaf out of that hairstyle and did a garden-version of it on my yard. I mowed a narrow strip along the edge of my meadow, and suddenly it looked intentional and much more cared for. Best of all? My mom approves." Everybody laughed.

The mayor said a few words at the end, expressing his interest and promising to bring up the topic of being more ecologically friendly at the next town meeting. "I'm looking forward to incorporating some of what I've learned today in Summerfield's parks and green spaces this season, and for years to come," he said in his slightly pompous way. Afterwards, people milled around to visit, look at the photos of rewilded yards with fresh interest, eat some more baked goods, and talk to the speakers and each other about what they'd just heard.

Justina came over to Clementine, Valerie, and Marjorie. "We've just heard from at least half a dozen people from Pleasant Hill that they want to make changes to their yard!" Justina told them excitedly. "They're wondering what to do about the HOA. I said I'd talk to you and get back to them when we have a plan."

"We'll discuss it later," Marjorie said in an undertone. "There are a few board members hanging around still, and I'd rather not have them overhear us talking."

"There are?" Valerie asked in alarm, looking around wildly. "Who?"

Marjorie nodded towards the food table. Sure enough, three older men were loading up their plates with brownies and slices of cake, and Valerie recognized one of them, Don Blake. The other two must be his cronies Dick and Doug. "What are they doing here?" Valerie hissed.

"Checking out the competition, aka us," Marjorie said. She looked immensely pleased. "Don is a cunning old bugger. He's only on the board of the HOA because that's where the power is. He always bets on the winning team, and in Pleasant Hill the HOA has been the winning team for a long time. If he's still hanging around here for all the world to see, he must think that we have a real chance of changing that power dynamic. His presence signals to everybody that we are the horse to watch in this race now."

As if he could feel them watching him, Don turned around, looked in their direction, and doffed his hat in greeting. Then he started heading towards them, big belly leading the way, Dick and Doug in tow. "Good afternoon, ladies," he said charmingly when he was close enough. "You've organized quite the event here."

"We're glad you like it," Clementine replied, smiling at him. "I remember you had quite a few questions about rewilding at the AGM a couple of weeks ago. Did we manage to answer them all today?"

Don grinned. "All but the most important one: how are you planning on getting it approved by the HOA?"

Clementine grinned back. "You just wait and see, Don. We don't want to spoil the surprise."

* * *

Two hours later they collapsed onto Marjorie's comfortable couches in her living room. They had cleaned up the community hall after saying goodbye to the last stragglers, dropped off the coffee and tea urns at Tilly's diner, and then driven back to Marjorie's house to discuss the events of the day.

"Phew," Marjorie said, rubbing her sore hip.

"You took the word right out of my mouth," Valerie agreed.

"What a day!" Justina added.

"It couldn't have gone any better!" Clementine glowed. "Ladies, we have a smashing success on our hands!"

They looked at each other and then started laughing.

"We do, don't we," Marjorie grinned. "A reporter from the *Summerfield Gazette* was there, I talked to him about the article he's publishing on Monday. He was very taken with it all and promised to write a rave review."

"That's great! Well done Marge. Did you mention that you're a fellow journalist?" Valerie asked.

"I didn't need to; the clever boy knew. Told me he was a fan of my work."

"You're an incredible writer, of course he is," Valerie said to Marjorie.

"Your speech was amazing, Clem," Justina told her. "You really had the audience going."

"Especially Holly and Homer – they left when you got to the part about HOAs policing us," Marjorie laughed. "It's a shame, because they missed you saying that you're not interested in telling people what to do. But then again, it's such a foreign concept to them that I doubt they'd even understand what it means. Telling people what to do is all they know."

They discussed at length the fact that the three Ds had been there, and what it might mean that the Ho Hos had shown up but then left before Clementine had even finished her speech.

"You mentioning HOAs must have confirmed their worst fears," Marjorie said. "I'm pretty sure they see our event as a direct attack at them."

"Yes, because they left before they could hear the important part that we all should let people live their lives the way they want," Clementine replied. "That should be the slogan of Pleasant Hill: 'Live and let live'."

"You'll get an opportunity to say it again when we call a meeting with the board. A few changes need to be made to the CC&Rs in the garden section," Marjorie pronounced.

"What? Is that really necessary?" Valerie was taken aback. "I thought after today we were done."

The other three women looked at her compassionately. "No, dear, we are not done yet. Today was only step one. Our goal was to get people interested in an alternative to the traditional yard with a green lawn. I think we've accomplished that. The next step is to get some of the rules changed to include a more open-minded approach to our outdoor spaces within the HOA," Marjorie explained gently.

Valerie looked upset. "I never thought beyond today. Guys, I don't know if I can keep doing this. First the AGM, then today's event. The constant tension, relief, tension, relief has me completely worn out. I need a break. Can you continue on without me?"

Clementine exchanged a look with the other two before

making a decision. "Listen, Val, why don't we go to my place and have a sauna together? Just you and me. To relax and hang out. Let's sweat all that fear out and talk about next steps. How does that sound?" Valerie hesitated for a long moment, but then agreed. They decided to meet in a few days to figure out how to best approach the HOA, said goodbye to the other two, and left.

At Clementine's they sat down in the cozy living room after Clementine turned on the sauna outside. "It takes about half an hour to warm up, we can wait in here. You want anything to drink?"

Valerie shook her head at first, but halfway through she changed the head shake to a nod. "You know what, Clem? I do. Right now I *really* want a drink. But not tea or water or iced tea. I want wine, and I want to down at least half a glass in one large gulp, and then I want to refill it all the way to the rim and continue to sip on it. And after that I want to refill it again and continue until I stop feeling so fucking scared and worried all the time." Tears filled her eyes. "I've never told that to anyone. It's so shameful to admit, but I know you won't judge me."

"No, that's not my style. Judging others doesn't help anyone, ourselves included. Besides, we usually judge in others what we don't like about ourselves, and I've made peace with my imperfections. I'd much rather try to understand why someone is doing something instead of making a judgment about them. And as you know, I'm intimately familiar with using substances to escape reality. I get the attraction. For me, it was purely about losing weight at first. But once I realized how drugs also temporarily took away my self-loathing about how I looked and my insecurity about my sexuality, I used them more and more. The pills were self-esteem on demand for me – I took them whenever I felt bad about myself. What does alcohol do for you?"

Valerie thought it over before answering. "I drink when I can't stand being me anymore. It's a break from my life and current situation. The thought of other people not liking me or talking shit about me is literally unbearable to me, Clem. I honestly think that I will one day collapse under the weight of what I imagine their terrible opinion about me is. It makes me feel like I'm a truly despicable person, and that every bad thing anyone has ever said about me is true. Drinking numbs the fear and the self-loathing. For a few hours, I can forget about it all and stop being me."

"Who would you rather be instead of you?"

Valerie smiled ruefully. "You. Or someone like you."

Clementine took her seriously. "Let's unpack that. What about me is it that you want for yourself?"

"That's easy. I want your confidence, your courage, your way of standing up to people. Nobody seems to scare you, and I honestly can't imagine what that's like. Just for a day I'd like to trade places with you and see the world through your eyes and with your mindset. You never seem to worry about what other people are thinking of you. What's that like? I want that, but I don't think I'll ever get it."

Clementine pondered that for a moment. Then she said: "I think we stop worrying about other people's opinion of us when we are at peace with ourselves. When you like who you are and you stand behind your decisions, it simply ceases to matter if someone else disagrees with you. Intellectually, you know that it's impossible to be liked by 8.1 billion people, right?"

Valerie smiled. "Yes, of course."

"I think we worry about others when there are things about us we don't like ourselves. And if I've learnt one thing in therapy, it's that this belief usually originates in childhood. No child is born with low self-esteem. We learn that when we encounter disapproval and judgment from our caregivers. Kids need adults for survival, so it's essential that we have their protection and approval. If it's being withheld from us there are only two possible reasons in the mind of a child: they're bad people, or we are. It's inconceivable for a kid to consider that the people they rely on for survival are unreliable, so kids always choose option two: they must be bad. Kids are little narcissists who make everything about themselves; it's how their brains are wired. I think you should explore your childhood with your therapist and see what comes up. How do you like her anyway? I haven't had a chance to ask you yet with everything going on."

"Gwen? I like her a lot. I mean, I've only had one session with her, so I don't even know yet how I feel about therapy, but she's great. She definitely made me feel comfortable."

"Were you totally exhausted after the session?"

"Yes! I felt like a wrung-out towel. It's more draining than I thought to talk about yourself."

"Yeah, I remember that. It gets easier once you're used to it. If you're anything like me you've probably shoved all the stuff you didn't want to deal with deep down inside you and unearthing it will take some time and effort. But I *promise* you that it's worth it. One day that dark place inside you that's currently filled with shame, guilt, self-loathing, and insecurity will be a source of strength and warmth. Just you wait."

Valerie looked at her doubtfully. "I'll have to take your word for it, because I can't imagine it."

"Have faith! It will happen. Now, the sauna should be ready, let's go outside. I usually get undressed in here and go over in just a towel. You okay with that?"

"Uhm, sure. Just so you know, I didn't shave my legs, I didn't plan on going to the sauna today."

"Girl, I couldn't care less. Never apologize for the natural state of your body, okay? It's a construct of the patriarchy, and it's about time we stop playing by their rules. Body hair is normal, there's nothing shameful about it. Besides, you'll be matching my legs, they're also unshaven."

They got undressed and wrapped themselves in large towels, and when they were ready they hurried through the dark backyard to the softly lit barrel sauna. It was chilly, and they squealed as they cool air hit their naked flesh. Stepping into the dry heat of the sauna felt heavenly after the cold night air, and they both stretched out on the wooden benches inside. For a while they didn't speak, simply enjoying the heat that enfolded them like a warm hug.

Eventually, Valerie whispered into the semi-darkness: "Do you ever miss it?"

"Miss what?"

"The drugs? The high they gave you? The forgetting?"

Clementine didn't need to think about her answer. "Never. Don't get me wrong, the first year was really hard, and I had a lot of cravings. But once I got through that I knew I'd never use again. I wasn't living before I got sober. I was just existing, trying to survive, scared all the time. You see, the thing you want to escape when you start using is still there, because you haven't dealt with it. But now you have all these new problems that come from doing drugs piled on top of the old ones, and you get more overwhelmed and stressed out, so you need to escape even more. Plus coming down from uppers is horrific, you get so depressed, it's awful. No, I've never missed it. I love being alert and fully aware, to experience life 100 percent without blurring it. That's why I don't drink. I wasn't addicted to alcohol in the clinical sense – uppers were my thing, and booze being a depressant always made me feel sluggish. But I don't like feeling any impairment. Without sobriety I would have never learnt to deal with my problems straight on, I would have never gotten to know myself, and I would certainly never have learnt to love myself. I'm convinced that every single person in the world has all the strength and wisdom they need already inside them. It's a gift given to each of us at birth. It's life and circumstances and bad experiences that block our access to them, and using substances to distract or soothe ourselves will block it even more. I didn't start discovering my inner strength and wisdom until I stopped looking for answers outside of myself."

Valerie was quiet for a while. Then she asked: "Do you know the quote that the definition of insanity is doing the same thing over and over again and expecting different results?"

Clementine smiled. "Yes, it's attributed to Albert Einstein. Who knows if he's the one who really said it."

"Well, that's what I've been doing. I drink to feel braver, but it makes me more anxious and scared, so I drink more in the hopes of feeling braver."

"Been there, done that," Clementine said affectionately. "It's never too late to try something new. If you need support, you know I'm always here for you."

"I've never even done dry January before. The longest stretch of time that I didn't have a drink for was a week, and I was hating every minute of it."

"You probably weren't ready then. We have to be ready for a change – it won't work when the time isn't right. Just try it again and see what happens!"

Then Clementine looked at Valerie mischievously. "Now, speaking of trying something new – it's time for us to go outside and cool off. I have an outdoor shower, but the temperature is cool enough that we don't need to use it. I have a little ritual where I strip off my towel and run around naked under the moon. Wanna join me?"

Valerie hesitated. "I don't know ..."

"Come on, nobody is going to see us, it's pitch black out. It's liberating! First step towards living a braver life?" Without waiting for an answer, Clementine stood up and walked to the door. With her back to Valerie she let her towel fall to the floor, opened the door, and stepped outside. The light next to the door bathed her briefly in a golden glow before she disappeared into the darkness. Valerie sat motionless for a moment. A mess of conflicting emotions battled inside her: a desire to do something crazy; self-consciousness about her body; fear of being seen; and a recklessness that she didn't care if she was. At last, she made a decision.

"Fuck it," she said aloud, dropped her own towel, and followed her friend outside.

Clementine was swaying under the moon, her arms raised high into the air. It looked like she was dancing to music only she could hear. At first Valerie stood hunched into herself, her arms put protectively in front of her body as if to hide behind them. But when she saw that Clementine was paying her no attention, she straightened up, let her arms fall to the side, and looked up. Countless stars twinkled from a velvety sky, surrounding a full moon. The cool night air felt amazing on her overheated body, and before she knew it, Valerie was dancing too. She closed her eyes, giving herself over to the moment: the sensation of cold meeting hot; breathing in the smell of the damp earth; hearing the frogs in the distance croaking a concert just for them. And for the first time in her life, Valerie felt absolutely, deliciously, wildly, *free*.

Chapter 19

Holly was in a panic. "What are we going to do?" she asked Homer as they were driving home from the community hall. "You heard her, she's attacking the HOA! We have to stop her!"

"What do you want me to do? She's gone public, it's too late to do any of our usual tricks. Not that they would work on her anyways; she's impossible to intimidate because she doesn't get scared. And now she has half the town behind her, so I wouldn't cross her if I were you."

"Well, what if we sue her? She's broken several of the covenants, with parking her bus on the road, that dog of hers, and now it sounds like she's going to do the same thing to her yard as Valerie has ..."

"No lawyers," Homer said curtly. "You know my opinion on that."

"But why? If we would have sued people like Valerie and Luke in the past it would have never gotten that far. What's your deal with no lawsuits anyway? You've never explained it to me, and frankly, I'm getting sick and tired of you acting like you're the boss in this marriage. 'I'm the man, what I say goes and I don't have to explain myself'," Holly mimicked, thoroughly aggravated now. "How about I act like you for once and do whatever the hell *I* want? And what I wanna do is sue these obnoxious women, mousy Valerie Park whose idiotic husband started it all, and fat Clementine Harrison who's ruining everything I've worked so hard for!"

"*We* worked for, you mean," Homer corrected her, irritably. "I've had enough of you acting like you're doing all of this by yourself. Without me, you wouldn't be where you are today."

"What's that supposed to mean?" Holly retorted angrily. "Who's walking around every day keeping an eye on the neighbourhood? Who came up with all the CC&Rs? Who has to enforce violations? Who organizes the meetings and keeps the board members in line? It's me, all me! You don't do fuck all, because when you come home from work you're too tired and can't be bothered with the tedious little details of your tedious little wife's life. All you do is park your lazy ass in a chair, waiting to be waited on by me like I'm a 50s housewife. Do you know how hard I work? Do you know everything I do in a day? Do you know what I've given up for you? Do you even fucking *care*?"

The car suddenly jerked, and Holly was thrown against the middle console as Homer turned the steering wheel hard to the right and slammed on the brake with so much force that it squealed. She had done it now, she knew it. One glance at Homer told her that she'd gone too far. He whirled around in his seat to face her and grabbed both her arms roughly with his large hands. "Don't you ever talk to me about what you've done for me," he said through clenched teeth. "If you knew what I've done for you, you'd fall on your knees and thank me, you ungrateful bitch!" Spit was flying from his mouth and hit Holly on the cheek. She stared at him wide-eyed, frozen in fear.

"I-I'm sorry, honey, I didn't mean it. I was just babbling, you know me. Of course you've done lots of things for me, I know that and I'm very grateful!"

Homer was still breathing heavily, but gradually the painful grip on her arms slackened. He slowly dropped his hands, turned away from her and leaned against his seat, closing his eyes. "Jesus, Holly, why do you have to provoke me like this? I really don't need your shit right now."

Holly rubbed her arms surreptitiously, knowing that there would be bruises tomorrow. That had been close. "Yes, I'm fine," she lied. She knew that the next few minutes were crucial. They would decide the state of their relationship for the near future, making him either an ally or an enemy. Holly exhaled shakily, trying to gather her wits. Homer hated losing control and inevitably always blamed it on her when he did. If she took the blame for his outburst and managed to mollify him then they could focus on the problem at hand, which was those bitches who were trying to destroy her life's work.

"I'm sorry for losing my temper like that, honey. Clementine makes me crazy, and I forgot myself. I was letting my frustration with her out on you; that was uncalled for. Can you forgive me?" The unfairness of having to apologize to him left a bitter taste in her mouth, and for a horrible moment Holly was afraid that she was going to throw up. Luckily, the sensation passed when she rolled down the window and gulped in several lungfuls of fresh air.

Homer didn't reply right away. Holly didn't dare look his way – she sat very quietly, breathing as evenly as possible, waiting. At long last, he spoke. "Alright. But don't let it happen again, okay? You know it makes me crazy when you get hysterical." She was so relieved at these words that she swallowed her annoyance at the injustice of them.

"I won't," she promised. His hand was snaking over the armrest between them, searching for hers. Everything inside her recoiled at the thought of his touch; she wanted nothing more than to open the car door, jump out, and run as far away as possible, never to be close to him ever again. Instead, she let him take her hand, and when he squeezed, she squeezed back.

* * *

Homer had a temper. He'd had it for as long as she'd known him, and it had gotten him into lots of trouble over the years. His road rage had cost him his licence for three months for reckless driving when they still lived in Vancouver, and he had to take the bus to work. During one of those bus rides he got into an altercation with another man that got so out of hand that the police had been called, and he ended up having to take anger management classes. To Holly's surprise they seemed to have helped somewhat, or at least humiliated him enough that he kept a tighter leash on his temper from then on.

He never hit her. That's what she kept reminding herself every time she was in danger of feeling sorry for herself for being in a loveless marriage. He was a yeller, a grabber, a shaker. Taking hold of her upper arms was somewhat of a signature move, and if he was really mad he'd shake her so roughly that it felt like he was rearranging her internal organs – but that was as physical as he got. One time he'd punched the wall she was standing against so close to her head, that for one terrifying moment she thought he *had* hit her. Even though he hadn't, the fear and panic she had experienced in that moment didn't know the difference, and she felt as violated and humiliated as if his fist had struck her flesh. He had broken his hand that time, and he was on his best behaviour for a long time after that. Holly believed that he'd scared himself by how close he had come to hitting her.

But all that had happened years ago. Now in his sixties, Homer hadn't had an episode like that in years, and Holly had thought that his outbursts of anger were a thing of the past. Today had shown her that they weren't.

Homer restarted the car and drove home carefully, staying exactly at the speed limit and obeying every traffic sign. Holly glanced over at him. His face was unreadable, but she noticed the whiteness of his knuckles, indicating the hard grip he had on the steering wheel. He was more troubled by what had just happened than he let on, which was good. She needed him feeling guilty, because she needed his cooperation.

Once at home she headed into the kitchen. "I'm making tea, do you want some?" she called over her shoulder, feigning normalcy.

"Sure," he replied absentmindedly. While Holly went through the familiar and comforting ritual, she considered how to proceed. Usually after an incident like the one in the car she would keep her distance for a while. Homer would be sullen and remorseful, tiptoeing around her and waiting for her to forgive him. She always did, at least on the outside; on the inside she hadn't forgiven him since that night after the party more than forty years ago.

Today had to be different though. Clementine and her merry band of wily women were threatening her beloved HOA, and time was of the essence. Holly needed to stop her, and she needed Homer's help to do that.

Holly carried a tray with two mugs of tea, sugar, a small pitcher of cream, a wedge of lemon, and a few cookies into the living room where Homer was sitting in his favourite recliner, a drink in hand. She frowned at the glass, knowing it contained Scotch, but thought better than to mention it. They had bigger worries than his drinking problem. He'd turned on the TV, which was what he always did when he was home. Having the TV on at all times was the glue that kept their marriage together. It prevented them from having to talk to each other, and it covered the silence that took up so much space in their home it was threatening to suffocate Holly.

But this time as she entered the room, she asked him to switch the TV off. He looked at her in surprise. "Why?"

"We need to talk."

His face clouded over. "Give it a rest, Holly. I don't want to talk about it anymore."

"Me neither. I'm referring to Clementine Harrison and her little speech today. She's a real problem, Homer. Her mere presence is challenging our authority. From the moment she arrived in Pleasant Hill she's been nothing but trouble. If we don't find a way to either shut her up or get rid of her she might destroy the HOA. With her gift of getting people on her side she's a real danger to us."

"Holly, there's nothing we can do. With her public exposure it's too risky to use some of the methods that worked in the past. And like I said, she doesn't scare easily. Besides, she's so tall and big, she could probably kick my ass."

Holly chose her next words carefully. "What are some of those methods you're referring to? How did you get rid of Taylor Kirby and her drug addicts all those years ago? You never told me how you did it."

214

"It's better that you don't know," Homer muttered darkly. "But let me assure you that it wouldn't work on Clementine anyways, so there's no point in telling you what I did."

"You didn't beat them up, did you?" Holly laughed nervously, not sure if she was joking.

Homer just looked at her. "Drop it, Holly."

For a moment Holly was paralyzed. Who was this man she had lived with for over forty years? Was he really capable of doing something like that? Did she know him at all? How well do we really know anyone?

There was no time to mull over these unsettling questions now. She had to focus on the problem at hand. In an effort to move on and act like she wasn't disturbed by the possibility that her husband had beat up a woman, she was thinking out loud when she said: "How about if we get to her through her friend Valerie? We have more than enough grounds to sue Valerie for noncompliance with at least half a dozen covenants, not paying fines, and not doing anything at all to cooperate. She has completely ignored us for the past year-and-a-half, and I think we have a great chance at winning a lawsuit. It would set an example that we are serious and mean business."

Homer exploded. "For fuck's sake Holly, don't you get it? I can't go to court. If a lawyer pokes around in my personal life they'll find a few things that will not only ensure that the other side wins, but that can send me to prison. Is that what you want?" His eyes narrowed. "Maybe it *is* what you want. Get rid of me so you can be the reigning queen of this house and neighbourhood and the HOA?"

Holly stared at him. "What do you mean, you could go to prison? Is this about what you did to make Taylor leave?"

Homer had been raking his hands through his hair, a sign

that he was worried. With his hair sticking up, his eyes wild and breathing heavy, he looked like a mad man. "I don't know if I can trust you," he muttered. "Better not to trust anyone."

"Homer, of course you can trust me," Holly said soothingly. "Taylor and her druggies all walked out of here alive and well, it can't have been that bad." At least she thought they all did – surely if one of them would have been injured or harmed in any way, she would have heard about it? "Besides, it happened almost thirty years ago, it must be way outside the statute of limitations. Even if it was– " Holly stopped for a moment to search for the right word "*unlawful* what you did, it's long over and done with. You have nothing to worry about anymore, right?"

Homer looked wretched. As Holly was watching him fight an internal battle, it occurred to her that he hadn't been sleeping well in quite some time. How long had it been? Months? Years? She had been so distracted by Clementine and Valerie that she hadn't paid attention. Getting older was so riddled with ever increasing uncomfortable bodily sensations that she hadn't even considered that something else might be going on that was causing his insomnia. For the first time she noticed that he'd lost weight. His face looked ashen, and there were dark circles under his eyes. Holly tried to analyze the complicated swirl of emotions she was feeling. She despised her husband – for what he had done to her, for having to marry him because he got her pregnant, for having the career she had wanted so desperately and had to give up for him and their son. But you couldn't feel only disdain for someone you shared a life with. Right now she pitied him for his obvious pain and despair, while at the same time she couldn't help thinking that if he was about to confess a crime to her, she might finally get her revenge.

Homer was visibly struggling with making a decision. Holly decided to try to help him along, excited by the idea that he was about to reveal something incriminating about himself. "I can see that you're suffering, honey," she began. "I'm sure you would feel better if you told me what's going on. Two heads think better than one, and together we can find a solution for whatever is troubling you."

He looked at her with tortured eyes. "Nobody can help me, Holly. It's better if you don't know, trust me. Just promise me that you'll drop the idea of a lawsuit, okay? Especially against Valerie, of all people. Promise me!"

"Okay, okay, I promise," she said in frustration, furious that he hadn't told her what he'd done. "And you are sure that you don't want to talk about it?"

"Yes, I'm sure. It's for your own good. The less you know, the better. Now, can we drop this? I wanna turn on the TV and not think for a while. Is that okay with you?"

"Sure, whatever." Holly's mind had just registered what she hadn't paid attention to before. What had he meant when he said, "Valerie of all people"? She had thought that whatever he had done had been to Taylor Kirby or one of her addicts. What did Valerie have to do with his bad conscience?

Chapter 20

Valerie was deep in thought. She was walking George on her favourite hiking trail outside of town, reflecting on what they'd talked about in therapy today. Valerie had started going for regular walks with George three weeks ago when she hit the pause button on her drinking, because moving her body helped with the restlessness she was experiencing. Besides, she found that going for walks after her therapy sessions helped to organize her thoughts and let the lessons sink in better. Today had been her fifth session, and they had talked about courage.

"Do you consider yourself to be a brave person?" Gwen had asked.

"No," Valerie replied immediately. "I'm scared of everything. I'm scared of other people's opinions, their judgment, what they think of me or might do to me. I'm scared of the future, of ending up alone, of getting sick, of losing my job, of losing my home. I'm scared all the time, Gwen, of everything. No, I'm definitely *not* a brave person."

"Let me ask you something," Gwen replied. "Who do you think is the braver person: the one that feels completely at ease going into a new situation, or the one that is afraid but goes in anyway, even if it is with trembling legs and butterflies in their stomach?"

Valerie was taken aback. "Uhm, the scared one is braver," she said in surprise.

"Exactly," Gwen smiled. "You have been telling yourself that you don't have any courage, when the opposite is true. It takes tremendous courage to show up despite the fear, and you have been showing up continuously all your life. Take a moment and think about it: you moved away from home as a young woman despite your fear. You married a man who not only was nine years older than you, but also from a different cultural background, which comes with its own challenges. You have faced harassment and discrimination, on top of losing your husband, which is one of the most painful experiences a person can go through; and you still have continued to show up for work where you care for others. And now you've made new friends, which is not an easy thing to do as an adult, *and* you are standing up to the people who have made your life miserable. You have shown enormous courage all your life, Valerie. You are not a weak person; you are one of the bravest people I've had the pleasure to treat. All you have to do is believe it, and I will help you with that."

Valerie was still in a state of stunned disbelief about this revelation. She, a brave woman? It was too bizarre to be true. But then again, what Gwen had said made sense. How brave was someone who was unafraid? They were basically just chillin' in their comfort zone, while she was outside of her comfort zone all the fricking time. "It's all about how you look at things, Georgie-boy," she told the dog who had trotted up to her to check where she was. She had him off leash because he would never run away. George liked having his people close by. "Sometimes it feels like I've looked into a funhouse mirror all my life, and Gwen is holding up a normal mirror to show me how things really are. Stuff I believed to be true turns out to have been distorted by a worldview I was given in childhood and never questioned. That worldview worked for my parents, but it isn't working for me. Or maybe it's just that I've outgrown it; I don't know. They're so conservative, and Luke was too. But guess what, George? I am not! I think I'm turning into a rebel, just like Clementine."

Valerie squatted down, put one hand on each side of his furry face, and looked into his beautiful brown eyes. "Can I tell you a secret, Georgie-boy?" she whispered. "I'm starting to believe Gwen. I think I actually may be braver than I ever thought. And I don't know if I would have come to realize this with Luke around. He was so overpowering. Not in a bad way, in an overprotective way. Luke liked that I was timid, it made him feel like the protector. I guess what I'm trying to say is that he liked to be needed by me. He shielded me from stuff I didn't want to deal with, and I was more than happy to let him do it. I'm pretty sure he did it out of love, but sometimes I wonder if part of the reason was that I was easier to control that way. I didn't have much of an opinion, I just went along with everything. But not anymore; it's time for me to find my voice."

At that moment, George's ears pricked up, he looked alertly over Valerie's shoulder, and then he let out a loud, low bark. Valerie, still squatting in front of the dog, turned around to see what he was looking at. "You've got to be kidding me," she said in astonishment when she recognized the person approaching them. It was Holly.

"I feel like I'm on candid camera," she muttered to herself as she got to her feet. "I guess the universe wants me to prove that I can walk the walk, not just talk the talk."

The nervous fluttering in her stomach had started, so famil-iar from the thousands of times she'd felt it before. Valerie's first impulse was to turn around and speed walk away without acknowledging Holly. That was what the old Valerie would have done; that's very much what the current Valerie also wanted to do. But Valerie stood her ground, her hand gripping tightly onto George's head, and while she watched Holly coming closer, she clung to the two mantras she kept repeating in her mind: *what would Clementine do?* and Gwen's advice, *courage can be learned.* Her knees were trembling, her stomach churning, but Valerie stayed put, determined not to run away from her enemy for once.

Holly had slowed down significantly, and it occurred to Valerie that she probably thought she was Clementine because of George. She was wearing a hat, which hid the fact that her hair wasn't a brilliant silver but an ordinary dark blond. The thought that Holly was wary of her, even if it was because she thought she was someone else, gave Valerie a shot of confidence.

"Hey neighbour!" she called out, her voice shaking only a little. She saw the exact moment when Holly realized it was her, not Clementine, because her shoulders dropped in relief, her steps quickened, and her face took on a determined expression. The butterflies in Valerie's stomach performed a few somersaults, but she clung to the knowledge that a moment ago, Holly had been afraid too. Besides, she had George with her, so it was two against one.

"Well, well, well," Holly drawled as she stopped in front of them. "If it isn't the keeper of the eyesore who's trying single-handedly to bring the neighbourhood down."

"Not single-handedly," Valerie retorted, rankled by Holly's taunting tone. "In case you haven't noticed, I have people on my side."

"*Now* you do," Holly spat. "It was a lucky day for you and a sad one for the rest of Pleasant Hill when Clementine Harrison rolled into town. Why don't you two pack your things and move to some place far away where you can have your hippie commune without bothering decent people with it?"

"We have as much a right as anyone to live in Pleasant Hill!" Valerie retorted angrily.

"No you don't, " Holly shot back. "You are selfish and inconsiderate, and you care more about yourselves than the people around you. People like you don't deserve to live in a nice neighbourhood like Pleasant Hill. You refuse to follow the rules that are in place for the good of the community, rules that seem to work for everybody else except you two. If you can't fit in you should leave."

Holly was hitting all of Valerie's insecurities, and for a long, paralyzing moment she couldn't speak. Was Holly right? *Was* she a horrible and selfish person? Were they wrong to fight the HOA? Should she have tried harder to fit in like everybody else?

But then Valerie remembered what Louise had told them about the woman who had lived here until something horrible happened to her, something that was connected to Holly and Homer. And Marjorie's list she called "Infractions and reactions" that was filled with petty, unjust, and downright evil acts they had done to others over the years, like leaving that poor old woman lying in her driveway and then fining her.

Valerie took a deep breath. "If wanting to honour my late husband's passion project is selfish, then that's what I am. I didn't plan on becoming a widow at forty-three, and it's been really hard. Not that you would know or care, since you've done your best to make my life even more miserable than it's already been since he died. You care more about appearances than people, more about how something looks than how it feels. We've been trying to explain to you several times how beneficial Luke's approach to gardening is to the environment, for animals, and for people, but you are either too stubborn or too dumb to get it."

"Are you calling me dumb?" Holly erupted, outraged.

Valerie fought the ingrained impulse to take it back, and said instead: "Did you hear anything else I said, Holly? You are not a nice person. You have treated me and others horribly, and you kick people when they're down instead of reaching out a helping hand. I never wanted this fight, but you started it the moment you laid eyes on my husband and saw that he was Asian. You are a racist, and a power-hungry, heartless, cold bitch to boot. Who harasses a grieving widow? Most people send casseroles instead of written warnings, but not you, Holly Kent. You were trying to use the most painful and vulnerable time of my life against me to get what you want. I would have done almost anything to avoid having to engage in this confrontation, but you know what? I'm done with that. I finally get that some people can't be reasoned with." She stepped closer, and since George moved with her, Holly took an inadvertent step back, keeping a wary eye on the large dog.

Valerie said slowly and clearly: "We are not going to rest until you and Homer are off the board. We will change the rules to include rewilded yards. And I'm done being scared of you. You are a pathetic woman, Holly Kent, and I pity you."

Without waiting for a response, Valerie turned around and

223

walked away, leaving a speechless Holly in her wake.

* * *

"You should have seen me!" Valerie was in Clementine's kitchen, pacing up and down with adrenaline pulsing through her veins. She had gone straight to Clementine's house after the encounter, to return George and tell her friend all about it. "I was giving it to her, Clem! I told her that she's a terrible person, I called her a heartless bitch and a racist, and before I walked away I said that she's pathetic and that I pity her. It was amazing!"

Clementine laughed and gave her a spontaneous hug. "Well done, Val! I'm so proud of you. It must have felt incredibly empowering."

"You have no idea. I've never felt so alive. At first I was so nervous I thought I was going to puke, but once I started, the nervousness disappeared. And you know what I kept thinking as I was waiting for her to come closer and felt so scared I was shaking? *What would Clementine do*; it was like a mantra. And I know that you'd never run from anyone, so I stayed put. Having George there with me helped too, I don't think I could have done it without him." Valerie danced to George's bed where he was having a nap and gave him a big kiss on the head. "You're the best, Georgie-boy," she told him affectionately.

Clementine laughed again. "You are high as a kite, girl."

Valerie giggled. "I'm drunk with power, and I love it! If I would have known it feels that good to stand up to someone I would have done it ages ago." She finally sat down, suddenly exhausted. The adrenaline was rapidly draining out of her body, and she felt deliciously tired, as if she'd just finished a hard workout. "She's scared of you, you know," Valerie said suddenly.

"Who? Holly?"

Valerie nodded. "Yup. When she was still some distance away she must have thought I'm you because of George. She slowed way down, as if she would have liked to turn around. It was only when she came closer and recognized me that she sped up again."

"She's probably not used to anyone standing up to her," Clementine mused. "Which has done her more harm than good. We all have to learn boundaries, but it seems that Holly hasn't. This is not going to be easy for her."

"Getting booted off the board, you mean? That's what I told her we would do. And that we were going to change the rules. Good thing she didn't ask me how we are planning to do that, because I have no idea."

"Oh, stuff like that is always done the same way. Meetings, votes, majority rules. With Marjorie's detailed document and the general mood in the neighbourhood, I don't think it will be that difficult to do. I'll feel out Don the next time I see him; he's always at Tilly's. And a bunch of people who've been at our *Born to Rewild* event have come up to me and told me that they want to incorporate some of the rewilding techniques into their yards this year. Change has already started to happen, and it's too late for Holly to stop it, no matter how much she's going to fight it."

"I've chosen a different day and time again for my next appointment with Gwen. Maybe this time I'll meet the woman whose friend used to live here."

"Oh, that would be good. We really need to know what happened. If those fuckers hurt someone they need to be held accountable for it. When is your next appointment?"

"Next Thursday afternoon. I have to say, even if we'll never find her, those sessions are life changing. I'm so grateful that you all talked me into it. I feel like I've always been the passenger, and now I'm finally learning to sit in the driver's seat and to take over the wheel of my own life. It's empowering."

Clementine squeezed Valerie's hand and beamed at her. "I'm thrilled for you! Sounds like Gwen is an excellent therapist and a great fit for you. Not all therapists suit all people, I'm so happy that you found the right one for you on your first try. You deserved a break; I'm glad you got it."

* * *

Five days later, Valerie parked her car in front of the therapist's office. She was nervous, as she had been every time before an appointment, but she knew that her nerves would dissipate once she'd settled in and started talking. She walked into the waiting room, expecting it to be empty, as it had been before all her previous appointments. But this time it wasn't.

A woman was sitting in one of the comfortable chairs, reading a book. She looked to be in her early forties, with curly dark hair, and when she looked up to nod a greeting, Valerie saw a serious face with dark eyes and an unsmiling mouth. She fit Louise's description, and Valerie's heart started to race. That was her! They'd finally found the friend, and it was up to Valerie to get her to give them the identity of the former Pleasant Hill resident. She couldn't mess this up, it was too important. Valerie took a seat across from her, her mind racing. She glanced at the clock on the wall and saw that they had ten minutes before her appointment started. Not a lot of time.

Despite hoping and wishing for this moment, Valerie hadn't prepared for it. She had tried to come up with a strategy, but with so many unknowns she'd given up and decided to wing it. Now she regretted that decision bitterly. She wasn't a winger; she was someone who needed to be prepared. *Too late now*, she told herself firmly. *Pull yourself together, you can do this. What would Clementine do? She would just talk and be honest. Be honest.* She took a deep breath. "Excuse me, sorry to interrupt your reading. We don't know each other, but I think you've talked to a friend of mine here in this waiting room before. Do you have a friend who used to live in Summerfield a long time ago, in a neighbourhood called Pleasant Hill?"

The woman looked at her warily. "Why do you ask?"

Valerie hesitated for a moment, but seeing as they only had eight minutes left, she threw caution to the wind. "My name is Valerie Park. I live in Pleasant Hill, and I've been harassed and intimidated by Holly and Homer Kent for over two years. They've bullied me and made my life hell, and it got so bad that I developed a drinking problem and fell into such a deep depression that I didn't want to live anymore. My new friends pulled me out of the well of despair I was in, and we are now fighting Holly and Homer. They're the president and vice president of the HOA and they've been acting like the king and queen of our neighbourhood for thirty years, but we are determined to put an end to that. When Louise told us that your friend was also a victim of their cruelty, we thought right away that we wanted to talk to her, to find out what happened and to tell her that we are doing everything we can to make them accountable." Valerie stopped, not sure what else to say.

The other woman looked at her for a long moment, letting

everything she just heard sink in. Then she closed her book, stood up, and offered her hand to Valerie. "My name is Rhonda Wallace. Thanks for telling me your story." She sat down in the seat next to Valerie. "I think Julia might be interested in talking to you. If you give me your phone number I'll pass it on." She handed her phone to Valerie and waited for her to type in her number before continuing. "She doesn't like to talk about that time of her life. Hearing that those people may finally be brought to justice might be helpful for her. Julia hasn't been able to find closure, and I hope that talking to you may give that to her. I'll leave it up to her to contact you, but let me just tell you one thing: her experience was way worse than bullying and harassment. It was criminal. I've always told her that she should have gone to the police, but she didn't for her own reasons. If she decides to confide in you, can you promise me that you will do everything in your power to try to convince her to press charges? He deserves to be in prison for what he did."

Valerie looked at her wide-eyed. "It's that bad?"

"It's that bad."

"And you can't tell me anything?"

Rhonda shook her head firmly. "No, it's not my story to tell. But I can do one thing for you: if she asks my opinion if she should talk to you, I'll tell her that I think she should."

The door to the office opened and a lanky teenage girl came out, wiping her eyes. Rhonda got up, took her daughter's arm, and walked out without another word.

Chapter 21

The phone rang at 6 am. "Who died?" Julia mumbled sleepily into the receiver. "There can't be another reason for you to call me at this ungodly hour. It's six in the morning here."

"Sorry, Julia, I waited for as long as I could, but I've been sitting on this news for six hours, and I couldn't stand it a moment longer."

Julia sat up. "What's going on, Rhonda? Everything okay?"

"Yes, yes, everything is fine. But I met a woman earlier today who lives in your old neighbourhood in Summerfield. She told me about the problems she's been having with this couple, but that her and her friends have started to fight them. You will never guess who the couple is she was talking about: Homer and his wife. They're still running the HOA, and it sounds like they're an absolute nightmare. The woman – Valerie – and her friends would like to talk to you about what Homer did to you all those years ago, and I think you should do it. I only spoke to her for a few minutes, but it didn't sound like they had anything truly incriminating on him, not like you do. This might be good for you, Julia! If you told them what he did, justice could be served at long last, and you could finally find peace."

Julia stayed silent for a long moment.

"Are you still there?" Rhonda asked.

"Yes, I'm here, just absorbing it all. You really think I should call them?"

"I do. It never sat right with me that he got away with what he did to you. I understand why you did it; you were badly wounded and fragile, and you needed to get away from him to start over and heal. But you're a different woman now – you're a lot stronger than you were thirty years ago. It's time."

"There's no statute of limitations for his crime," Julia said quietly.

"I know there isn't," Rhonda replied seriously.

Julia made up her mind. "Give me the number."

Chapter 22

"She called, Clem!" Valerie burst through the front door, vibrating with excitement. They had stopped ringing each other's door bells several months ago and just came into each other's houses. Valerie had given Clementine a key, and Clementine didn't lock her door since she had her dog. "Nobody sneaks in uninvited with George on the job," she liked to say, and she had a point. As good-natured and loving as he was, when strangers entered the property he turned into a fierce, intimidating watch dog. Since he was the size of a small horse, he provided much better protection than any lock ever could.

Clementine didn't answer, so Valerie walked through the house and out into the backyard, assuming correctly that her friend was there. She liked to practice yoga outside now that the weather had warmed up – but today she wasn't doing yoga. Valerie stared at her in amazement. "What are you doing?"

Clementine was lying on her back on a yoga mat, her long skirt hiked up and bunched around her waist, knees bent and open wide, feet on the ground. Her eyes were closed, and she was breathing slowly and rhythmically. When Valerie took a closer look, she saw that her friend wasn't wearing any underwear.

"I'm sunning my yoni," Clementine said serenely, keeping her eyes closed. Valerie didn't know what a yoni was, but using context clues she had a pretty good idea.

"Okay," she replied slowly, trying not to laugh. "Why?"

"Yoni sunbathing is an ancient and potent tool for awakening dormant energies. By exposing the darkest part of our body to sunlight we bring harmony and balance to our energy system. It boosts the immune system and kills bacteria." Clementine opened her eyes and grinned up at Valerie. "It also feels *really* good. Wanna join me? I can pull up another mat."

"No, thanks, maybe another time," Valerie said quickly. "You do know that your yoni is pointing straight to the Ho Ho's house, don't you?"

"A happy coincidence," Clementine smiled. "Maybe gazing into the opening of my sacred space will give them clarity and wisdom." She laughed. "They can't see anything unless they get out their telescope, and if they feel the need to do that, they have my blessing. Our yonis are miracles to behold."

Valerie sank down onto the ground, making sure she was sitting next to Clementine's upper end. "You got me sidetracked for a moment. Clem, Julia called! She's coming here!"

Clementine's legs snapped together, and she sat up. "She did? She is? That's amazing! Tell me everything!"

"She lives abroad – she wouldn't tell me where, just that it's in Europe – and she mainly asked me questions about the Ho Hos, what's been going on here, and what they have done to me. She sounds really nice, but she was reluctant to go into detail about what happened to her. All she would say is that Homer assaulted her, and that she didn't go to the police because she was convinced that they wouldn't have believed her."

232

"I can understand that. Women are being doubted a lot when they report a sexual assault. It's as if we have to prove that it really happened, and there's always the risk of being blamed for it because of the way we dress or behave. It's awful. Besides, when you report it you have to relive the ordeal again by telling them everything, and that must be so traumatizing. I don't blame her for not wanting to go through all that."

"Yes, and don't forget that she was a recovering drug addict and Homer is a pharmacist. Who are the cops going to believe? There's so much stigma around addiction, I see it at work all the time. A lot of cops and healthcare workers treat addicts as lesser humans. It's terribly unfair and sad, but reality."

"You're preaching to the choir, girl. That's one of the many reasons why I did my photography project, to show that addicts and sex workers are people just like you and me, but with more pain and trauma in their lives. They're deserving of respect and compassion, not prejudice and derision. It breaks my heart that Homer brutalized her when she was so vulnerable. Is she coming here to press charges?"

Valerie looked thoughtful. "I don't know, and I got the feeling that she doesn't know yet either. All she said was that she wants to talk to us, that no woman should go through what she went through, and that it's time to face her demons. Julia mentioned that she's carried around the shame of what happened for thirty years, and that she's exhausted. 'I haven't told anyone in my life about it,' she said. 'Rhonda is the only one who knows. Nobody else does, and I'm tired of the secret. It's finally gotten too heavy, and I need to get closure.'"

"I hope very much that she will find it. We'll do anything we can to help her. Did she tell you a little bit about herself? What she's been doing? If she found at least some happiness?"

"She said that she has a good life. She's an artist, divorced, one daughter. Clean and sober for twenty-nine years."

Clementine noticed the discrepancy right away. "Julia relapsed after the assault?" she asked quietly.

Valerie nodded. "Yes, she did. She said she almost died twice because of him."

"Fuck," Clementine said with feeling. "Poor girl."

They sat in silence for a moment, each lost in their thoughts.

"When is she coming?" Clementine asked eventually.

"In a week! I offered to pick her up from the airport, but she declined, saying she's going to rent a car. She wants to be alone for the 're-entry into her past', as she put it."

"I can't wait to meet her, she sounds amazing. Is she going to stay with Rhonda?"

"I assume so, she said she would stay with a friend. What's next? What's the plan?"

"Oh, I didn't tell you! Tomorrow I'm meeting with a bunch of neighbourhood ladies after my yoga class. They all want to implement some of the rewilding techniques we told them about, and we're going to discuss how to approach the board to include it in the CC&Rs. Can you come?"

"No, I'm working," Valerie replied regretfully. "Have you figured out a way to change the covenants?"

"Justina looked into it. First we'll have to formally propose the amendment, and then there needs to be a board meeting that's open to all homeowners so everyone can provide input. Then there's a vote, and the majority wins."

"That's it?" Valerie was surprised. "That sounds pretty straightforward."

"It does, doesn't it. I hope I'll get an idea after tomorrow if we have a majority or not."

"Keep me posted, okay?" Valerie got up. "I gotta run, I have a massage appointment. Remember, Julia's going to be here in a week from today! Homer's days of walking around as a free man may be numbered."

"I wish it wouldn't have to come to that," Clementine mused. "Prisons are horrible places."

Valerie gave her an affectionate kiss on the top of her head. "My cute little hippie, you're such a softie. Not everything can be solved with yoga and sunning one's yoni. Come to think of it, maybe the lack of a yoni is why he's done such bad things? Men's penises tend to get them into trouble."

"We don't know yet what he's done. Let's wait and hear what Julia has to say."

"She said he assaulted her, Clem. The details don't matter; assault is a crime."

Clementine sighed. "I guess so. I can't help it, whenever I hear something like that I wonder what happened to the person to become that way. Did he have a terrible childhood? Did he get hurt? Has he never learnt how to self-regulate his nervous system?"

Valerie paused for a moment. "Probably all of the above. Hurt people hurt people. But that doesn't mean that he shouldn't be held accountable for what he's done, whatever it is. He's a grown man. He's made choices, and every choice has consequences. Anyway, I really have to go or I'm going to be late. Love you!"

"Love you too! Talk tomorrow." Clementine laid back down, hiked up her skirt, and opened her legs again. Her energy system could use some more harmony and balance.

* * *

235

A week later, Clementine was cooking dinner when the doorbell rang. She hadn't made plans with anyone, so she wondered if it was Jehovah's Witnesses at her door. She felt sorry for them for the no doubt rude welcomes they must receive often, and decided to invite them inside. Clementine wiped her hands on a kitchen towel and headed to the door, George by her side. When she opened the door with a flourish and a ready smile on her face, she was prepared to see a couple of modestly dressed, conservative people with leaflets clutched in their hands. The person she found in front of her was completely unexpected.

"Jules!" Clementine stared at her friend in astonishment. "What are *you* doing here?"

Her best friend Jules stood at her doorstep with an uncertain expression on her face. "I never knew how to tell you, Clem. I'm the Julia you've been looking for."

Chapter 23

"What in the–?" Clementine was speechless. It took a moment before she recovered enough to pull her friend into a hug. "I can't get over that you're here, in front of me, and not in France. *You* are the woman we have been looking for all these months? You used to live here, in this town, that I randomly chose to settle down in?"

"Yeah, tell me about it," Jules said dryly. "I almost had a heart attack when you told me. Of all the towns you could have chosen, you ended up here, in the last place on earth I wanted to be reminded of. Why do you think I haven't visited you sooner?"

"The universe works in mysterious ways," Clementine muttered in awe. "Shit, we're still standing on my doorstep like fools, I'm sorry Jules. You've taken me so by surprise, I don't know what to do with myself. Come in, come in!" Clementine ushered her friend into the living room, taking her suitcase off of her. She burst out laughing when a thought occurred to her. "Am I by any chance the friend you told Val you'd be staying with?"

Jules looked sheepish. "I hoped you wouldn't mind."

"Of course I don't mind! I'm thrilled that you're here. Why didn't you tell me that you were coming though?"

Jules grew serious. "I couldn't, Clem. I've never told you about this chapter of my life because I'm so ashamed of it. I wanted you to think of me the way you know me, as the strong, independent woman who chases her dreams and is fearless in the face of adversity. In this town, I was a victim. I was at the lowest point of my life, a recovering drug addict, fresh out of rehab with no self-worth and no prospects. Except for Rhonda, nobody knows about this part of my life, Clem. My daughter Paula doesn't know, my closest friends don't know, and neither does my family, and I wanted to keep it that way. Every time you told me about your friend Valerie and what she's been through with Homer and his wife, I felt so guilty for not coming forward, but I hoped that you would figure out a solution without me getting involved. It was only when Rhonda called me and encouraged me to tell you guys what Homer did to me to bring him to justice that I knew I couldn't stay out of it any longer. But I've been dreading it, and I'm scared, and I'm really worried that you'll look at me differently from now on." Tears had started to fill Jules' eyes and were now silently rolling down her face. Clementine pulled her friend into her arms.

"How could you think that I'd ever think less of you? I love you. Besides, you know all about my history with drugs; why in the world did you think I'd judge you?"

"You're different. You're so strong and brave, and you own your past. You're not embarrassed about it like I am. I have so much shame about my drug use and what I did when I was young that I don't want anyone to know about it." Jules grew quiet for a moment and then whispered: "I always felt that I deserved what he did to me. I was such a shit when I was a teenager."

Clementine took her by the shoulders and looked at her friend fiercely. "Listen up. No matter what you did or how much of a shit you were, nobody deserves to be assaulted. You didn't deserve whatever Homer did to you. You don't have to be ashamed of any mistakes you made when you were younger. We all make mistakes, and we're all dumb shits when we're kids. No matter what you did, I won't think any less of you. It doesn't matter to me, do you hear me? I love you for who you are, not for what you did or didn't do." She pulled Jules back into her arms and let her cry for a long time. When she finally quieted down Clementine said: "How about we have something to eat? You must be starving."

Jules smiled a watery, surprised smile. "You know what? I actually am. I didn't think I'd be able to eat after all this."

"Crying always makes me hungry," Clementine said and pulled Jules to her feet. "Come on, I'd started dinner when you rang, it won't take me long to finish it."

They went into the kitchen where Clementine poured Jules a large glass of pineapple juice and finished the stir fry she'd been in the process of making. While they ate, they caught up on their recent lives, chatting about Jules' art, Clementine's photography, the people they'd met and the projects they'd planned. Clementine looked at her friend fondly. "You look great, you know? Bags under your eyes aside, you look really happy."

"I am. I'm finally living the life I always wanted to live. It took a few detours to get there, but I made it. Part of the attraction of moving to a new place where nobody knows you is that you can reinvent yourself. I can decide what I want to share about my past, who I want to be, and how I want people to see me. All throughout the winter and spring, when you told me about Valerie, the HOA, and Homer and Holly, I pretended that these people had nothing to do with me. I almost convinced myself that I'd never laid eyes on them, that the town of Summerfield was nothing more than the place where my best friend had settled down in. Thirty years is a lifetime – I told myself that the person I used to be then doesn't exist anymore."

"What changed your mind about helping us?" Clementine asked gently.

Jules sighed. "I got tired of pretending. Lying to yourself all the time is exhausting, and once I started remembering that time, I couldn't stop thinking about it. There have been long stretches of time in my life where I didn't think about it. I shoved it all in a box, locked it, and threw away the key – or so I thought. But despite my best efforts it would come spilling out once in a while, and there was nothing I could do about it. I was triggered when #MeToo happened, when Paula was a teenager, anytime you mentioned your history with drugs or rehab, when you did your photography project in Toronto about the women living on the streets, sometimes by seemingly nothing at all – a smell, a sound, the mention of medication. And I've never been able to watch *The Simpsons* or go into a pharmacy, and frankly, I don't care about *The Simpsons*, but not being able to fill your own prescription is embarrassing. So I decided to be like you, to own my story instead of hiding from it, and to make sure the fucker gets what he deserves."

Clementine reached over the table and gave Jules an awkward, fierce hug. "I'm so proud of you, babe," she whispered. "You are a fucking hero, and the strongest woman I know."

"Right back atcha," Jules replied, hugging Clementine back. "Alright, I better get it over with and tell you the whole sorry tale." She took a deep breath, and then she began. "You know how I told you that I'm an only child? That's actually not true. I used to have a little brother, Josh. He was four years younger than me. He died when he was three." Clementine squeezed her hand but didn't interrupt. Jules' eyes filled with tears. "He drowned. We were at the beach that day, and I was impatient to go into the water. My mom wasn't ready yet, but I kept on whining that I wanted to go into the water, and she finally snapped and told me to go, but to wait at the shore for her. I had my floaties on, so I guess she wasn't too worried. Josh had been digging in the sand, and I ran off without waiting for him. All I could think about was feeling the water on my skin and looking for seashells. Without me or my mom noticing, Josh must have followed me. I never even saw him. I was playing by the water when suddenly my mom came running, screaming Josh's name. 'Have you seen him, Julia? Is he with you?' she yelled, but I had no idea where he was. The whole beach started looking for him, and after a while they found him." Jules stared into space, not seeing her surroundings. She was back at the beach, reliving that horrendous day.

"There was nothing they could do. He was dead, and our family died with him. My dad couldn't forgive my mom, and he moved out after six months, remarrying a year later. He had another couple of kids and basically forgot about me. My mom never said it out loud, but I knew that she blamed me for Josh's death and my dad leaving. She became cold and withdrawn, stopped hugging me, stopped being a mom, really. I tried to be good, to make her happy, but it didn't work. So then I started acting out when I was a teenager, drinking and smoking weed and sneaking out. I started hanging out with the bad kids, because being good hadn't gotten me anywhere, so I

241

might as well be bad. They introduced me to oxies, and it was love at first try. I felt happier and calmer than I had since the day Josh died, and I was hooked immediately." Jules paused to take a sip of her juice.

"You know how these things go. At first it's fun and feels good, and then it isn't. I had a few dark years there, doing things I'm not proud of–" Jules paused again before looking up and smiling. "Do you know who convinced me to go to rehab?"

Clementine shook her head, guessing that it hadn't been her parents.

"It was a doctor. I got really bad pneumonia one winter and ended up in the hospital. The ER doc who looked after me was amazing. By this point I was used to people treating me like dirt, especially in healthcare, and I had no expectations when it came to authority figures. Or, to put it more accurately, I only expected the worst. But this doc was great. Once he'd told me my diagnosis and treatment, he asked me about myself. That was the first time in years that anyone had shown any interest, and it really meant a lot. He told me that he could help me get into rehab if I was willing to go, and that I was worth getting better. He said I deserved to get healthy, and that no matter what had brought me to this point in my life, the best days of my life hadn't happened yet. It's corny as hell, but I couldn't stop thinking about it. He left me alone for a few hours, and when he came back in the morning I told him I wanted to go. He started me on methadone right away because I was starting to withdraw, and promised he would find a place for me. And he did, not far from here. That's how I ended up in this neck of the woods.

"As you know, they strongly recommend in rehab to con–

tinue some sort of treatment on the outside. I heard through the grapevine that a lot of halfway and sober-living houses were pretty shitty, but that there was a lady who ran an independent place that was supposed to be amazing. I asked around and found out that the lady's name was Taylor Kirby, a tough-love kinda woman who was by all accounts pretty eccentric but incredible. She was an artist who used art as a recovery tool, and as soon as I heard that, I knew that I wanted to get into her place. She came for a visit towards the end of my stay, and we hit it off immediately. Two weeks later, I moved into her place in Pleasant Hill." Jules stopped talking and took another sip of juice. She looked pale, but determined, and Clementine gave her hand an encouraging squeeze.

"You got this, Jules," she said reassuringly.

Jules nodded, took a shaky breath, and continued. "I didn't know it then, but the year before, the HOA had been founded, and most people in Pleasant Hill had voluntarily joined. Taylor didn't, obviously, because her having up to ten people living with her at a time was a violation of the new rules. We were a real dark stain on their shiny new plan of creating a picture-perfect suburbia with uniform houses, yards, and minds. We were always smoking outside, there were easels in the yard or people creating huge art pieces, and the house needed a paint job that Taylor couldn't afford. I can almost understand that they didn't want us – we didn't fit in. We were like a giraffe in a herd of sheep, standing out a mile."

"I bet the Ho Hos were furious," Clementine ventured. Jules knew who she meant from their previous phone conversations.

"You bet your ass they were," Jules confirmed grimly. "Taylor had been getting anonymous letters for months, saying stuff like 'nobody wants you here, move away'. She knew they came from Holly, and she always acted like it didn't bother her, but I'm not so sure. She acted tough, but she was a sensitive, caring person – it must have gotten to her. Who likes being told that they're not wanted? But maybe I'm projecting, I don't know. I asked her once if she'd ever consider moving away, and she just laughed and said, 'it takes a lot more than a few letters to scare me off, kiddo'."

Jules fell silent and squeezed her eyes shut for a moment, as if trying to shut out what was coming next. "Well, they came up with something that was a lot more effective than letters. I was in the yard one day, working on a painting, when this guy comes up to the fence. He calls over, 'excuse me, could you help me?', and I put down my paintbrush and go to him. 'Sure, what's up?' He sticks out his hand and introduces himself– 'Hi, I'm Homer, I'm your neighbour, can you give me a hand for a sec?' I hadn't met him before, because we were keeping to ourselves, and Holly was the one always prowling the neighbourhood, not him. I guess he was at work all day and then went straight home, or maybe I just didn't pay attention, but either way, that was the first time I laid eyes on him. He looked totally ordinary, just a regular guy. He says, 'my dog got out of the yard, can you help me find her?', and I don't even think twice about it, I just say 'sure', and follow him down the road. It's evening, twilight, but it feels safe, because this is a safe neighbourhood in a small town. He keeps talking, I don't remember what about, but I remember he was chatting up a storm, and at some point I wonder why he isn't calling his dog's name, but before I can ask him about it he opens the gate to an empty house that's for sale and walks around it to the back, saying that his dog ran into that backyard. I follow, and see that there's a garden shed. He opens the door, saying 'I bet she's in there, she's done it before', and he beckons me to follow him. Like a fool, I do."

Jules stopped, closed her eyes again, and then continued in a rush, keeping her eyes shut tight. "As soon as I step into the shed he slams the door behind me. He throws me on the floor, tears at my clothes, undoes his belt, and unzips. And I'm frozen. I'm so stunned that I don't even fight him – I just lay there. I can't move. While he's doing it he says the nastiest things to me – that I'm a whore, that I'm worthless, that this is the only thing I'm good for. I dissociate, separating myself from my body, floating above the person this is happening to. I look at it from above, and I'm so disgusted by her lack of fight, by just taking it, that I think, 'maybe he's right. Maybe she is worthless.' Why else wouldn't she fight?'

"When it's over he pulls something out of his jacket pocket. 'I have a message for Taylor,' he says, and then he grabs my arm. He ties a tourniquet around it so fast, I don't realize at first what he's doing. Then he pulls something else out of his pocket – a loaded syringe. 'You know what this is?' he whispers, holding it close to my face. 'It's a hotshot. There's enough oxy in here to kill a horse, more than enough to snuff out a worthless little life like yours. Tell Taylor that if she doesn't leave, she's going to start losing her beloved little junkies. You'll be first, but definitely not the last. Nobody will be surprised that a junkie OD'd, and the police won't care. Taylor's halfway house will look like an experiment gone predictably wrong, because druggies can't be rehabilitated. Once a druggie, always a druggie.' He pricks my skin with the tip of the needle, and I'm terrified that I'm going to die. But then he suddenly gets up and walks out without looking back, leaving me lying there on the dirty floor, the syringe still stuck in my arm."

"Oh my God," Clementine whispered, staring at Jules, wide-eyed. "Oh my fucking God. What a horrible thing to go through. He's evil! He's truly evil!" Clementine's eyes were shiny with tears, but she didn't allow them to fall. Jules needed her strength right now, not her falling apart.

"I lay on that floor for a long time. I'm drowning in shame, because I feel so stupid for having gone with him, for not having fought back, for believing I ever had a chance to leave my past behind me. I keep looking at the syringe, and the urge to use it is so powerful, it scares the shit out of me. I know that all the pain and shame could be over in seconds; that I could sink into oblivion and float away, never having to experience pain ever again."

"But you didn't do it," Clementine said fiercely. "Your will to live was stronger."

"No, that wasn't it," Jules said, shaking her head. "I wanted nothing more than to die in that moment. The reason why I emptied that syringe onto the dusty floor and not into my vein was that I knew I had to warn Taylor and the others. I didn't want what he'd done to me to happen to anybody else.

"It's dark by the time I leave the shed, which is just as well because I'm an absolute mess. My dress is torn, I'm bleeding, and my hair is a bird's nest. I remember worrying about someone seeing me because of my *hair*." She laughed a short, humourless laugh. "The things we fixate on when the unspeakable has happened. Anyway, let me finish the story, it's almost over. I tell Taylor what has happened, refuse to go to the police even though she begs me to go, and she decides that it isn't safe anymore to stay in Pleasant Hill."

Jules paused for a moment and took another sip of juice.

"She put the house on the market, and even though she promised she would continue the sober house in a new location, everybody started to drift away. I think a couple people may have found another placement in a halfway house, but the rest just left, probably going back to their old lives. Even though I had sworn Taylor to secrecy, she had to warn the others that Pleasant Hill wasn't safe anymore, and nobody stuck around. I went back to Vancouver for a while, back to my old life. I needed to forget, and what's the best way to numb yourself? Oxy.

"I cleaned up my act a year later when I moved to Toronto, went to school, and got my degree. I painted all the time during those years, and that's what saved me. Nobody knew my history, and I pretended that the person all that had happened to was someone else. I hoped that I had shed her like a snake sheds her skin, emerging as a brand-new, better version of myself. Unfortunately, the insecure part of myself was still very much alive and kicking, which led me to Matt. I know now that I would never have started dating him if I wasn't so desperate to be loved and taken care of. I never told him about my past, about the drugs or rehab or the assault. With him I tried out the 'normal' life we're all supposed to want, with a 9-5 job, mortgage, child. You know how that turned out: depression, divorce, single mom. Still, in a way I revelled in it, because it was so *normal*. There were hundreds of thousands of women in the same situation as me, and I liked feeling as though I was just like everybody else. But as you know, I hated my job as a dental hygienist, and I was dying inside without art as an outlet. Thank God for my health scare. It woke me up from my stupor and reminded me that life was damn short, that I'd almost died twice, and that I should give happiness a real shot." Jules fell silent for a moment, gathering her thoughts.

"I've reinvented myself several times over my lifetime. I went from guilt-ridden child to rebellious teenager, from drug addict to bohemian art student, from traditional working mother and wife to single mom, to finally living life on my own terms. I've always run away from something, usually the previous version of who I used to be. My thing has always been to start over, to shed the old me. I'm done with running. I'm all the versions of me combined. I've grown as a person, but I'm still the scared child I used to be, the hurt teenager, the traumatized young woman, the desperate-to-please wife. Except I'm also a survivor, a mother, an artist, an independent and strong woman. I've overcome a lot in my life, and now it's time that I face the worst incident of my life and make the person who's responsible for it pay. I'm ready to go to the police and press charges against Homer Kent."

Chapter 24

Is it finally my turn? About time. The women have been blabbing on for much too long, feeling sorry for themselves, blaming men for everything. It's all *"poor me, men are so evil, I'm the victim, boohoo"*. I'm so sick and tired of this narrative. It's completely unfair to vilify us men simply because we're men. Talk about discrimination! Yes, it's me, Homer Kent, the so-called bad guy. But once you've heard my side of the story you'll change your mind about me, I can guarantee you that. Did I have to make a few hard choices? Sure I did. All men do. But I did what I had to do to protect myself and my family.

I'm the oldest of three – one brother, one sister. My old man was a high school principal, my mother a homemaker. We grew up Catholic, going to church every Sunday, saying grace before each meal, praying before bedtime. Father was strict, a real rules guy. Typical teacher, wanted everyone to obey without argument. He was a "kids should be seen, not heard" man, claiming that he had enough screaming kids during the day at work, he didn't need them at home, too. Makes you wonder why the man even had kids, but when I made the mistake once of asking him that question, my ass and I lived to regret it. There was still corporal punishment in schools when I was a kid, fully supported and regularly used by Father, which meant he had zero qualms using it against his sons at home as well. He had a strap in his office, and part of the punishment was to get it and bring it to him. That was always the worst part, because it made you feel complicit in your own beating.

Am I mad at him for that? Not really. That was just how things were done back then. Most kids I knew got slapped around by their parents, by teachers, often even by their friends' parents. Nobody thought much about it. Besides, have you read the Bible? It's loaded with verses about discipline. Father had one hanging in his office at school, I think it's from Hebrews.

> *"No discipline seems pleasant at the time, but painful. Later on, however, it produces a harvest of righteousness and peace for those who have been trained by it."*

He really believed that crap, and so did our priest. That old codger loved to preach about discipline, obedience, and punishment, the bloodier the better. Twisted old pervert.

My mother was a quiet, timid woman who never laid a hand on us. She was a typical 60s housewife who cooked, cleaned, and raised us kids. Father expected her to look nice as well, so every afternoon before he came home from work she'd change out of the housecoat she wore all day into a pretty dress and heels, do her hair and put on some lipstick. I always thought that was nice. Why not make an effort for your husband who provides for you and your children? She was the real religious one in the family, always confessing and repenting, carrying around a rosary at all times. If we were getting too rowdy and she didn't know what else to do she would threaten us with

Hell, as in "if you don't stop fighting with your brother you'll go to Hell". Other mothers used "I'm telling your father" as a threat, but Mother never did. I think she hated the strap even more than we did, but she would never have dared to contradict my father. His word was law, and we were all expected to follow it to the letter.

The downside of Mother's use of Hell as threat was that I was terrified of going to Hell as a kid, and when I was younger I tried really hard to behave and be good. Inevitably I would mess up and get either the strap or the Hell talk, and as I got older I finally had enough of constantly trying and failing, and I rebelled. I started chasing girls when I was fourteen, losing my virginity at fifteen to an older girl, and from that moment on I was crazy about girls. It was the 70s – the time of disco, drugs, hot pants, and no bras, and I was in heaven. Chasing tail was all I was after, and it was only a matter of time before my parents found out. One of their church friends ratted me out, telling my father that they'd seen me making out with a girl in her daddy's car by the lake, a favourite make-out spot for kids. I have no idea how they could have seen me with the windows all steamed up, but when my father confronted me I was too startled to challenge the accusation and admitted it on the spot. Bracing myself for the worst, the old man surprised me.

"Son, you're a young man now," he began. I was seventeen. "I understand that you have needs. Men are different from women in that way; we have urges that demand to be satisfied, compulsions that are impossible to ignore. If you sow your wild oats now, while you're young, you will have gotten them out of your system by the time you get married, so you can be faithful to your wife. But there are two important rules you have to follow: be discreet, and don't get the girl pregnant, understood? If you get her pregnant you have to marry her, so you better be careful."

He then attempted a clumsy speech about condoms and preventing pregnancies, but I cut him off and told him I got it. You could have knocked me over with a feather, so surprised was I by this turn of events. My father, the Catholic, condoning sex before marriage *and* the use of condoms? What a hypocrite. But I wasn't complaining.

Not that he was that lenient with my sister Betsy. When she started dating a boy at sixteen and my father found out, the shouting in our house rattled the glass in the windows, and she was grounded until basically forever. Didn't keep them apart though; the fool climbed in through her window one night, got her pregnant, and off to the altar they went. I guess Tommy could have benefited from the condom talk my father tried to give me, but it was too late by then. The marriage didn't last, and when Betsy got divorced, against our parents' strict rule to "lay in the bed you made for yourself", they more or less cut her out of the family.

Anyway, back to me. This is *my* story, remember? I got into pharmacy by accident. Not knowing what to do after high school, I simply copied my best friend Brian. His parents were pharmacists, and they had a huge house with a swimming pool, brand-name groceries instead of the knock-off stuff that we had at home, and a new Buick every two years. Their salary was much better than my father's, so I decided to become a pharmacist.

I barely got in because my grades were more mediocre than good, but Brian's dad knew the guy in the admitting office – the university was his alma mater –and with his help, I squeezed in. He gave me a stern talking to, saying that from now on it was up to me, I had to put a lot more hard work in than I had in high school, blah blah. I was used to sermons from a lifetime of listening to Father and the priest, so I adopted my most earnest expression, nodded seriously, and promised that I would work harder than I ever had before, sir. He lapped it up, as I knew he would. The old geezers are all the same, want to feel important, and if you bow and scrape enough they'll mistake that for respect.

I picked up where I'd left off in high school, asking a different girl out every week, with the goal of getting her into bed. The number of girls I'd slept with was high in the double digits by then, and my goal was to reach triple digits by the time I graduated. Life was filled with parties, girls, and fun. And then I met Holly.

I had to repeat second year (no need to give me a hard time, the geezer club already did that) which meant joining a new class, and there she was. Blond, slim, studious, gorgeous. She had that sexy secretary thing going with her horn-rimmed glasses she wore to read the board in the front, and she was the smartest girl in class. She was also completely uninterested in male attention of any kind, which only made her more irresistible. My buddies and I had a bet going who would land her first, and I was determined to win it. It wasn't hard for me to get girls back then because I was a handsome son-of-a-gun who could charm the socks off even the most uninterested females. Except for Holly. Asking her out and her turning me down became a game, and I was sure she was just playing hard to get. Wasn't that what the women's magazines told them? I was confident that I could wear her down if I persisted, and guess what: I was right.

Holly wasn't one for parties, but her girlfriends had dragged her to the Christmas party, and I was determined not to waste this golden opportunity. I brought her drinks, listened patiently to her go on about school (who talks about school at a party? But I pretended to be immensely interested), and when she was ready to leave I offered to walk her home, ever the gentleman. She was definitely tipsy, and I was pretty sure I'd get lucky that night. She didn't invite me in, so I told her I had to use the bathroom. Once inside her dorm I kissed her, and she was still playing hard to get, trying to push me away. "You can stop pretending now, I know you like me," I murmured, grabbing her ass. She had a great ass. She kept fighting, but women did that sometimes, probably to preserve their virtue or something. She'd talked to me all night, let me walk her home, invited me up to her room – her words may have said no, but her actions said yes.

We had sex that night, but to be honest, it wasn't that memorable. I'd never have gone back for seconds if she hadn't tricked me. How was I supposed to know that she wasn't on the pill? All the girls were on the pill then, but Holly wasn't. I'd knocked her up, and the crazy bitch was talking marriage. Abortion wasn't legal then, but there were ways to get one. My Catholic upbringing made me uncomfortable at the idea of it, but not as uncomfortable as getting married and becoming a father at twenty-three. I'm pretty sure I could have talked her into getting rid of it, but Holly had other ideas. She contacted my parents and told them about their upcoming grandchild, and as my father had promised, baby equalled marriage.

I'm not going to lie; I was resentful as hell in the beginning. I wanted to continue partying and hooking up, not playing house with a wife. But to my surprise I fell head over heels in love with the baby. Cutest little boy I'd ever seen, and what man doesn't like having a son? Holly dropped out of college to look after the baby – I stayed in school, and to be honest, I was soon back to my old tricks. Holly had no interest in sex, and with her working nights to support us and me gone during the day, we barely saw each other. Most days I didn't feel like I was married, and there were many nights where I crashed at my old dorm when I was too pissed to go home. I settled down when I was done with school and started working. Sure, there was the occasional fling, but most men have them, they don't mean anything. A man has needs, and if he doesn't get it at home he'll get it outside the marriage. Holly never said anything, except when I hooked up with the neighbour's wife. Too close to home – she was worried what our friends and neighbours would think. That's how we ended up in Summerfield, and at first it seemed like a good move. We could afford a bigger house in a better neighbourhood; the high school was great for Christopher – not so many immigrants like in Vancouver – and I found a job right away. But then we founded the homeowner's association, and that's when the trouble started.

If there's one thing I can't stand it's bleeding-hearts liberals. Like that Taylor Kirby woman who ran the junkie house in our neighbourhood. If you want to waste your time on druggies, be my guest, but don't do it in my backyard. Go to Downtown Eastside or something and keep them away from decent people like us. Holly, who had *insisted* on being the president and was suddenly drunk with power, tried to get rid of her, and I decided to wait and see if she could do it. I didn't think for a minute that she'd succeed, but I thought I'd let her come to me and ask for help, not offer it. She was getting ahead of herself, and it would be good for her to remember who the man in the house was. Sure enough, after a year of sending useless letters the woman probably laughed at, Holly came to me asking for help, just as I knew she would.

I hadn't planned on having sex with that girl. My plan was to rough her up a little and threaten her with the loaded syringe that had enough oxy in it to kill half the junkies of that damn halfway house. But – well, what can I say? I got turned on, and she was probably a prostitute anyway. What was one more client? I even paid her, if you count the oxy, which I stole from work by taking a few pills here and there from patients' prescriptions. And it worked, didn't it? They moved away, and I was sure I would never see any of them ever again.

We did a good job running the board. Pleasant Hill is flourishing, the property values have more than doubled, and we kept the troublemakers under control. You have to if you want to be an effective leader, that's just the way it is. Carrot and stick, and there are people who only understand the stick. Remember the verse on my father's wall about discipline? About how it's painful, but later on it *"produces a harvest of righteousness and peace for those who have been trained by it"*. Most people get that. But people like Taylor Kirby and Luke Park don't. You can try the carrot all you want, but only the stick will work. Luke kept provoking us with his travesty of a yard, his refusal to fall in line, his *otherness*. I was worried that his rebellion would spread, that others would join him. And I was right, wasn't I? I stopped him, but it was too late. Those women got infected by his cancer, and now it's spreading all over Pleasant Hill. We have lost.

An hour ago I saw the girl arrive at Clementine's place. I recognized her right away despite the thirty years it's been since I last saw her; she's still very tall and skinny, and there's

256

something about the way she moves that is very distinct. I've thought of her often over the years. An encounter like ours isn't something you forget. I don't know what she's doing here and how Clementine could possibly have found out, but it can't be a coincidence. If she's here to go to the police and press charges against me then I have to disappear. Especially since that's not all I've done.

I have to leave now. I don't have much time.

Chapter 25

Homer was panicking. A suitcase was lying open on his bed, and he was randomly throwing items in: clothes, socks, underwear, shoes. He needed to get out of here, but where to? Why had he never come up with a contingency plan for a situation like this one? Because he thought there never would be a situation like this one, that's why. He'd been so careful with Luke, and the thing with the girl had happened so long ago, he had been convinced that she was either dead or far away. He was still in shock that she was *here*, in Pleasant Hill, at his archenemy's house. In an attempt to calm himself down he'd just swallowed a few extra Ativan, a medication he started taking eighteen months ago when he couldn't sleep after – well, after he did what he did. *That had been weird. He had slept like a baby after the thing with the girl.*

Anyway. They weren't working, which was no surprise seeing he was so agitated. Homer thought a medicinal slug of Scotch might do the trick, so he abandoned his packing and went downstairs into the kitchen to the liquor cabinet. Holly was sitting at the table, doing nothing. That stopped him in his tracks. Holly was never not busy. "What are you doing?" he asked.

She looked at him. "Thinking."

"What about?"

"You."

A chill ascended his spine, settling like an icy hand around his heart. "Oh?" he managed. He went to the liquor cabinet and pulled out the bottle of Scotch, noticing that his hand was shaking. Not bothering with getting a glass, he took a long swig right from the bottle, spilling some liquid down his chin. Why was he so clumsy? He didn't feel right. Taking the bottle with him, he sat down opposite Holly. "So, whatcha come up with thinkin' bout me?" Why was he slurring his words? The icy hand around his heart squeezed tighter.

Holly's stare was as frosty as his insides. "I've been thinking about Luke Kent." Her gaze bored into him as she mentioned the name, waiting for a reaction. Had she seen him flinch? *Had* he flinched? He didn't know for sure what his body was doing. It felt separate from him, as if it belonged to someone else.

"How come a healthy, fit man in his early fifties suddenly drops dead? You told me yourself that he was taking heart medication. People live for decades when they're on meds for heart disease. It's weird, isn't it." Holly hadn't thought that Luke's death was suspicious until recently. Men in their fifties died of heart attacks all the time, particularly when they had heart disease. But Holly had reflected on Homer's behaviour over the last few months: his weight loss, the bags under his eyes, his jumpiness. He drank more and had started taking Ativan, which was very unlike him. In Homer's opinion, pills were for other, weaker people, not men like him.

Holly thought long and hard about when his odd behaviour had started, and it suddenly struck her: it was right after Luke's death. And she knew — she just *knew* — that he was somehow involved in it.

259

Homer cleared his throat nervously. "Not tha' weird, no," he mumbled. He suddenly noticed that he was sweating profusely. He took another swig of Scotch, desperately hoping it would calm him.

Holly leaned forward. "Here is what I think. I think you had something to do with his death. You've been a bundle of nerves since he died, and unless it's because you're grief stricken over our dear neighbour's death, it's because you did something you shouldn't have. Because that's what you do, isn't it, Homer. You do things you shouldn't, but it doesn't matter, because it always works out for you. You're a white man with an education and a white-collar job, and you've always been able to do pretty much whatever the hell you want, with no consequences. You can stomp through the world like an elephant in a china shop, breaking and destroying things, raping and cheating, and nobody cares. The world indulges you overgrown boys, telling the rest of us that 'boys will be boys', that a 'youthful indiscretion' shouldn't ruin a promising career, that we should be understanding and forgiving. Your sleeping around is fondly labelled 'sowing wild oats', while the women you do it with are called whores, their lives ruined."

Holly's eyes narrowed, and she leaned in even closer, until her face was only inches away from his pale, sweaty one. "You ruined my life, Homer Kent. All I ever wanted was to have my own career, my own house, and my own life. You took that away from me the moment you forced your dick inside of me. I never wanted to become this person who measures other people's front lawns! The crazy lady who's controlling other people's lives just so she doesn't have to think about her own. You made me become this way, and now you're going to pay for it. What did you do to Luke? Tell me!"

260

Homer tried to focus on Holly, but her face was swimming in and out of focus. He felt sick, and when he attempted to swallow his throat didn't seem to work. What the hell? He tried again, but his throat wasn't complying at all. Homer started to panic.

"H-Holly? Somethin' iss wrong wiss me. I-I think I needa docta" he slurred. In his panic he was dimly aware that there was something he was supposed to do. He tried to remember. He had the nagging feeling that he was in a hurry, that he didn't have time to get checked out by a doctor. Better get up and get going. Go where? He had no idea. Hopefully it would come back to him once he was moving.

Homer tried to stand up, but his legs were like wet noodles, and he crumpled to the floor. Holly loomed over him. "You don't look so good, dear husband. You want me to call help?"

Homer wanted to nod, but his muscles didn't obey. He stared helplessly up into his wife's cold eyes. Why was she so mad at him? Didn't she see that he needed help? Holly lowered herself down onto the floor next to him. "I know about the pills. You've been swallowing Ativan like Skittles since the time Luke died. Strange coincidence, isn't it? And ironic, too, given the way you feel about drug addicts. Are you aware that *you* are a junkie now, Homer? You probably don't see it that way, but you've become pretty dependent on your little helpers. Anyway, I can see that time is of the essence here. You really don't look good, Homer. It's been a long time since I was in college, but I still remember the adverse effects of Ativan. Confusion, loss of muscle control, difficulty swallowing, low blood pressure, slowed breathing, sedation. These are increased by age and mixing them with alcohol. You are sixty-five years old, and you've been drinking heavily all

261

your life, so you're ticking all the boxes. Let's get down to business. I will call 9-1-1 in a moment, Homer. But before I do you have to do something for me. You are going to tell me what you did to Luke, and I am going to record it. Then I'll get you help. Deal?"

Homer's head was spinning. The girl was here, Holly knew about Luke, he was dying, Holly hated him? He was dying, so what did it matter, he was dying, he was dying ...

He didn't want to die. That thought swam to the surface, clearer than the others. He didn't want to die, and she would get him help if he did just one thing. What was that thing again?

"Tell me what you did to Luke Park, Homer." Holly's voice was clear and soothing. "Unburden yourself and you'll feel better."

Oh yes, that was it. She wanted him to tell her about that night. The night he went to Luke's house with the bottle of Scotch under the pretense of ending the feud. The night he knew Luke's wife Valerie was working the night shift and wouldn't be home until the next morning. The night he took charge and did what was best for them by removing a threat to him and his family.

It had been surprisingly easy. Luke filled his prescription at Homer's pharmacy, so Homer knew that Luke was on digoxin for atrial fibrillation. Digoxin could be fatal in high doses, which was the first thought that had popped into his head when he came across Luke's name and medication.

He hadn't acted right away. They had always managed to get people to fall in line, and they tried all their usual tricks first. But Luke not only turned out to be a stubborn son of a bitch, he'd also started asking questions and digging around in Homer's past. There were a few too many skeletons in

Homer's closet to be comfortable with that, and when Luke wouldn't quit, Homer got worried and decided he needed to do something about him. He'd called Luke up and pretended that he wanted to talk, and Luke agreed.

Homer took the small bottle of liquid digoxin he had swiped from work and the bottle of twelve-year-old Glenlivet and went to Luke's place, not sure if he'd really go through with it. But it had been so simple. So surreal. He'd left before the digoxin took effect, when Luke was still alive. It hadn't felt real. Except that his body knew that he'd done something terrible, because it had been punishing him ever since with insomnia, migraines, abdominal pain, the shakes, and an ever-increasing need for the pills and booze in a futile attempt to numb himself from the nightmare he couldn't wake up from. Maybe saying it out loud would help? Even if it didn't, he didn't have a choice, because he could feel his consciousness ebbing away, his heart rate slowing, his breath becoming shallow ... "I killed Luke Park," he whispered into the phone Holly was holding out to him, before everything went dark.

Chapter 26

The Summerfield police station sat peacefully in the morning sunshine on this quiet Friday morning. Kenny Reid, the constable on duty, arrived as usual at five minutes to eight, looking forward to his first cup of coffee and then, ten minutes later, a leisurely trip to the bathroom. Kenny liked to start his day slowly, and having his morning poop at work was a beloved part of his daily routine. However, to his dismay there was someone already waiting for him in front of the locked door. One look at the woman's determined face told him that today he wouldn't be able to indulge in his usual morning regime. Kenny suppressed a sigh. Constipation and no coffee – the day wasn't off to a great start.

"Good morning," he greeted her resignedly. He tried not to let his consternation show, but he wasn't sure if he was succeeding. "Are you waiting for me?"

"Are you the officer in charge?" she asked briskly.

Kenny nodded.

"My name is Holly Kent. I want to report a crime," the woman said.

Probably a neighbour mowing their lawn too early in the morning, he thought uncharitably. He didn't know the woman, but she looked the type.

"A murder," she added crisply, and Kenny's head shot up.

"Really?" he asked in surprise. "Do you have any evidence?"

"I have a recorded confession. The perpetrator is currently in the hospital, but I suggest you get someone up there fast to guard him. He's a flight risk. Before he collapsed last night he was packing a suitcase in preparation to run.

"He's my husband," she added when she noticed Kenny's confused look. "Can we get on with it, please?"

Kenny gaped at her for a moment before pulling himself together. "Of course, let's go inside and I'll take your statement."

They were still in the middle of it when the door opened, and three more women entered the station. Kenny couldn't believe it. What was going on today?

"Excuse me for a moment," he said to Mrs. Kent. She turned around to see who had entered the room, and when she saw them her eyes narrowed.

"What are *you* doing here?" she asked the trio derisively. All three looked over at her in surprise.

"We could ask you the same thing," Clementine replied.

"It's none of your business what I'm doing," Holly said shortly.

"Ditto," Valerie fired back.

Jules turned to Clementine. "Is that his wife?" she asked in an undertone. Clementine nodded.

"She needs to know," Jules said quietly, but firmly. Clementine gave her a reassuring nod. Jules walked over to where Holly sat and held out her hand. "Mrs. Kent, my name is Julia Gibson. You probably don't remember me, but I used to briefly live in Pleasant Hill, thirty years ago. What I'm about to tell you will come as a shock, but you will find out anyway, and I'd

265

rather you hear it from me."

"You were one of them, weren't you," Holly stated abruptly.

"One of whom?" Jules asked in confusion.

"One of Taylor Kirby's addicts."

"Oh." Jules was taken aback by Holly's bluntness but nodded. "Yes, I was one of them. Your husband raped me, Mrs. Kent. That's why I'm here. I was too scared and too ashamed to go to the police after it happened, but I'm neither of those things now, and I'm here to report the crime he committed."

Holly's entire demeanour had changed at the mention of the word *rape*. She seemed to deflate, as if someone had let all the air out of a balloon.

"I always knew he must have done something terrible back then," Holly whispered. "I'm so sorry he did that to you. You still look young, how old were you then? A teenager?"

"I was twenty-one," Jules said, exchanging a surprised look with Clementine and Valerie. After everything she'd heard about Holly, she hadn't expected this sympathetic reaction from her.

"Just a year older than I was," Holly murmured, tears filling her eyes.

Clementine stepped forward and put her hand on Holly's. "What do you mean, Holly? Did Homer hurt you, too?"

Holly put her face in her hands and started sobbing. "Yes, he did. He got me pregnant when I was twenty, and I had to marry him for the baby's sake. I hate that son of a bitch." She looked up at Valerie, tears streaming down her face. "Valerie, I swear, I didn't know anything about it. I had no idea that he was capable of doing something so terrible."

"What?" Valerie was confused. Why was Holly apologizing to her about Homer raping Jules and Holly? And holy shit, had

266

Holly really just admitted that she married her rapist because he had gotten her pregnant? This was crazy!

"Do you have any idea why I'm here?" Holly asked, her gaze still fixed on Valerie.

"No idea. I thought maybe somebody put a flower pot you don't approve of on their porch, and you want them thrown in jail."

Holly was quiet for a moment. "I deserved that." She took a deep breath. "No, it's much more serious than that. I'm here because Homer made a confession to me last night."

"About the rape?" Valerie asked, trying to keep up.

"No. About killing your husband."

* * *

It took Kenny a while to regain control of his station. He had never experienced anything like this before. A supposedly upstanding man of the community – a senior, no less! – accused of two rapes and a murder? Years or even decades after the fact? It was unbelievable. Kenny called his boss in early to get help with all the statements, and to take charge. This was way above Kenny's pay grade. His boss – a practical, calm woman named Mallory Moseley – had a gift diffusing highly charged emotional situations, and when she arrived she not only brought order and calmness with her but also two people: a doctor to give a traumatized Valerie something for the shock, and a social worker for support. Only then did she take Jules to a different room to take her statement and indicated to Kenny to finish with Holly.

When they were done, Inspector Moseley promised to open an investigation and to question Homer. She was also going to post an officer in front of his room at the hospital right away to prevent him from fleeing.

The four women were dismissed at the same time. Outside the police station they blinked in the bright sunshine, shell-shocked by what they'd all just learnt. Valerie turned to Holly; her face was swollen from crying. "You owe me an explanation. I want to know everything."

Holly nodded shakily. "Of course. Where do you want to go?"

"Not a public place," Valerie said, her voice wobbly. "I need to lie down while you talk. Whatever the doctor gave me is making my whole body feel like rubber."

"Let's go to my place," Clementine decided.

Fifteen minutes later they arrived at Clementine's. Valerie headed straight for the couch, Jules offered to make coffee, and Clementine told Holly to have a seat in one of the armchairs before sitting down close to Valerie, making sure she was comfortable. George, with his unerring instinct for who needed his comfort the most, went first to Valerie for an affectionate lick and cuddle, but then settled himself down next to Holly.

Smart boy, Clementine thought. *She's all alone here and her entire world just collapsed.* Holly sat stiffly erect, with a pale, drawn face and clenched hands that made Clementine suspect that they would be shaking if they weren't clasped so tightly. "How are you holding up, Holly?" Clementine asked gently. "You must be reeling from everything you just found out about your husband."

"I've had better days," Holly said wanly, trying to smile but failing.

"Why is he in the hospital?" Valerie asked.

"He took too many Ativan and mixed them with booze,"

268

Holly explained.

Valerie sat up. "Did he try to–?"

"Kill himself?" Holly gave a short, bitter laugh. "No, I'm not that lucky. My dear husband is very attached to living. I don't know for sure, but I suspect that he saw Julia and panicked. He must have known that the jig was up. He probably lost track of how many pills he'd already taken. I'm sure it was a mistake, not done on purpose."

Jules returned to the living room carrying a tray with four steaming mugs, a sugar bowl, cream, and a plate of cookies. "Help yourselves," she said as she carefully sat the tray down on the coffee table. They each took a mug, prepared their coffees to their liking, and settled down again. All eyes landed on Holly.

Holly nervously put her coffee down, spilling some liquid onto the floor in the process. "I'm so sorry, Clementine," she said shakily, getting up. "Let me clean it up."

Clementine waved her off. "Don't worry about it, Holly, we'll clean it later. Sit down. I know this is hard, but Val deserves to know the truth. Can you tell us exactly what Homer did?"

Holly sat down again, took a deep breath, and then she began. "I need to start in the beginning if that's alright. Just so you can maybe understand a little bit more about the kind of relationship we have. Homer and I met in college. He joined my class in my second year because he had to repeat it. His opinion of himself has always been higher than his actual achievements. He was a player, and he pursued me relentlessly. I had no interest in him, but he wouldn't give up. After months of that I went to a party. Parties weren't my thing, and because I was nervous I had a few drinks. I wasn't used to alcohol, and it went straight to my head. Homer was there, of course –

269

he never missed a party – and we ended up talking for hours. You know how alcohol can make even the most boring person appear interesting? That's what was happening that night. Anyway, when I told him that I wanted to leave he offered to walk me home. I said yes. When we arrived at my dorm I tried to say goodnight, but he asked to use my bathroom. It seemed impolite to say no to such a simple request." Holly closed her eyes for a moment. "We had sex. I didn't want to, but it happened, and he got me pregnant. When I found out a couple of months later, my entire world shattered. Getting an abortion was out of the question for me. I'm a Christian, which means that to me that's a sin. Also, abortions were illegal then, I wouldn't even have known how and where to get one. Besides, I don't think I could have lived with myself afterwards. I'd heard of girls who regretted it for the rest of their lives, whose lives were ruined by it. I had to keep the baby. But I also knew that I didn't want to be a single mother. There would be no support from my own parents, and I didn't think I could do it alone. So, we got married. I dropped out of college when Christopher was born, Homer finished his education, and we settled into a life together. I worked nights for a while to support us, but by the time we moved to Summerfield I hadn't done that in years. Christopher was a teenager by then and didn't need me as much anymore, so I was looking for something to do. I decided to make our new neighbourhood better."

"By starting the HOA," Valerie said quietly.

"Yes." Holly was defensive. "None of you were here then, you don't know what it was like. Pleasant Hill was run-down and shabby. There were rusting cars sitting in driveways, peeling paint on houses, garbage in the streets. It didn't feel safe to walk around at night. And that halfway house ..."

"Taylor was saving people. Houses like hers are absolutely essential to give addicts a chance. Without them, most of us are almost guaranteed to end up back where we started. Why can't you see that?" Jules asked.

"Nobody forces anyone to get hooked on drugs. If places like that halfway house have to exist then it should be away from decent neighbourhoods. They're corrupting our children and make a neighbourhood unsafe."

"Do you really think anybody *wants* to become an addict?" Jules asked incredulously. "Nobody chooses that! It's an escape, a desperate attempt to feel better when the pain becomes too much. Anybody who's ever been addicted to something has gotten there because they wanted to feel connection, or confidence, or happiness, or love. And at first, drugs feel good. You think it's working, and that you found the solution. By the time it's not working anymore it's usually too late. You probably won't believe me, but it truly can happen to anyone. There are not only sex workers and street people in rehab but successful people as well: lawyers, doctors, teachers, CEOs. Addiction can affect anyone."

Holly opened her mouth to protest, but Clementine interrupted her. "Let's not do that now. We have different perspectives, and it's not the right time to get into a long discussion about addiction and how to treat it. You were telling us how Homer ended up killing Luke."

Holly winced as if she'd been struck. "You're right, I'm sorry. I got carried away. Anyway, we wanted Taylor to move, and she wouldn't do it. I, uhm–" she blushed furiously– "sent her anonymous letters for a while." Jules shook her head at that in disgust.

271

"It didn't work. Then Homer said that he would take care of it. I had no idea what he did, I swear!" Holly pleaded, furtively glancing at Jules.

"Did you want to know?" Jules asked simply. Holly shook her head.

"That's what I thought."

"Tell us about Luke, Holly," Valerie interjected in a brittle voice that brooked no argument.

Holly bowed her head. "Like I said earlier, I had no idea that he would do that. I didn't know Homer had it in him, and when I heard of Luke's passing, I honestly thought it was just an ordinary heart attack. He was the right age group, and Homer had mentioned that Luke was on heart medication; he filled his prescription. At first I didn't notice anything different about Homer. I don't pay much attention to him, to be honest; even though we live under the same roof, we live next to each other, not with each other, if you know what I mean. But some time over the last year I noticed that he didn't sleep well. He started taking Ativan, and he drank more. He seemed moody and withdrawn, almost as if he was depressed. I've never seen him like that before. I questioned him about it a few times, but he was always dismissive and said that everything was fine.

"Yesterday I put it all together. His refusal to get the police or lawyers involved in HOA business. His odd behaviour that started around the time Luke died. His cryptic remark a few weeks ago that he would end up in prison if someone poked around in his life. I didn't know you existed or that he'd done something to any of you," Holly indicated Jules, "so I didn't attribute his panicked behaviour yesterday to you. I thought he'd finally snapped because of what he must have done to Luke, so I cornered him." Holly paused for a moment, understanding dawning on her. "I just realized something. If he hadn't taken too many pills yesterday I don't think he'd ever have confessed. He would have finished packing his suitcase and taken off, and I'd never known that he was capable of murder. But because he had taken too many pills and mixed them with booze he was experiencing acute overdose symptoms that scared him so much that I could get the confession out of him. Ironic, isn't it?"

"Substance abuse is everywhere," Jules confirmed quietly. "I told you."

Holly finished the rest of the story quickly, repeating what Homer had told her after he'd woken up at the hospital. When she was finished Holly stood up. "Julia and Valerie, I'm deeply sorry for what my husband – soon to be ex-husband – has done to you. And I'm sorry for how I treated you, Valerie. I see now that I took it too far."

"I–" Valerie searched for something to say, but when she couldn't think of an appropriate response that conveyed the amount of shock, grief, anger, and sorrow she felt, she closed her mouth again.

"Time for you to go, Holly," Clementine told her solemnly.

Without another word, Holly turned on her heel and left.

Epilogue

Two years later

Valerie poked her head out of the window and called to the young woman working in the backyard: "Rosie, I'm leaving in ten minutes. Do you want to come?"

"Yes, I'm almost done here. How dressy is this thing? Do I need to change?"

Valerie took in the young woman's denim cut-offs, peasant blouse, and the streak of dirt on her rosy cheek. Her feet were shoved into an old pair of gardening clogs, and there was no doubt a healthy amount of dirt under her fingernails. Pride swelled inside her at how far Rosie had come. "You look perfect," she told her. "Clementine will be thrilled to see you."

Ten minutes later, they left, Rosie having exchanged her gardening shoes for high-top Converse sneakers. They were on their way to Clementine's new photography exhibition *Rewildest Dreams,* a documentation of rewilded spaces. She had travelled all over Canada two summers ago to take photos of inspiring rewilded areas, from urban parks like the Corktown Common in Toronto or Parc Jean-Drapeau in Montreal, to private gardens, balconies, and window boxes.

Valerie had come with her for several weeks. After the

shocking revelation of Luke's real cause of death she had fallen into a serious depression that lasted months. The press covered the case extensively, and once they'd exhausted the murder and then the rape, they gleefully moved on to the HOA and how Holly and Homer had run it. For a crazy few weeks Summerfield was overrun with journalists and camera crews, camping out in Pleasant Hill to get quotes from residents and an interview with Valerie, who refused to talk to them. Clementine decided to take her away. She loaded up Matilda, told Valerie to sneak to her place through their backyards, and they took off in the middle of the night.

While on the road the two friends talked, cried, laughed, sang together at the top of their lungs, or sat in companionable silence. They did yoga together, and Clementine persuaded Valerie to go skinny dipping. After her initial reluctance Valerie became a big fan, relishing the feeling of liberation and freedom it gave her. She talked to her therapist Gwen once a week over Zoom, working through her grief and trauma about what had happened. She was angry at Holly for a long time. Valerie cursed her up and down for telling the truth about Luke's death. What good had come of it? It had re-opened her wounds, but this time with a ton of salt added to them thanks to Holly, and it made Luke's loss so much worse. The pain was magnified by knowing that his death had been a cruel and unnecessary one.

Gwen listened patiently, and over time she made Valerie understand that Holly was a victim as well. It didn't excuse her behaviour, but it made it understandable. During the media frenzy there had been a long article about Holly in a magazine that detailed her upbringing: the absent father, hoarder mother, the fact that Holly had to raise herself from a

275

young age. To Valerie's surprise she found that the fire of her white-hot anger burnt itself out over time. It cost too much energy to be so mad all the time. She had moved through the rage and emerged on the other side of it. Valerie understood that she would carry her grief with her for the rest of her life; but she didn't want this to be the only thing she carried in the suitcase of her life. She intended to add other, more pleasant things to her suitcase. But what?

For the first time in her life, Valerie asked herself what *she* wanted. Not her parents, or friends, or husband. What was it that would please *her*? Valerie took George for long walks, needing alone time to figure out what she wanted to do next.

And then, on a bright morning somewhere in Alberta, as Valerie was diving headfirst into the cool water of the glacier-fed lake they had camped next to, it came to her. "Clem, I know what I'm going to do!" she yelled as she ran towards her friend, naked as the day she was born.

"That's fantastic! What?" Clementine yelled back, poking her head out of Matilda.

"I'm going to open up my house to help recovering addicts," Valerie said breathlessly, grabbing a towel and falling into a seat across from Clementine. "I have this huge house that's way too big for me, I have the medical background, and I know that there is a need. I want to pick up where Taylor Kirby left off all those years ago."

"I think that's an excellent idea," Clementine said with a smile that could light up the world.

* * *

Even though the HOA had been dissolved in the aftermath of

all the publicity, Valerie wanted to make sure that she wasn't breaking any bylaws. She applied for all the required licences and permits, took classes in substance-abuse counselling, and switched from her full-time position at work to a part-time job.

Rosie was the seventh young woman that Valerie had welcomed into her home. Some had stayed for only a few weeks, others several months; Rosie had been with her almost from the beginning. Valerie and her hit it off right away, and when Rosie announced that she wanted to take evening classes to get her adult high-school diploma because she never graduated, Valerie offered her to stay until she was finished. Rosie gladly accepted the offer, and the two women had become close friends.

Homer was convicted of Luke's murder and Jules' rape and sentenced to twenty-five years in prison. Mary Potter, the long-time neighbour and friend of Holly's, had watched Homer go to Luke's house on that fateful night, and saw him return in a hurry half an hour later. She testified against him in court. The police also found the empty bottle of liquid digoxin in a locked drawer in Homer's study, stuffed to the very bottom.

Holly moved away soon after everything happened. The community's outrage at Homer's criminal acts spilled over to her, and she became the most hated woman in Summerfield. The last thing they heard was that she'd moved to Halifax, Nova Scotia, and gone back to school to finish her degree in pharmacy, forty-four years after she had dropped out of university. "Good for her," Valerie said when she heard it. She bore no more ill will against Holly, believing to her core that she'd been punished enough.

* * *

Valerie and Rosie pulled up in front of the community hall. People were milling about in front of it, laughing and chatting, and Valerie spotted Marjorie, who was waiting for her. Marjorie, long recovered from her broken hip and subsequent surgery, was proud of the fact that she still had her driver's licence at eighty-one and insisted on driving herself, regularly declining any offers of rides.

Several people greeted Valerie or waved at her as she, Rosie, and Marjorie walked into the hall together. Valerie smiled and waved back, greeting many people by name. Clementine was talking to someone in the front, magnificent in a floor-length black dress with big white and pink flowers printed on it, paired with cowboy boots and turquoise jewellery, her long grey hair in a braid. When she saw Valerie approach she excused herself and came towards her, beaming. "My three favourite girls are here!" She hugged them in turn, and when she reached Valerie she held on for a moment.

"Luke would be so pleased," Valerie murmured into Clementine's ear. "These are incredible. Once people get a look at these photographs, the other half of Summerfield who hasn't done it yet will also want to rewild their yards."

Ever since their information session about rewilding two years ago, more and more houses adopted at least some of the principles of letting nature do her thing. And seeing all the photos together like that, blown up and lit expertly, the effect was stunning: a symphony of colour, wild beauty – and hope. Clementine had not only photographed plants and nature, but also taken close-ups of butterflies, insects, bees, and birds, thriving in their natural habitats. And she'd included

278

portraits of the people who made it possible, who cared about biodiversity, saving wildlife, preserving nature, and reversing some of the damage humanity had done to the planet.

Seeing those extraordinary images gave Valerie a warm, optimistic feeling: that the world, despite its darkness, was also a bright, loving, and supportive place. Standing here, surrounded by her friends, her community, and possibilities, Valerie felt it in her bones: not only was she going to be fine; they all were.

About the Author

Miriam Verheyden is a Canadian nonfiction writer, novelist, x-ray technologist, and mental health advocate. Known for her honesty and deep vulnerability, she writes books about love, fear, mental health, and being a woman in the world.

Miriam was born and raised in Germany. During a solo trip at twenty-two to the wild west of Canada she fell in love with her husband, dropped everything at home, and moved to British Columbia to be with him. Twenty+ years later they are still happily married, living on a ranch in the interior of BC.

Miriam has published three nonfiction books. *The Home-owner's Association* is her first novel.

You can connect with me on:
- https://miriamverheyden.com
- https://www.facebook.com/miriamverheydenwriter
- https://www.instagram.com/miriamverheydenwriter

Subscribe to my newsletter:

✉ https://miriamverheyden.substack.com

Also by Miriam Verheyden

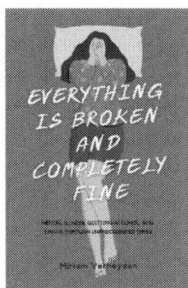

Everything Is Broken and Completely Fine
Miriam tried for most of her life to hide her mental illness. She hoped that if she pretended it didn't exist, nobody else would notice it either. Spoiler: that plan backfired spectacularly.

Unexplainable rage attacks, persistent intrusive thoughts, and a recurring overwhelming despair are difficult to hide. Working as an x-ray technologist through COVID-19 contributed to her declining mental health.

In a desperate attempt to numb the pain and cheer herself up she reached for what society endorses as the ultimate relaxant: wine. It was supposed to transform her from a chronic worrier with low self-esteem into a carefree, confident person.

That didn't happen.

Alcohol made her mental health significantly worse, increasing her anxiety and causing severe self-loathing. Instead of solving her low mood, it contributed to it.

Everything is Broken and Completely Fine takes you into the flawed brain of someone who's living with anxiety, depression, and PMDD.

Set in the unprecedented times of a pandemic, natural disasters, and life's unavoidable ups and downs, this book explores what happens when denial turns into acceptance, grey-area drinking transforms into sobriety, and one woman finds herself where she's never been before – at peace.

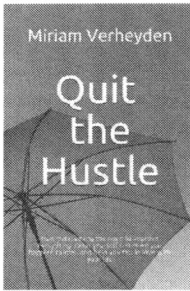

Quit the Hustle

Never has the hustle been more glorified than it is today. We have been told for decades that we have to do it all: have kids, a great relationship, a career, a Pinterest-worthy house, and a perfect body and face.

With the rise of the #bossbabes, even that is not enough anymore: we should also strive to turn our hobby into a side hustle, follow the latest healthy eating trends, and pretend that celery juice tastes better than coffee. But the tide is turning. We are fed up with the chase for perfection.

This book explores what happens when we stop doing and start being – and let me tell you, it's *magical*.

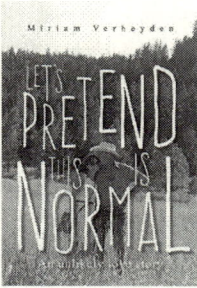

Let's Pretend This Is Normal

Life after high school wasn't at all how Miriam imagined it. Instead of having big plans and excitement for the future, she had no idea what she wanted to do with her life and struggled to find her purpose.

When the man she thought would save her from herself married her sister, she travelled to the wild west of Canada on a journey of self-discovery and found much more than she bargained for: she fell head-over-heels in love with Richard, twenty-five years her senior and a father of four.

When she introduced him to her shocked family, they tried to persuade her to leave him. Failing, they did the next best thing: they pretended it was normal.

Let's Pretend This Is Normal is a testament to what can happen when you listen to your heart instead of the opinions of others. This tale of romance and growing up is proof that even if you have no idea what the hell you're doing, with some patience and trust in yourself, you'll figure it out.

Manufactured by Amazon.ca
Bolton, ON